I0761616

AFTER
THE FALL

ALSO BY EDWARD ASHTON

Three Days in April

The End of Ordinary

Mickey7

Antimatter Blues: A Mickey7 Novel

Mal Goes to War

The Fourth Consort

AFTER THE FALL

EDWARD ASHTON

ST. MARTIN'S PRESS
NEW YORK

This is a work of fiction. All of the names, characters, organizations, places, and events portrayed in this work are either products of the author's imagination or used fictitiously.

First published in the United States by St. Martin's Press, an imprint of St. Martin's Publishing Group

EU Representative: Macmillan Publishers Ireland Ltd, 1st Floor, The Liffey Trust Centre, 117–126 Sheriff Street Upper, Dublin 1, D01 YC43

www.stmartins.com

Library of Congress Cataloging-in-Publication Data

Names: Ashton, Edward (Science fiction writer) author
Title: After the fall / Edward Ashton.
Description: First edition. | New York : St. Martin's Press, 2026.
Identifiers: LCCN 2025040749 | ISBN 9781250375650 hardcover | ISBN 9781250376220 ebook
Subjects: LCGFT: Science fiction | Fiction | Novels
Classification: LCC PS3601.S567 A38 2026
LC record available at https://lccn.loc.gov/2025040749

First Edition: 2026

10 9 8 7 6 5 4 3 2 1

To everyone's best pal, Claire!

AFTER
THE FALL

CHAPTER ONE

"John!" Martok bellows as he bursts through the door. "I have news, my friend—wondrous, wondrous news! You'll not believe what fell to me in the markets today!"

John turns away from the window, the only one in the bare boardinghouse room he and Martok have shared for the past two months, where he'd been passing the afternoon watching the machinations of a murder of crows as they attempted to scavenge the carcass of a dead rat from beneath the wheels of the passing trundlecars in the street below, to see his patron hanging his formal sash on the hook by the door. Martok's three-fingered hands are trembling with excitement, so much that it takes him two tries to get the sash to stay, and the crest that runs down the center of his broad bald scalp is flushed a happy pink.

"John!" Martok says again, then crouches so that his head is nearly level with John's and spreads his arms wide. "Come to me, my friend! This has been a truly wondrous day!"

John hesitates a bare moment, then sighs, crosses the tiny room in three strides, and steps into the gray's crushing embrace. Martok lifts him, thick hands pressing John against the hairless, wrinkled skin of his chest, spins him half-around, and sets him down again with his back to the door.

"Ask, John! You must ask!"

John takes a deep breath in and lets it out slowly, mostly to make sure Martok hasn't cracked his ribs in his exuberance, then says, "Please tell me, Martok. What wondrous thing did you find in the markets today?"

He's expecting to hear something about a new sash, or a refurbished handheld, or perhaps a particularly ripe piece of fruit. Consequently, he has no idea how to react when Martok says, "A home, John! I have found us a home!"

THE INTRICACIES OF the grays' economic system have never been remotely clear to John. What education he received in the crèche was mostly structured around learning ways to serve a future patron in practical ways. He was taught to cook, to clean, and to shoot (small-caliber weapons only, sufficient for hunting native game, but not remotely suited for penetrating the leathery, three-centimeter-thick hide of a gray). He knows there are some humans at work in the markets. He's seen them there from time to time, has even seen Martok forced to barter with one of them on a few occasions. Whatever arcane knowledge of debit and credit that those humans have gained, however, did not come from the crèche, and Martok has never shown the slightest interest in passing along to John any small understanding of economics that he might have.

John has seen enough, though, to know one thing for certain: He and Martok are poor. If he's being honest with himself, that much was clear to him even on the day Martok took him away from the crèche. John was not one of the children who lined up eagerly to show off their skills for the grays who came by shopping for a bond. He was small for his age, with a high, piping voice and a slight stammer that came and went, with timing seemingly designed to maximize his embarrassment. Awkward with his peers and mostly terrified of the grays, John hung back as far as the nursemaids would let him when visitors came to the crèche—and as a consequence, he was passed over, time after time after time.

He still remembers the moment when he realized that he was dooming himself. He was twelve, and a girl named Tila had just aged out without a bond and had been unceremoniously put down in the alley behind the crèche. As one nursemaid heaved her body into the refuse bin and two others herded the children back into the building, it struck him suddenly, with the force of a physical blow: *That'll be me someday.*

By the time Martok came by, John was, strictly speaking, already past the age where he should have been declared permanently un-bonded. The only reason he was still there, the only reason that the nursemaids kept shoving him out in front of every gray who came by, was that he was still small enough to pass, and the nursemaids in his crèche, despite their general indifference and occasional cruelty, didn't actually enjoy putting humans down. Martok has never said exactly how the two of them wound up walking out of that place together, but John strongly suspects that when the nursemaids realized that Martok was just window-shopping, that he didn't have enough credit for the processing fee, let alone for the purchase of a bond, they offered up John for precisely what he was worth—which is to say, for nothing at all.

"I DON'T UNDERSTAND," John says. "A home? Isn't this our home?"

"This? A home?" Martok crosses over to the pantry in two

short strides, reaches inside to pull out a protein brick, and tears off a bite half the size of John's head. "This squalid hovel?" He gestures broadly with the hand holding the brick, spraying crumbs from both his hand and his thick, wrinkled lips in an arc half the size of the room. "This cramped, wretched hole? No, John. This is no home. This is a place of bare subsistence, sufficient only to keep our heads dry and our bodies warm as we wait for the gods of fate to hand us the opportunity that we have been awaiting." He takes another bite, chews, and swallows. "And now, my friend? Now they have."

Martok drops onto the big bed that takes up a quarter of the room's floor space, pops the remainder of the protein brick into his mouth, and then flops backward with his hands folded behind his head. "We leave this place tomorrow. I shall settle accounts with our twice-cursed landlord once we've had our breakfasts—it wouldn't do to tell him before he's fed us one last time, of course—and we shall be on our way. I have already secured a trundlecar to take us as far as the central terminal. From there, I've booked passage to the terminus at Lake Town."

John waits a beat for him to go on, then says, "Lake Town? That's where we're going?" John has never seen Lake Town. He's never seen much of anywhere, honestly, other than the bits and pieces of Farhome, the city that still houses nearly eighty percent of the grays on the planet, that Martok has seen fit to show him. He's heard of Lake Town, though. It's the farthest western extension of the grays' footprint on this world, a barely populated outpost on the southern shore of a mostly frozen freshwater sea. He's not sure what sort of home Martok might have found there, but he's hard-pressed to imagine that it could be any better than this place.

"Oh no," Martok says, his chest rumbling with laughter. "Lake Town is a terribly depressing place, John—a refuge for miscreants and ne'er-do-wells who have been driven from the more polite society of Farhome, mostly for perfectly good reasons. I spent two thoroughly unpleasant years there when I first made landfall on this world, and I have no interest in ever returning. Lake Town is not our destination. It is simply the farthest extent of the transport network. I intend to stay there for the shortest time that we can possibly manage."

"Oh," John says, then reaches up to scratch the back of his head. "I'm confused."

Martok sits up again, and his lips fold back from his thick, square teeth and two stubby upturned tusks in a parody of a grin. "As well you might be. You would not know this from our time together, John, but I was not always the soft city dweller that you see now. Years ago, I was considered quite the adventurer, and I expect that experience will serve us well now. Upon reaching Lake Town, we shall strike out southward, away from the lakeshore. Our destination is some fifty kilometers along, over hill and bramble, across rill and stream, and through trackless wilderness."

He leans back, and the bed groans as his weight settles onto his elbows. "As I have already implied, I had a most fortuitous meeting in the markets today. In particular, I met a worthless scion of the Greatfoots, a distant descendant of the Chief Administrator himself—Daro Lia née Greatfoot by name. It seems this wretch had acquired a great deal of property beyond the reach of polite society, south and west of Lake Town in what was once an agricultural region of sorts. He purchased this property not because he had the slightest idea what to do with it, of course, but merely as a speculative investment. Such follies are common among the more useless members of the wealthier clans, you know. They have abundant credit, but they lack the wit to imagine how to invest it usefully. It seems he had some idea that Lake Town was due to expand greatly, and that when it did, he would be in a position to profit massively."

With that, Martok gets to his feet again and begins pacing—a singularly unsatisfying thing to do in such a tiny space, but John knows by now that when Martok is excited about something, he has a great deal of trouble holding still.

"This ignorant Greatfoot has such an impoverished imagination that he could see no use for land such as this beyond the construction of more of what we already see around us. When it became clear, as it should have been from the outset, that no expansion in the direction of Lake Town was in the offing, he had no ability to see other possible avenues of progress."

He stops pacing then and turns to face John, arms spread wide. After a moment's hesitation, John hazards, "But . . . you did see some such opportunity?"

"Yes!" Martok says, and starts pacing again. "Of course! I am no failed third nephew of a wealthy clan, John. All my life, I have had to earn my way by my wits, and as this dullard poured out his tale of woe over a half-full tankard, I could already see what he could not. I let him ramble on for an hour or more, and then, my voice dripping with sympathy and fellow-feeling, I offered, strictly as a favor to both him and his noble clan, to relieve him of the burden of his misbegotten investment."

Martok seems about to burst with self-satisfaction. John, though, is beginning to feel a familiar, gnawing unease. This isn't the first time that Martok has had a brilliant idea, one sure to bring him the wealth and acclaim that he clearly deserves.

A quick glance around their squalid room tells the tale of how those other opportunities ended.

"So . . ." John says. "This Greatfoot, he just . . . *gave* you the title to this property?"

That stops Martok's pacing again, and when he turns to face

John, his face has lost some of its smugness. The gnawing in John's belly turns abruptly into a sharp, stabbing pain.

"Well, no. Of course not. Even a decadent Greatfoot dandy would not be foolish enough to simply hand over an opportunity like this to one he'd just met, would he?"

John closes his eyes and breathes in, then out slowly. When he opens them again, Martok's gaze has dropped to the floor between them. "Martok?" John says. "What did you give him?"

"Well," Martok says. "Nothing, really. A pledge, only. He was in such desperation to be rid of the property that he lent me the credit to take it from him. I had only to pledge him collateral."

Collateral? John's eyes sweep the room. Everything Martok owns is here. What could he have . . .

Oh gods.

"Martok?" John says, slowly, evenly. "Did you . . . no, you couldn't have. Please tell me you didn't pledge him my bond?"

Martok turns away, flops back onto the bed, and covers his face with his arms. "What does it matter what I pledged? I tell you truly, John. At the rate he offered me, this property will pay for itself a thousand times over."

John drops back into his seat by the window and buries his face in his hands. His heart seems to be trying to pound its way out of his chest, and when he speaks again, his voice is trembling.

"When is the first repayment due to him, Martok?"

"Sixty days," Martok says. "An eternity, really."

John knows the answer to his next question, but he asks anyway. "And do you have it? Do you have enough credit even to cover the first payment?"

Martok doesn't answer. Outside the window, the crows have given up on what remains of the carcass in the road and have fallen to fighting among themselves over a hunk of protein brick that's been dropped by a passing gray. John closes his eyes again and breathes in, breathes out.

"Oh come now," Martok says as John climbs up onto the high stool that the master of the house has set out for him at the common table. "How much longer do you intend to continue this miserable sulking? This is a great day for us, my friend. I should have thought you would greet it with a bit more enthusiasm."

John stares across the heavy wooden table at Martok for a bit too long, then takes a hard roll from the platter sitting between them, bites into it, and chews. It's early enough that they're still alone in the dimly lit, wood-paneled dining room, other than the bondsman servers who come and go, laying out food and drink for the other boarders who will presumably be along shortly. The thing that he would like to say—that, while Martok has done foolish, impulsive things many times in their years together, this is the first time that he's led John to believe that he does not, in fact, care a whit whether John lives or dies—is not a thing that he can say.

John has spoken with the bonded employees of other grays. He's heard stories. He knows that the way Martok interacts with him, the way he speaks to John as if he were another living, sentient being—as if he were, in fact, actually a friend, and not just a cheap, meaty automaton—is far more the exception than the rule in these relationships. Because of this, he knows better than to push. He knows that there's a line that he might cross that would change their relationship irrevocably, and he knows that change would not be for the better.

That doesn't mean he has to be cheerful about the prospect of being sold off to some Greatfoot degenerate, though. He finishes his roll in silence, pours himself a glass of water, using two hands to manage the gray-sized pitcher, and drinks that down in silence as well. Martok watches him this entire time, chewing absently on a hunk of dried meat, his crest slowly darkening.

Just as Martok's expression is beginning to shade over from annoyance to actual anger, John says, "The part of this that I don't understand—the part that, in fact, makes me question the accuracy of how you've presented this story to me—is this: What could this Greatfoot you met yesterday possibly want with me? He wants out of his investment? Sure, I get that. We all make bad bargains sometimes. He wants out badly enough to extend credit for the buyout to someone with no visible means of repayment? That's a bit more of a stretch, honestly, but I guess I'll go along with it. But the last bit? The idea that he's willing to accept the bond of a single non-famous, not-particularly-skilled human as collateral? You must see that's nonsense, Martok. Let's say you wind up defaulting on that payment in sixty days. How does taking on my bond serve as compensation? What possible use could this person have for me?"

"Ah," Martok says, and glances around the room. A pair of grays have taken seats at the opposite end of the table, but they're carrying on a conversation in rumble-speak and paying no attention whatsoever to John and Martok. "I see. Your confusion stems from your lack of understanding of the workings of business—hardly your fault given your station—but, apologies; I had not considered the depths of your ignorance when I explained our situation. You seem to be under the impression that your bond is intended to serve as *financial* collateral in this arrangement. As you say, this is nonsense. Even if you were a specialist—one of those insufferable bondsmen we occasionally encounter in the markets, say—your bond would not remotely serve in this capacity. When one offers financial collateral against a loan, the value of the thing offered must obviously be commensurate to the value of the loan. How could *any* human's bond stand as collateral against the sum this Greatfoot has advanced me?"

John starts to mention that Martok has not, in fact, told him how much credit he's been offered up against. He quickly thinks better of it, though, as Martok continues.

"Obviously, such an idea does not bear discussion. It should be clear, moreover, that in this case, the property itself serves as financial collateral. If I fail to repay our foolish benefactor in a timely manner, the rights to the land will revert back to him immediately." He pauses to take a long pull at his breakfast ale, wipes his mouth with the back of one meaty arm, and lets loose a gut-rattling belch that brushes John's hair back from his forehead. "So, you might ask, why is any other collateral necessary? Why, to ensure that I am properly motivated to do what is necessary to make this investment pay appropriately, of course—which is to say, your role in this endeavor is that of *motivational* rather than *financial* collateral. Do you see?"

Unfortunately, John does see—or at least, he's beginning to. The pain in his stomach has returned with a vengeance.

"So what you're saying is that this Greatfoot isn't actually interested in taking me into his service if you default?"

A shrug ripples through Martok's massive shoulders, and his ears flip in negation. "It seems unlikely, does it not? One of his station could have his choice of bonds directly from the crèche. To break in a new bondsman, one who is already of your relatively advanced age, would likely be more trouble than it was worth."

"So . . ."

Martok throws back the last of his ale and gestures to the server to stop his pointless poking at the fire and bring another. "As I said previously, in order to reel this fish into the boat, it was necessary for me to form a personal bond with him. We drank together for a long while before getting down to our business, and in that time I spoke glowingly of you. I went out of my way, in fact, to emphasize how highly I prize your service—and more than that, your companionship. I am clanless on this world, you know, and I led him to believe that I see you not as a servant at all, but rather as true family." Martok sees John's face change at that, and hurries to add, "This was not deceit, of course. You truly are all the family I have here. It is no exaggeration to say that I would be utterly devastated to lose you."

"But if you default . . ."

Martok takes a fresh ale from the server, tips it back, and drains half of it in one go. "Yes, John. You see our situation correctly. This is why we must both now do our utmost to ensure that I do not default."

CHAPTER TWO

John still dreams of the crèche.

He knows the dreams aren't strictly accurate. He's seen plenty of crèches as an adult. Martok has taken him along to window-shop for the new bonded employee that he doesn't need and can't afford on at least a half-dozen occasions. They've always struck him as neat, orderly places, with the children old enough to bond out lined up on display in the viewing rooms, and younger ones peering from windows and half-open doorways, trying desperately to get a glimpse of the visitors without drawing the notice of their gray nursemaids. The children are sometimes eager and sometimes sullen, but they're always subdued and respectful when Martok questions them, and they always try their best when he asks them to show off for him in one way or another, jumping or running, dancing or singing or doing sums in their heads.

The crèche John dreams of is not an orderly place at all.

Even while he's dreaming, John knows that, bad as things might have been, the other children weren't really fang-toothed demons chasing him down darkened hallways, that the gray nursemaids weren't really lumbering, murderous monsters, snatching children up in their massive three-fingered hands and squeezing them until their eyes popped from their heads—not most of the time, anyway. Dreams have their own logic, though, and that knowledge doesn't ease the terror in the slightest, doesn't stop him from waking soaked in sweat and panting, hoping desperately that his thrashing hasn't disturbed Martok's sleep.

He needn't worry about that, of course. The grays' hearing is mostly in a register far lower than John's peeping, and more than that, Martok has grown fond of putting away a flagon or two of thick, dark ale before turning in. Most nights, it would take a gunshot to rouse him.

"Wake, John. We have business here."

John hadn't actually been sleeping—at least, he doesn't think so. He'd been resting his eyes, curled up in the massive, padded carriage seat that Martok had booked for him, presumably as an apology for suspending John's life by the thin thread of Martok's business acumen.

All in all, he might have preferred to ride the way he ordinarily did on the rare occasions when the two of them have traveled together, seated on the floor between Martok's feet, and to have Martok apply the cost of this cozy seat to that first repayment note. Needless to say, however, John was not consulted on the matter.

Martok is on his feet already, gathering his bags. John sits up, stretches, and hops down to the floor. His own bag, a backpack containing a toothbrush, a comb, a spare pair of shoes, and three changes of clothes, is tucked under his seat. As he's pulling it out, the gray sitting across from him, an older, heavyset female wearing the thick black sash of a Greatfoot administrator, nudges him with one foot hard enough to knock him to his knees and rumbles something indistinct but clearly rude in the grays' language.

Martok, who'd been struggling to wrestle an oversized bag from the luggage rack over their seats, stops what he's doing and turns slowly to face her. The grays' language is conveyed mostly in frequencies that are below the audible range of human ears, but John is able to pick out a word here and there from the exchange that follows. *Friend. Leave. Strike. Ruin.*

That last one, which came from the Greatfoot as she rose from her seat, her crest dark with anger, leaves John hoping Martok will just let this go. It's not as if she actually hurt him.

Martok puts one thick hand to her forehead and gently but firmly shoves her back into her seat. Apparently he isn't interested in letting this go.

The two grays are stomping their feet and shouting at one another now, their voices so loud in the cramped compartment that John has to cover his ears as he scrambles back up onto his seat to avoid being crushed. The Greatfoot attempts to stand again, but Martok is looming over her now, and she doesn't have the leverage, so instead she *slaps* him, her right hand striking the side of his head with all the force she can muster.

Martok slowly straightens then, and the compartment falls silent. This is a dangerous moment. John has rarely seen one gray strike another—even lightly, even in jest—for the simple reason that grays are prone in such situations to enter a state that they call *absenting*. Grays in general lean toward the overcourteous, at least when dealing with one another. An *absent* gray, though, is a crazed animal, a five-hundred-kilo bundle of rage and aggression. Once, in the crèche, an older boy named Michael tried to sneak into the kitchen, hours past the evening meal. When he was caught, because of course he was caught, he struck the nursemaid who found him with a cooking pot he'd snatched from a countertop.

John and all the other children in the crèche at the time were roused from their beds and marched into the kitchen that night, were forced to see what little was left of Michael when the nursemaid was done with him, when she had finished stomping his bones into splinters and come back to herself. *This is what happens*, they were told. *We are kind when we are* present. *When we are* absent, *though?*

You must always make sure not to make us absent.

It seems, however, that this Greatfoot never got that memo—or perhaps she was simply driven somewhere close to that state herself by Martok's provocations. John watches in horror as Martok visibly struggles to remain *present*. He imagines that he can see Martok's mind flickering in and out in the twitching muscles of his face. The Greatfoot too seems to have just realized what she's done. She sits very still now, eyes wide, arms held up in front of her. John has never actually seen two *absent* grays tearing into one another, but he remembers what Michael looked like, and in this close space, even if they both completely ignored him to focus on killing one another, he can't imagine that he'd survive.

Gradually, though, over the course of ten seconds or so, Martok masters himself. It's an impressive display of self-discipline, one that John doesn't imagine most grays would have been able to manage. When it's done, when his face relaxes and John is able to breathe again, Martok says, "In any case, I will thank you not to touch this human again." He turns away, yanks the stuck bag free, staggers briefly under its weight before steadying himself, then looks back over his shoulder and says, "He may seem nothing but a bondsman to you, madam—but to me, he is a friend."

THE BUSINESS THEY have here, in a nameless cluster of warehouses and shelters midway between Farhome and Lake Town, is a visit to a crèche.

Like all crèches, the building is a massive stone edifice, with tall, narrow windows and a heavy, ironbound wooden door. It's set just past a crossroads at the center of this . . . John hesitates to think of it as a town. The entire settlement huddles around the rail station, as if the buildings themselves are afraid of what lives in the surrounding forest. The land here is like a blanket on an unmade bed, with long, narrow ridges alternating with deep, wooded valleys. This place is near the bottom of one of the deeper hollows. John can hear the tinkle of running water in the near distance, and the air smells of must and pine needles. When he sees where they're going, John says, "Martok? What are we doing here?"

Martok glances back at him. He has one massive bag slung over his shoulder, and the other—the one that got stuck in the overhead—rolls along on wheels behind him. "Why, John," he says, "I should think this would be obvious."

A neat concrete walkway leads from the sidewalk to the crèche's door. The grass to either side of it is winter-brown and beaten down by years' worth of children's feet. Martok drops the bag from his shoulder, leans it against the stone wall next to the door, and knocks.

"You can't afford a bond," John says.

"Is this so?" Martok says without looking back. "Have you become an economist now, John?"

John recognizes the mocking tone in Martok's voice, knows he should be quiet now, but all he can think is that in fifty-nine days Martok will need to produce some unknown amount of credit to prevent John from being taken, and then presumably killed and fed to Daro Lia née Greatfoot's animals, and that every bit that he's spent over the past twenty-four hours makes the possibility that Martok will actually be able to pay his debt even more remote.

"I'm not an economist," John says, "but I'm not an idiot either. You said yesterday that we—"

"I said that we had a great opportunity before us," Martok says, all mockery drained from his voice now. "In order to earn credit, it is sometimes necessary to expend a bit first." After a moment's silence, he adds, "I am very fond of you, John. You know this. However, I do not employ you for your fiscal advice."

John is still trying to decide how to respond to that when the door swings ponderously open, and they enter.

John strongly suspects that even if he lives to be a hundred years old, which of course he absolutely will not, he will never step across the threshold of a crèche without feeling his breath come short. This particular crèche is no worse and no better than others he's seen. The doorway opens into a dim vestibule. To the right and left are doors that must lead to the viewing rooms. Before them are stairs rising up to the dormitories. The nursemaid who admitted them gestures for Martok to leave his bags in the corner, then rumbles something to him in a register so low that John can't make out a single word. Martok replies in the same tone, and the nursemaid turns and stomps up the stairs, her footfalls echoing on the heavy wooden treads.

"What's happening?" John says. "Haven't you arranged a viewing?"

Martok glances down at him. His facial expression, which John has become acutely sensitive to over the years, is unreadable. "I have not. This is but a brief stopover. Fortunately, no viewing will be necessary."

John opens his mouth to ask what that's supposed to mean, but before he can form the words, indistinct shouting echoes down the stairs, first in the voice of a human girl, and then in the subterranean rumbling of the nursemaid. This goes on for almost a full minute, long enough for John to ponder the fact that he's fairly sure he's never actually witnessed a human screaming at a gray before, until finally the heavy beams of the ceiling shudder under what must be the nursemaid's threat-stomps, and the voices fall silent. Thirty seconds later, the nursemaid comes back down the stairs, a human girl-child trailing behind her.

As she steps down onto the floor of the vestibule, John mentally revises his estimate of the girl's age. She's older than he'd first assumed—maybe, as he was in her situation, close to or even over the age at which she should have been put down. She has long black hair pulled back from her face and trailing down past her shoulders, ghost-pale skin, and a sullen set to her features that falls somewhere between petulant child and seething adult. The nursemaid rumbles to Martok. He answers, then sinks to his knees and says, "Hello, Six. My name is Martok. This is my friend John. We've come to take you away from here."

THEY'RE BACK AT the terminal, sitting on a cold steel bench while they wait for the next transport bound for Lake Town to roll up, when Six finally speaks for the first time. She's sitting between John and Martok, feet dangling a half meter off the ground, staring down at a dead leaf wending its way across the platform toward the tracks, when she turns to John and says, "Just so you know, I don't like you. I'm not sure what Martok thinks is happening here, but you and I? We're not going to be friends."

John, who'd been staring down the tracks, eyes narrowed against the stiff cold breeze, turns to her and says, "Is that so?

I don't think you know me well enough yet to decide whether you like me or not. Maybe give it a day or two before you write me off?"

She shrugs and returns her attention to the leaf. "Don't have to know anything more about you than I already do. You're a pet. I don't like pets."

"John is not a pet," Martok rumbles. "He is my friend. This is an important distinction, which you must learn to appreciate."

Six squints up at him, then shakes her head and says, "If he's your friend, then he can stop being your friend whenever he wants. That's how friendship works. Isn't that right?"

"John?" Martok says. "Do you wish to stop being my friend?"

John looks up at Martok, then down at Six, and says, "I do not."

"Doesn't matter," Six says. "You couldn't if you wanted to. If you tried to leave him, they'd catch you and bring you back. If you tried again, they'd call you a feral and put you down." She turns to look at him then, her eyes narrowed. "That's not friendship. That's *ownership.*" She cuts her eyes back to Martok, then drops her voice an octave and a half and adds, "This is an important distinction, which you must learn to appreciate."

The three of them sit still and silent for a moment then, and John finds he's holding his breath, waiting to see how Martok will react. John hasn't often seen a human openly mock a gray, but on the few occasions back in the crèche when one of the other children crept up to that line, the response from the nursemaids was invariably swift and severe. Martok has never punished John in any serious way—but then, John has never really given him reason to, and he knows how other grays treat their bonded employees. Once, in the markets, he saw a hulking female kill one of her bonds with a single casual backhanded blow over a dropped and broken vase.

Six, for her part, doesn't seem particularly concerned. After the space of three or four heartbeats, her insouciance is justified as Martok breaks into laughter. "You see, John? Never question my eye for talent. This one will make an excellent addition to our little company."

A HALF HOUR later, the wind has risen from stiff to biting, while the temperature has dropped by at least ten degrees. Six is wearing nothing warmer than her standard crèche-issue black shift over a thin linen shirt and loose trousers. Over the past fifteen minutes or so as the temperature has fallen John has watched her gradually shrink into herself, pulling her feet up onto the bench and hugging her knees to her chest, eyes narrowed to slits and teeth now beginning to chatter.

Martok, of course, is oblivious. The grays are built for the cold, huge and thick-skinned, with a metabolism capable of cranking itself up like a coal furnace at need. Their world of origin, from what John has been able to gather, is a miserable ice ball, frozen over nearly from pole to pole most of the year and barely able to support a biosphere. Despite this, they never wear clothing beyond their formal sashes, and mostly spend the brief, wan summer months here shuffling as quickly as possible from one air-conditioned space to another, complaining bitterly of the heat all the while. John has tried to impress on Martok that humans aren't made that way, and he's succeeded at least to the extent that Martok reluctantly splurged on a jacket and knit hat for him midway through their second winter together. The idea that Six might be suffering at this moment, though, clearly hasn't occurred to him.

John is beginning to shiver himself, heat leaching gradually out of him and into the cold metal of the bench. Six's entire body is trembling. She hasn't actually asked anything of him, though. It's possible, even probable, he tells himself, that she doesn't want his help.

He looks up into the slate-gray sky, takes a deep breath in, and lets it out in a put-upon sigh. "Hey," he says, and unzips his jacket. "I'm not sure how much longer we're going to have to wait, but it could be a while yet. You should put this on before you freeze."

She turns her head to look at him when he holds the jacket out to her, but makes no move to take it from him. After an awkward five seconds, she says, "I said I don't like you. You heard that, right?"

"Yeah," John says. "I heard."

She hesitates for another long moment, then says, "Okay, then." She takes the jacket from him and wraps it around herself like a cloak, legs still drawn up and hood pulled over her head, then returns to her silent contemplation of the tracks without so much as a thank-you. John's shirt is thick fleece, objectively much warmer than what Six was wearing, and at least he's still got his hat. Even so, though, as the wind kicks up again and cuts through to his skin and the cold begins to sink down through fat and blood and muscle and bone, he takes a moment to wish that Martok had just dozed off on the train and missed this stop. He glances over at Six. She seems to have stopped shaking, anyway. John grits his teeth to keep them from chattering, hugs himself tighter, and settles in to wait.

After the train finally comes and the three of them make their way to an empty compartment, John has another two hours, as the muscles in his jaws unclench and his core temperature slowly returns to normal, to contemplate the question of why, exactly,

Martok felt the need to add another bond to his portfolio at this exact moment. Given her apparent age and, more importantly, her demeanor, John suspects that the direct cost of bringing Six out of the crèche was probably roughly the same as John's own bond fee—which is to say, the next-nearest thing to nothing. Still, next to nothing isn't *exactly* nothing, and even if it were, Six is still another mouth to feed. Every credit that went to the nursemaids, every credit that goes toward caring for this girl over the next two months, is another credit that won't go toward keeping John from ending his days being hunted for sport on Daro Lia née Greatfoot's private estate.

Martok still hasn't explained how he expects this property he's acquired to yield up the profits he'll need to pay his notes. If the plan involves manual labor, perhaps John should be grateful for the extra pair of hands. John has never known Martok himself to have any particular talent for or inclination toward hard work, physical or otherwise, so anything that needs to be done on the property will presumably be done mostly by John—and now, perhaps, by Six as well.

John spends an unpleasant while contemplating the idea of spending his days toiling in a field somewhere with only this sullen girl for company. She's sitting across from him now, perched on the edge of the carriage seat with his jacket still around her shoulders and her feet dangling a half meter above the floor, staring past him with a look of mild disgust on her face. Martok is sound asleep in the seat beside her, legs splayed and mouth dangling open, with his head leaning back against the wall. Six is so small next to him, and John finds it hard to believe that she'd be much use plowing a furrow or digging a trench or whatever it is Martok has planned for them. So why . . .

Oh.

In a flash of insight, John realizes that Six almost certainly isn't here because Martok thinks she'll help prevent him from losing John.

She's here as insurance, in case Martok does, in fact, lose John.

She's not intended to be John's helper. She's intended to be his replacement.

With a sigh, John pulls his legs up onto the seat, rests his forehead against his knees, and closes his eyes.

CHAPTER THREE

Lake Town, as it turns out, is barely more civilized than the huddle of buildings where they found Six. The station is a single stone building set a dozen meters back from the ground-level platform at the rail line terminus. Only two other passengers get off with them, both young male grays wearing the white sashes of laborers bound to clan Ice River. The wind is sharper here, rolling off the frozen lake in bitter, ice-laden gusts as John scuttles from the carriage to the shelter and ducks inside. Martok and Six follow at a more leisurely pace, Martok dragging his wheeled bag and shouldering the other, Six walking beside him with John's jacket wrapped tight around her.

"So," Martok says as the door slides shut behind him. "I have some business to conduct here in town before we can be on our way. I see no need to drag the two of you along with me, however. Lake Town can be an unruly place, and I would just as soon keep you innocent of it. Are you content to wait here for my return? I should be no more than an hour or two."

Six glances over at John and seems about to speak, but before she can, John says, "Before we leave this place, Six needs at least one change of clothing, probably two. And a jacket. And boots, if your plans have us spending any amount of time outdoors in this kind of weather."

Martok glances down at Six and says, "Hmm. Is this so?"

"I don't know," Six says. "I'm warm enough right now."

John narrows his eyes. "You won't be once I take my jacket back."

Martok gives a rumble of annoyance, then shakes his head and says, "I will never understand how your species managed to be so poorly adapted to survival on your own world, but I suppose it is what it is. Six, you may accompany me on my errands, and I will add a stop at the bondsmans' supply. With luck, they may have a few used items that we can acquire without putting too great a strain on my already overburdened finances. John, you will remain here and guard our baggage. Is this acceptable?"

After a long pause, John realizes that this wasn't a rhetorical question. "Yes, Martok. Thank you."

"Very well," Martok says. "Come, Six. Let us find you a wardrobe."

It isn't unheard-of for humans to be out and about in public without a gray escorting them, but it's certainly not common. Some grays allow certain specialists, like the ones John has seen in the markets, or repair workers the labor companies use for worming their way into spaces too tight for a gray to access, to move about freely when conducting clan business. Even those, though, are generally required to be accompanied by an employer when not working—and even when they're on the job, they always labor under the constant threat of abuse or even physical violence from passing grays. John once saw one of the market clerks subjected to a bellowing tirade from a low-status gray who didn't like the way the fellow was haggling over a case of protein bricks. If Martok hadn't intervened, stepping between the two and talking the gray down off the ledge, things might have ended badly for the clerk. As it was, the man was clearly shaken, and he ended up handing over the goods at half the price he'd been asking.

John himself has rarely been alone in public, with his outings mostly limited to errand-running, and almost always to times when few other grays would be out and about to harass him. He has never been left alone in broad daylight in a place as public as a transport station, not since the day Martok brought him home from the crèche.

Not until today, in any case.

After Six and Martok have gone, John climbs on top of Martok's bags, tugs his hat down over his ears, and puts his back to the cold stone wall. The room he's in is twenty meters square, with a door on one side leading out to the tracks and another opposite it presumably leading to the road into town. Across the way, a screen for booking passage set into the wall blinks silently from red to green, red to green. John wastes a moment fantasizing about buying a ticket back to Farhome and being done with this nonsense—but, as Six pointed out, even if it didn't require a gray's huge handprint to activate the terminal, an unaccompanied human in Farhome would sooner or later be picked up as a runaway and either sold off or, much more likely, put down.

He's contemplating that thought, picturing himself stomped to jelly under the feet of some anonymous control officer, when the town-side door slides open and two grays come in.

It takes John a moment to recognize them as the white-sash laborers who'd arrived with them a half hour ago. The two glance around the room as the door slides shut behind them, then turn to focus on John. One of them gestures toward him.

"You see? All of his things, just left here. He must *want* them taken." He spoke in English. That was for John, not his companion, the gray's way of saying, *I'm going to rob you now. Don't get in the way*. A sudden jolt of fear twists John's belly into a knot, but he sets his jaw and gets to his feet. "You should know, sir, that these bags are the personal property of Martok Barden née Black Hand. He has business in town, but please be aware that he may return at any moment."

The gray faces him fully and lowers his chin to his chest in what could be taken, if one were inclined to take it that way, as a threat stance. "Is that so? And he's set you here as guardian, then, has he?"

John's breathing quickens and he can hear his pulse echoing in his ears now, but he keeps his voice calm and his body language neutral as he says, "My employer set me here as a watcher, sir. I would never think to challenge you, obviously, but it is my duty to observe and report."

The gray closes half the distance between them in two lumbering strides. "A watcher, eh? Is that what you'd do if I were to liberate a few items from those bags? Watch?"

John swallows bile, then says, "I could not advise that, sir. Martok Barden née Black Hand is protective of his possessions."

"Black Hand?" the second gray says. "I don't believe I've heard of that clan. Do they have a holding in Farhome?"

"They do not," the first one says over his shoulder, then turns back to John. "A word of advice, little fellow: If your goal was to intimidate us, you would've done better to avoid mentioning your employer's name. Even back home, a Black Hand is little better than a vagabond. Here, he may as well be clanless. You've practically invited me to take my pick of his possessions. Truly, at this point it would shame me to refrain."

John opens his mouth to dispute this—he's spent much of

the past several years listening to Martok recite the glories of the Black Hand clan—but even as he does, he realizes with an unpleasant start that he finds this stranger's assessment of their fortunes more credible than Martok's. While he hesitates, the gray steps forward and spreads his arms wide, palms out. He's seen this pose before. Among close friends or family it can be an expression of welcome. Martok uses it that way often with John, though he's never seen his employer use it with another gray. To a stranger, though, this same pose is an overt threat, often coming just before a gray *absents*. John's mind races. Obviously, he should retreat now. This gray could kill him with a swipe of his arm, and he knows full well that there would be little that Martok or anyone else in this miserable town would or could do about it if the gray claimed provocation.

Does it really matter, though? If Martok fails to pay the note on his newly acquired property in fifty-nine days, John is likely to end his days being hunted for sport, a far worse fate than being splattered against the cold stone wall of the station building. Martok defaulting on his debt is probably more likely than not under the best of circumstances. How much more so, then, if John allows these louts to make off with whatever valuables Martok actually owns?

John doesn't have any good cards to play.

Time to bluff.

John slides down off the bags and onto the floor in front of the gray. He folds his arms across his chest, juts out his chin, and says, "What you say is true, sir. My employer is as good as clanless. Moreover, you are correct to suppose that these bags contain much wealth. You could take them now, and clearly my humble self could in no way hinder you." The gray lowers his arms then, and his face relaxes. He seems about to speak, but John hurries on. "However, sir . . . however, before doing so, I would ask you to please consider this: How is it that my clanless employer has managed to survive on this world, and indeed to thrive? I see from your sashes that you are of the Ice River clan, second in numbers and power here only to the Greatfoots. And yet, despite this great advantage, you appear to be simple laborers, so lacking in property that you look to steal from my employer like crows picking at scraps in the road."

This last was a calculated risk, and for a moment John thinks he may have taken the ruse too far. The gray's crest darkens and his breath comes faster, and John knows he's one more slip from dying. He runs his tongue around his suddenly bone-dry mouth, bows his head, and says, "Humbly, sir, please consider: How has my employer managed to accumulate this wealth, which includes even a stable of servants such as myself, when you who should clearly be greater than him have not? We have come to this sorry place to survey a new property that my employer has purchased—many thousands of rich acres, just to the south of here. What skills would allow a vagabond, as you say, to acquire such things?"

And this is the crux. Nothing John has said so far has been a lie, in the strictest sense. He and Six comprise a stable of sorts, and the bags do contain whatever meager wealth Martok owns. This is vital, because for a human to lie to a gray is death, and at least to his own mind John has up to now avoided crossing that line. What he implies with this last bit, though? He hasn't spoken the words, but both he and the gray know that there is only one practical way to accumulate real wealth without the benefit of a powerful clan's support.

Grays may kill humans and other animals at a whim, but they are congenitally incapable of doing real violence to one another without becoming *absent*. This presents a serious problem in circumstances where doing a bit of violence without losing all self-control might be advantageous. Criminal organizations and the authorities who are tasked with controlling them both are heavily dependent on that vanishingly small part of the population for whom the neural circuitry that drives grays to *absent* is somehow broken. A gray with the ability to hurt or even kill while *present* can more or less command his price as an enforcer for either side. Such ones are often both wealthy and revered.

Revered, yes—but also deeply, deeply feared. An enforcer can kill at will, and for all practical purposes can do so without consequence as long as he's discreet about it. For a gray, getting crosswise with an enforcer is the next best thing to suicide.

John holds his breath now, as this Ice River lout glances back over his shoulder to his friend. If he asks, will John answer truthfully? To lie outright would be to condemn himself if Martok returns while these two are still here and they realize the truth. To admit that Martok is no more an enforcer than he is a Greatfoot, though, would most likely be to lose whatever hope he has left of living out the year.

A low rumble passes between the two grays as John feels his life hanging in the balance. He knows he's missing at least half the individual words, but nonetheless he's able to gather the gist. *If the rogue is no more than he seems, then the bags are worthless. On the other hand, if he has anything worth taking, then we dare not.* John finally lets his breath out slowly as the gray takes two steps back, and then favors him with a mocking bow.

"You speak well," he says, "and I must allow that you're a brave little fellow—but then, what could we expect from a bondsman who keeps company with an enforcer? I hope that your employer is giving you your worth."

After they've gone, John finds himself dwelling on that last bit. Has Martok been giving him his worth? He treats John well, for the most part. Some grays think nothing of physically correcting their employees for even minor errors, occasionally to the point of real injury or even death. Martok has never struck John in anger, not once in all the time they've been together. That absence of cruelty isn't to be discounted, but now that he considers the matter, John has to admit to himself that this is the extent of what Martok has been able to provide him.

It's not material things per se that John thinks of when he considers whether he's been fairly compensated for his time with Martok. They have little enough, it's true, but whatever Martok does have, he's always shared with John. They've been hungry at times, and once spent nearly a month without a roof over their heads, but it's not as if Martok were feasting then while John suffered. When he thinks about the market clerks or the pipe cleaners, it's not their clothes or their gear or their suppers he envies. It's not even their relative freedom. The thing he envies is their *purpose*.

John is twenty-nine years old. He's been with Martok now for nearly half his life, and for all that time his days have followed a single simple pattern. He wakes. He feeds himself, if food is around to be had. He accompanies Martok on his often-inscrutable errands or he doesn't, depending on Martok's whim of the day. He eats again. He goes to sleep. None of this is *bad*, really, at least if you can overlook the occasional day of fasting or night spent freezing on the streets because Martok wasn't able to scrape up the credit for a room, and John doesn't feel any particular envy when he considers the specifics of what those other humans are doing with their days. Neither worming his way through a sewage pipe looking for a fat-and-feces-laden blockage or haggling with irritable grays over the price of a new sash has any particular appeal when he really thinks about it.

Still, though, he can't escape the thought that his life ought to be about something more than it is.

He's still ruminating on that thought when Six and Martok return from their errands an hour later.

"John!" Martok says as the town-side door slides closed behind him. "We had the most wonderful fortune in town! Six, show him what we were able to find for you!"

Six glances up at Martok, sees the excitement on his face, then gives John a half-hearted twirl. She's wearing a black leather coat now that hangs down past her knees, a thick fleece hat, and bright red woolen mittens. "You can have your jacket back," she says, and hands it up to him. "I like this one better."

"Thanks," John says. He slides down off the bags, takes it from her, and pulls it on with a grateful shiver.

"I am sorry to have left you alone for so long," Martok says as he gathers his things. "I trust you had an entirely dull time waiting here?"

John has already opened his mouth to say that no, his time here wasn't dull at all, and that this was not in any way a good thing. Before he can, though, some scrap of self-preservation instinct kicks in. Did he lie to the two grays who tried to raid Martok's bags? No, not exactly.

Did he *not* lie to them, though? Again, not exactly.

In that ambiguity lies the possibility of John's head cracking open under a constable's foot.

"No," John says. "Of course not. I performed my duty, which is never boring."

That's not technically a lie. It's not the full truth either, of course, but some things can't be helped.

Martok laughs, gives a mocking half bow uncomfortably

reminiscent of the one the roustabout gave him, and says, "A very formal answer, sir. Very well said indeed. In any case, and despite your protestations that your time here was no burden, I am sorry to have forced it on you. I am certain, however, that you will forgive me when you come outside and see what I've obtained for us." He bares his teeth and tusks in an approximation of a grin as he settles the bag over his shoulder. "It seems, my friend, that we shall not be walking to our new home after all."

CHAPTER FOUR

"You . . ." John manages, before realizing that nothing he could say right now will help his case, and many things he might say could hurt him.

"Ha!" Martok says. "You see, Six? Just as I predicted. He is struck dumb with joy!"

Standing at the curb directly across from the terminal entrance is a trundlecar.

It's not a *good* trundlecar. John can see that at a glance. The exterior is a dull, mottled black and the four hulking off-road tires are mismatched and badly worn. A crack runs the length of the window above the rear door, and the handle hangs away from the body of the car in a way that suggests to John that he'll probably need to walk around to the street side if he wants to get in. Still, though.

"How, Martok?" he finally manages. "How in Greatfoot's name did you get the codes to this thing?"

"This is not for you to worry over," Martok says as his grin widens. "The point of this, the thing that should have drawn your notice, is that we are now the owners of this fine vehicle.

This means, my friend, that rather than trudging footsore for days, braving the wilds and the weather and possibly being set upon by bears and wolves and who knows what else, we will instead be able to travel to our new estate in comfort and style."

"You *own* it?" John doesn't know what a trundlecar—even one as clearly decrepit as this one—costs compared to, say, a week's worth of food or lodging, but he strongly suspects that it must be a large multiple of either, and he has never known Martok to have enough credit at any one time to cover anything close to that level of expense.

"*We* own this car," Martok says. "If I have been unclear on this, please allow me to correct any misperception now, John. Your contribution to this venture has been as great as mine, and I suspect the same will be true of Six soon enough. We are a team, we three, and from this day forward, everything we hold is held in common."

What about my bond? John thinks to say. *Do we hold that in common?* He doesn't, though. Even in a mood like this, there are limits to how far Martok can be pushed. Instead he says, "I appreciate that, Martok. Honestly, I do. Please, though . . . it would comfort me greatly to know how you managed to pay for this vehicle."

Martok's crest darkens and his face falls briefly, but after a moment the grin returns. "Oh, if you must know, John, I did not pay for it at all. It was gifted to me."

John waits a beat for the punch line, then turns to Six. She shrugs. "It's true. Some huge old gray in an Ice River sash rolled up on us while we were on our way back to the station." She gestures behind her. "Just down the road there. Got out of this wreck and said something to Martok in rumble-speak, then patted him on the shoulder and walked away."

John gapes at her, then turns back to Martok and says,

"That's . . . that makes no sense, Martok. What did he say to you?"

"Well," Martok says, "I did not intend to go into these details, for fear of sounding boastful; however . . . it surprises me to say this, though it really should not, but it seems that my fame has preceded me. The worthy who gifted us this carriage, who is, just by the by, the senior administrator of the local Ice River holdings and Chairman of all of the Western Province, first asked if I was in fact Martok Barden née Black Hand. I allowed that I was the very same. He seemed most pleased at this, and asked if I would care to take ownership of this delightfully character-filled trundlecar. I told him that I would of course be very pleased to do so, given that we have a long journey ahead of us, but that my finances were regretfully illiquid at the moment. This, however, did not dissuade him in the slightest. He gave my shoulder a friendly pat, just as our new friend Six said, and turned over the access codes. When I asked to what I should attribute his fine generosity, he said that his clan had great need of one such as I in this area, and that I could consider the car a down payment of sorts, to be credited against future services."

It takes a moment for that to sink in. When it does, John's belly clenches and his heart lurches into a new, faster rhythm. Six is watching him closely, one eyebrow raised. He opens his mouth to speak, closes it, and then tries again. "Did he, ah . . . did he specify what, exactly, he meant by 'future services'?"

"No," Martok says, and his face falls momentarily before brightening again. "However, one can assume. I was hardly shy, after all, in telling the various merchants we dealt with today of our recent good fortune and our plans for our new property. Word must have spread, as it tends to do in such a place. The Ice River clan is powerful here. They hold sway in Lake Town just as surely as the Greatfoots do in Farhome. They certainly have the resources to purchase the sort of leisure experience I plan to provide once we've settled into our new home. I'm sure this fellow will expect a few days of gratis service once our establishment is up and running, which we shall be more than happy to provide him."

It takes John a moment to realize that Martok has just told him how he plans to earn the credits that will be needed to prevent John from ending his days fleeing from a Greatfoot hunting party. He had assumed it would be something ridiculous, but this . . .

"Luxury experience? That's your idea for this property? What does that even mean? I thought we'd be . . . I don't know . . . farming or something?"

Martok laughs. "Farming, John? Tell me, my friend—have you ever farmed?"

John rolls his eyes. "You know I haven't, Martok."

"Yes, I do know that. What you may not know is that I, however, have. In my youth I once spent most of a year planting and harvesting grain, and I can tell you that, here even more so than on our home world, it is absolutely beastly work. The sun is unbearable, and when it fails to shine the mud is worse—and the heat! This may surprise you, but much of the work of farming must occur during the summer months, when anyone possessing the least bit of sense will obviously remain indoors at all costs.

"More to the point, farming requires capital to purchase seeds, fertilizer, and equipment, and the repayment, if it ever comes, is months past the investment. How did you suppose we would recoup the credit needed to pay the note on your bond? Selling the promise of future corn to passersby in the markets?" He lumbers around to the rear of the car, lifts the hatch, and drops his bags inside. As he does, John can see that the space there is filled with packages and parcels—more things purchased with credits that Martok doesn't have, each box and bag another rung on the already horrifyingly tall ladder they'll need to climb to pay John's note two months from now. "No, John. Such a course would be foolish in the extreme. We will extract credits from the scions of the Ice Rivers and the Greatfoots and any other of the wealthy clans that come our way directly. You'll see. Once word of our hospitality spreads, we shall have more credit than ways to spend it."

He slams the hatch, then comes back around to open the rear door for them. He tries to work the handle back into place, twists it one way and then the other, then tries to pull the door open, only to have the handle come away in his hand. "Well," he says after staring at the thing for a moment. "Here is one thing we can do with all the extra credits we'll soon be receiving, I suppose." He drops the broken handle to the curb, then opens the front door, bows grandly, and says, "Come, my friends. Our future awaits."

"You have to admit," Six says as they bid farewell to Lake Town, "this is better than walking."

John isn't entirely sure about that. If they were walking, he wouldn't have quite so large a pit in his stomach right now. He has to admit, though, that the car is much nicer on the inside than he would have suspected. The rear compartment has two deeply padded gray-sized benches, one forward-facing, where he's currently sprawled on his back with one arm tucked behind his head, and one rear-facing, where Six sits cross-legged with her hands on her knees. The windows are tinted, leaving the black-upholstered interior a dim but strangely cozy space. The motor purrs quietly beneath them, almost drowned out by the thump and rumble of the wheels picking their way across broken pavement, and warm air rises silently from vents in the floorboards.

"John may not appreciate the level of comfort we have achieved," Martok says from the front, "but I certainly do."

"Sorry," John says. "I don't mean to seem ungrateful. I just . . ."

"You worry," Martok says. "This is unsurprising, John. You have always worried. Do you recall the summer I came into my birthright? It was just a year or two after the beginning of our partnership. The Black Hand clan is an ancient one, Six, with a storied past. However, our holdings are currently sadly diminished, and my share, when I received it, was barely enough to secure us a rented room and a flagon of ale. John would have had me squirrel my little pile of credits away, and then dole them out to vendors and landlords until they were gone. That might have bought us a bit of comfort, to be sure—but for how long? A year? Perhaps less? I, however . . . I understood that, little though it was, my birthright was capital, and capital is not meant to be hidden away. Capital in the hands of a wise investor is like seeds in the hands of a farmer. Capital is meant to grow.

"My stake was too small, of course, to seed a grand venture of the sort we are currently engaged in—but as chance would have it, there was an election that summer. The old Greatfoot Administrator, Garun Garundi, had somehow managed to *absent* one of his underlings during a staff meeting—unsurprising, really, if the stories of his utter lack of courtesy are to be believed—and had ended with his skull cracked beneath that worthy's foot. The wide expectation was that Garun's deputy, a fellow by the name of Tund who had been waiting patiently for years for someone to make an end of the old tyrant, would be chosen to replace him. However, unknown to most, there was another contender for the office. This one was younger, in the second tier of clan leadership, and from a slightly disreputable Greatfoot branch, but he was as brilliant as Tund was blockheaded, and as charismatic as Tund was dull. I heard the talk in the markets, and as the election approached, all the movement was away from Tund and toward his young challenger. So, I found a mark, and I placed a wager: all of my birthright, every single credit, that Tund would never sit in the Administrator's chair.

"Now, you may think, Six, that you have come into the employ of a madman. John certainly did. All that week as the election approached, he paced around our boarding room, pestering me to find the one I'd entered into this wager with and call it quits—as if that would have been possible! Oh, how he worried! How he moaned! Was there a chance I might have lost? Certainly! But great gains must always keep company with terrible risks. This is simply the way of the world. My counterpart had offered me odds of eight-to-one, which I judged to be more than fair. A victory would convert my birthright from a pittance that would keep us fed and dry for a few measly months to a true nest egg, one which might form the foundation of a fortune. All that was required to grasp that future was a dollop of courage and a steady hand."

"Wait," Six says into the silence that follows after Martok has wound down. "I'm confused. The current Administrator—isn't he named Tund?"

"He is," John says wearily. "Tund received over ninety percent of the voting shares. We lost everything."

"Well," Martok says after a long, awkward pause. "Not quite everything. We still had one another, John. This is the most important thing, no? And in any case, my point was . . . well . . . hmm. I'm not sure I recall exactly what point I was making, but it certainly wasn't that."

"You were trying to say that John worries too much," Six says.

"Ah. Yes! Thank you, Six. That's it exactly. John nearly made himself sick with worry over that election, and as you can see, it was all for nothing. The event came and went, worse came to worst, and despite all that, here we are, on our way to a fortune far greater than that silly wager would have brought us."

John has no idea what to say to that, and after thirty seconds of silence it becomes clear that Six doesn't either. After another minute, Martok begins humming tunelessly to himself. John closes his eyes.

Sleep would be nice now. John hasn't been sleeping well recently. Even before he learned that his life now hangs on Martok's ability to turn a quick profit on a half-baked . . . no, half-baked is far too generous. This idea of his is a raw, wet, ill-conceived ball of dough, sitting on a counter somewhere and being slowly carried away by a swarm of ants. Even before that, though, he'd been having trouble falling asleep at night, and trouble waking up in the morning. His life with Martok has always seemed precarious, always seemed to be just on the verge of collapsing into completely abject poverty. Lately, though, he's seen changes in Martok. As his prospects have dimmed, one by one, his ambitions have seemed to grow in proportion. This newest scheme, from John's perspective, is just the culmination of what had already been a clear trend. He'd imagined that it would end with Martok's head under a constable's heel. In retrospect, though, he probably should have known that it'd be his.

Sleep, unfortunately, clearly isn't going to happen on this trip. They've barely left Lake Town before the roadway, which was cracked and rutted even near the station, becomes something more like a rocky forest path. Peering out the window, John can see that this must once have been a grand highway. There are stretches, here and there, of intact pavement more than twice the width of their car, and past a deep, heavily overgrown ditch to their left he catches glimpses of another road of similar size parallel to their own. Now, though? Grass has grown up through wide cracks in the pavement, as tall as the windows in places, and the trees crowd close to the roadway on both sides, leaning in as if eager to finish the job of reclaiming this strip of artificiality for nature. The fat, knobby wheels of the trundlecar labor up and over cracked slabs and through ruts that more than once threaten to swallow them whole. At one point, Martok has to carefully push off of the roadway entirely and halfway into the ditch to work his way around a fully grown tree that's sprouted up through an eruption in the pavement.

"There's something I don't understand here," John says as Martok eases them fully back onto the road. "This road is huge. I mean, it's bigger than anything even in Farhome. Why would the grays have built something like this and then let it fall apart again?"

Six stares at him blankly for a solid five seconds before saying, "You can't possibly be this stupid."

"I assure you," Martok says from the front, "John is not in any sense stupid. He has, however, perhaps led a more sheltered life than you have, my newly acquired friend."

John's eyes jump from Six's face to the back of Martok's head and then back again. "What are you two talking about?"

"The grays didn't build this road," Six says, her voice dripping with condescension. "Humans did. The reason it's getting swallowed up by the forest is that it's from before, and the grays haven't had any reason to take care of it."

"Six speaks the truth," Martok says. "My understanding is that Lake Town is near the site of what was at one time a sizable human city. This road was presumably a major artery, shuttling goods and humans in between the city and the agricultural lands to the south. It must have been truly impressive before The Fall."

John opens his mouth to respond, but nothing comes, so he finds himself gaping out the window as Martok gooses the engine and they roll on. He'd known, in an abstract sense, that this had been a world of humans prior to the coming of the grays. He'd never really grappled with what that meant, though. If he thought about it at all, he supposed he would have imagined a world full of servitors like himself, just sitting here waiting for someone like the grays to come along and give them a purpose.

He'd never considered that humans might be capable of building something like this.

He's still contemplating that thought when he looks up to see that Six's face has settled into a hard, narrow-eyed grimace. "Hey," he says. "What's with you?"

She stares him down, then cuts her eyes toward Martok and says, "Nothing's with me, pet. I'm totally fine."

Martok glances back over his shoulder, then hastily returns his eyes to the roadway as they shudder through a particularly deep rut. "Is our new friend in distress, John? Sickened by the motion of the car, perhaps? I apologize for the state of the roadway, but unfortunately there is little to be done about it. I could stop, however, if poor Six requires a rest."

Six closes her eyes, and John can see the muscles in her jaws bunching as she grits her teeth. "I do not need a rest," she says, then opens her eyes again to glare at John. "Let's just get where we're going, okay?"

"Very well," Martok says. "Do try not to be sick onto the upholstery, though. I would hate to spoil this fine car so soon after acquiring it."

"I'll do my best," Six says. John raises one eyebrow in question, but she's not looking at him. After a moment's hesitation, he decides not to push the matter.

THREE HOURS AND an unknown distance from Lake Town later, Martok eases the car off of the remains of the highway and down a short curving track that leads to another road. This one is smaller, barely wider than the trundlecar itself, and is if anything in even worse condition, with a wall of trees looming over one side and a steep slope on the other that appears to have stolen half or more of the old roadbed in places.

"You know," Six says as Martok maneuvers around a particularly worrisome gap, pushing close enough to the trees on the car's right side that the trunk of one scrapes along the outside of the door with a squeal of protest, "I'm having a hard time picturing the upper-ups of Lake Town society braving this trip for a *leisure experience*."

"Oh," Martok says, "fear not, Six. Our clientele will not be limited to the rude provincials of Lake Town. Why, I won't be surprised to see the Administrator himself joining us at some point, with his entire retinue in tow! This sort of experience is currently unknown to our society. The services we provide will be entirely unique, and it is a truism of business that that which is unique quickly becomes sought-after."

Six gives John a disbelieving look, then says, "Did you ever think that maybe there's a reason this experience is unknown to your society?"

"Of course!" Martok says, then curses as one wheel slips off the edge of the road and he yanks the wheel hard to the right to keep them from tumbling down the hillside. "The reason, as you say, is that it has never occurred to one of us to provide such a thing. Our people are far too industrious to conceive of an enterprise dedicated entirely to leisure. I, however, have an unusually open mind, and I have researched this topic thoroughly. Resorts such as the one I propose to found were quite common among humans before The Fall, and were by all reports beloved by all." The car jolts as the left front tire drops into a rut, then spins its way back out. Martok glances back at them, then continues.

"It is common wisdom that our society is superior in all ways to the one that your ancestors lost. I, however, believe that, while this is obviously true in *nearly* every respect, there may be some small things that we could learn from your history. In particular, your people seem to have had an unparalleled talent for entertaining themselves—an area where, as I mentioned, my folk may actually be somewhat lacking. No doubt this characteristic, which in abundance will render a people lazy and unproductive, contributed greatly to The Fall. However, all things are poison in too great a dose, and I have concluded that in smaller measure this particular toxin represents one aspect of ancient human culture that we might occasionally be wise to emulate."

"Huh," Six says, and rolls her eyes so aggressively that John wonders whether she might have injured herself. "Humans might actually have been good at something? That's very big of you to admit, Martok."

"Yes," Martok says, "I know. It is a heresy of sorts to suggest that any part of native human culture might have had true merit. Your utter incompetence at managing your own affairs is the primary moral justification for our presence on this world, after all. I, however, believe that it is best to see the world just as it is, and it cannot possibly be that every single aspect of the society your people built here was bad."

"Stop," Six says. "Please. I'm blushing."

John tries to give her a warning look—he knows Martok can

come across as a genial goof at times, but he is still a gray, after all—but Six just folds her arms across her chest and lets her face settle into a smirk.

"At any rate," Martok says, "it is obviously imperative that any reference to human culture should be kept strictly among we three. If anyone inquires as to the origins of our little venture, we shall maintain that the idea was entirely original and entirely mine. Is this clear?"

John recognizes the change in tone, even if Six doesn't. "Yes, Martok," he says. "I understand."

After ten seconds of silence, Martok says, "Six? Are we clear?"

Six sighs, shakes her head, and says, "Of course, Martok. Entirely."

"Excellent." The car slows to a stop, then turns sharply uphill onto what looks to John like little more than a game trail. As they turn, John catches a glimpse through the side window of a hulking structure at the top of the hill, half-overgrown with dead and dying vines. "Because, as you can see, we have arrived."

CHAPTER FIVE

"Well," Six says. "This is . . . something, all right."

"Yes!" Martok says. "Isn't it magnificent?"

John steps out of the car, stands and stretches and looks around.

He has to agree with Six. This place is . . . something.

They're standing at the summit of a broad, forested hill. It's clear that at one point the woods were pushed back well away from the massive brick-and-stone structure that dominates the space, but that must have been many years ago, because the trees are crowded in close now, with a few saplings pressing in almost to the building's walls. Behind them, the hill falls away steeply for two or three hundred meters to what looks through the mostly denuded trees to be a smallish lake. Before them, the house rises up like an apparition, three stories tall and at least twice as wide. A sheltered porch stretches the width of the building, and rows of still-intact windows stare down at them from the top two floors. The door, a solid-looking, arched thing of iron-wrapped wood, looks like it would be at home guarding the entrance to a fortress.

"I believe we can leave our baggage for the moment," Martok says. "Come, friends. Let us see what fate has brought us."

John's first impression was that this place must be a relic from before the coming of the grays. It seems too old and too clearly abandoned not to be. As they step up onto the porch, though, the scale of the place confuses him. He would have expected a human-built place to be built to a human scale, but the door is nearly as large as the entrance of the crèche where they found Six. The handle, a massive black wrought-iron thing, is chest-high on him, and the bottom of the door's arched window is over his head.

As Martok unlocks the door with a tiny metal key and pushes it open, though, John can see that this isn't a gray-built place either. Martok has to stoop slightly to get through the door, and once they're inside his head nearly bangs against a light fixture hanging from the ceiling.

"Behold!" Martok says, and spreads his arms wide. "Our new home!"

"Huh," Six says. "Could be worse, I guess." She runs one finger across the surface of a small table next to the door. It comes away almost clean. "I expected things to be falling apart in here. Looks like someone's been keeping the place up?"

"Of course," Martok says. "Surely you would not expect that I would bring us to a wreck? The Greatfoot from whom I obtained this property assured me that it was livable." He brushes his hand across a bank of switches next to the door, and lights embedded in the ceiling spring to life. "As you can see, it has even been provided with a power cell. We have heat, light, and water. What more could we possibly ask?"

Six crosses the foyer and takes two steps down into what looks like a sitting room. "I don't know. Food?"

Martok grins and lets the door swing closed behind him.

"Fear not, my small friend. All will be provided. I purchased at least two weeks' worth of provisions in Lake Town."

Six folds her arms across her chest and looks up at him. "Okay. What happens after two weeks?"

Martok's voice drops into the gray-rumble register that indicates growing annoyance. "Many things can happen in such a time, Six. Have faith, and perhaps we will all be rewarded." When he sees her dubious expression, he adds, "Food can be delivered at need, you know, and we have the trundlecar to go foraging for ourselves if we absolutely must. Focus, please. We have enough to concern ourselves with in the next two days. Two weeks from now must care for itself for the moment."

Six looks like she has more to say on the topic, but John manages to catch her eye and give his head a short, sharp shake. Her eyes narrow, but after a moment's hesitation, she apparently decides to keep her own counsel. Martok, for his part, isn't able to repress his good mood for more than a few seconds. His grin returns, and he claps his hands and says, "Now, friends, let us fetch our provisions and other assorted treasures. We have a great deal of work to do, and an early finish requires an early start, does it not?"

As he hauls load after load into the house from the implausibly stuffed rear of the trundlecar, John finds himself alternating between despair at how much all the gear and food and linens and knickknacks must have cost, at how much credit will now be funneled to pay off angry Lake Town merchants rather than to pay off John's note, and bewilderment at the scale of his new home.

He's spent his entire life, aside from his time in the crèche, in spaces designed for the height and bulk of a gray. He's used to having to climb up onto furniture, having to stand on tiptoes to see what's on a countertop. This house isn't quite like that. The ceilings are high enough and the doorways wide enough for Martok to pass comfortably for the most part, but he has to duck his head here and there to avoid light fixtures and lintels, and the furniture, while clearly too large to have been built with someone like John in mind, seems to John's eye to be overly dainty for the job of supporting a gray.

"I don't understand," he says as he and Six are struggling to get a crate of protein bricks onto a pantry shelf that's higher than John's head. "Who is this place for?"

Six turns to look at him. "Us, I guess? Or maybe the upper crust of Lake Town society? I hear that's an actual thing."

John snickers at that, then gives the crate one last shove onto the shelf. "Yeah, I heard what Martok said about the business plan. That's not what I meant, though. Somebody built this place. It obviously wasn't humans, and it doesn't look like it was the grays. So?"

Six gives him a half smirk as they turn and head back out to the car. "It's a real mystery, isn't it?"

"You know," John says as they clomp down the too-large stairs from the porch, "I'm getting kind of tired of your *I know things you don't know* routine."

Six shrugs. "Sorry. Maybe you should try knowing more things?"

"Oh please. You're fresh out of the crèche! You don't know anything."

"I dunno," she says. "Seems like I know more than you, mister man-of-the-world."

He catches her sleeve at that and pulls her up short just shy of the trundlecar. Martok is inside the house somewhere. John can hear the basso profundo of him singing to himself in rumble-speak wafting from the open door. "Okay," he says. "Fine. You know everything. You know exactly what's going on here. So, explain it to me. Feel free to use tiny words, so I can understand."

Six breaks into a grin. "Okay, dummy. This is actually very simple. How old do you think this place is?"

"I . . ." John begins, then hesitates and looks around. "That tree," he says. "The one growing up through the walkway on the side of the porch. It's got to be, what, fifty years old at least? Maybe more?"

"Very good. See? You're not so dumb after all. It's probably more than fifty, though. That's an oak. They're slow growers. If it weren't for the fact that this place has stone walls and a slate roof, it'd probably be a wreck by now. So, this house has been abandoned for a minimum of, what, sixty or seventy years? Factor in that the tree wouldn't have jumped up out of the ground the minute the original owners stopped taking care of the grounds, and it's probably at least a bit more than that. Call it around a hundred years. Now. What do we know of that might have happened around a hundred years ago? Something, maybe, that might have coincided with this place being abandoned?"

"You're . . . you think this place dates back to pre-landfall?"

She pats his arm. "Not so dumb at all."

"Wait," John says as she turns away to pull another bag from the back of the car. "That still doesn't explain anything. If this place is pre-landfall, that means it was built by humans, for humans. So why is everything so big?"

"You're so close," Six says as John grabs the other end of the parcel—dried, salted meat, from the smell of it—and they start back around the car. "Keep thinking."

John stops walking. Six almost loses her balance as her thighs bump into the package. "Stop," he says. "Just spit it out, okay? What am I missing?"

Six glares at him and bumps the parcel into him with her belly, then shakes her head and says, "Look, we already decided that this place has been around for a long time, right? It's probably been here longer than the grays have. Before the grays got here, there was only one animal on this planet that was into building houses as far as I know. So this place must have been built by those guys if it was built by anyone, right?"

"So you're saying this is human work?"

Six closes her eyes. When she opens them again, the expression on her face says that she's surprised he hasn't imploded in a blazing burst of idiocy. "Yes, John. Obviously."

"But then—"

"The part that you're missing—the part that should have been totally obvious to you the second that you walked into this place and had a look around—is this: Yes, this house was built by and for humans . . . but not for you and me. Because the two of us, John? We're not human."

When John was a child, years before Martok came into his life, the nursemaids brought a new boy into the crèche. That wasn't ordinarily the way things worked. Babies came into the crèche and were placed into bunk rooms with other babies. Grown children were taken away, and eventually their bunk rooms were emptied and repurposed for the next crop of babies. That was the cycle.

This boy wasn't a baby, though in some ways he acted like one. He was bigger than John—no surprise there, most of the children in his cohort were—but he spoke in a babyish pidgin and didn't seem to understand rumble-speak at all. The nursemaid who introduced him to the bunk room said that his name was Dee, which one of the boys who'd up until then spent most of his spare time tormenting John immediately announced was short for "Dimwit." The nursemaid gave him a warning rumble, but didn't make any effort to actually discipline him. When she was gone, Dee climbed into the bed she'd assigned him, lay down, and pulled the covers up over his head.

At first John was just happy to have someone else around for the bullies to focus their attention on. They were only given so much free, unsupervised time, and the more of it they spent harassing Dee, the less they had left over for John. Occasionally, John even joined in the teasing, in a half-hearted way. He had a vague idea that he might be able to worm his way onto the good side of the bully / victim divide, and for a while it almost seemed to be working. The worst of his tormentors, a tall, lanky, dark-haired boy named Kel, became so focused on Dee for a while that he seemed to have forgotten about John entirely. A few of his underlings still gave John grief from time to time, but without Kel's leadership their bullying had an almost perfunctory feel to it.

Dee, for his part, didn't seem much to care what Kel said or did. He ignored the verbal barbs, to the extent that John sometimes wondered how much of them he actually understood, and he seemed to shrug off much of the physical abuse as well. Mostly that was limited to small insults that wouldn't leave a mark and that the nursemaids wouldn't notice—shoulder shoves when Kel passed him coming in or out of the bathroom, the occasional finger-flick to the back of Dee's ear, and once in a while an effort to trip Dee coming up or down the stairs. For a dimwit, though, Dee was surprisingly nimble, and those efforts never seemed to succeed.

That's where things stood on a cold, dark winter morning, a week past the longest night, when the nursemaid who was doling out their breakfasts announced that today was Dee's molt-day. Humans didn't have a real molt-day, obviously, but the celebration was a big part of gray culture, and so the nursemaids assigned each of them a day once every eighteen months or so on what seemed to John to be a completely arbitrary schedule.

A gray on his molt-day was a petty tyrant. He could ask for anything, and by tradition it had to be given to him. This occasionally led to predictably ridiculous outcomes, with one gray, for example, demanding the codes to his neighbor's trundlecar on his molt-day, and the other demanding it back when his came along. Inter-clan feuds had begun over molt-day shenanigans, and the unreasonable demand was a staple of gray storytelling.

The children in John's crèche, for obvious reasons, weren't given quite so much latitude, but they were allowed to request a treat of their choice at breakfast. Dee asked for a cream pot, a rare bit of fatty sweetness that the nursemaids ordinarily only doled out in tiny servings and on special occasions. He was carrying it back to the common table, a blissful smile plastered across his face and his eyes pinned to the treasure in his hands, when Kel finally succeeded in tripping him.

There was a long moment of silence after the sharp crack of Dee's bowl shattering against the floor. Dee was sprawled on his belly, hands splayed out in front of him, face spattered with cream. Kel, who was sitting at the end of the bench with his back to the table, looked down at him and snickered. After a moment, a few of his minions joined in. Dee got slowly to his feet. He turned to face Kel, grabbed him by the front of his shirt, and lifted him half-off the bench.

Kel tried to push him away with one hand and swatted ineffectually at Dee's head with the other, but Dee hardly seemed to notice. He slammed Kel's head against the table, lifted him up, and then did it again. He might have kept going, might have literally beaten Kel to death, if the nursemaid hadn't stepped in, pulled Kel out of his grasp, and lifted Dee up with one massive hand around his neck.

"It wasn't his fault!" John found himself saying. "You can't punish him! He was *absent*!"

The nursemaid turned to look at him. Dee was flailing in her grasp, but already his movements were losing purpose, devolving toward random spasms. "Humans," she rumbled as Dee's eyes bulged and his lips turned blue, "do not *absent*." John saw her grip tighten. "Humans do not *fight*." She squeezed again, and something inside Dee audibly snapped. "Humans must be *good*." She held John's gaze until Dee stopped moving, then turned and walked out of the room, Dee's limp form still dangling from her hand.

IT'S BEEN A long while since John has thought about Dee. Some things are best forgotten, after all. He thinks about him now, though, as he's struggling to shove another box of provisions onto another too-high shelf. At the time he'd thought there was something wrong with Dee that made him seem years younger than the rest of the children in their cohort despite his size. What if that wasn't it, though? What if he *was* years younger? He was as tall as Kel, and at least in that moment he seemed impossibly strong. If he had been allowed to grow up, would he have been suited to this place?

If he'd been allowed to grow up, would the nursemaid have been able to squeeze the life out of him quite so easily?

That idea skitters around inside John's head like a drop of water on a hot griddle. Humans are docile. Humans are weak. Nearly every moment of John's life has reinforced those two facts in one way or another. But what if . . .

No, even in the privacy of his own skull John can't bring

himself to finish that thought. Even contemplating it, he feels the brush of the nursemaid's three-fingered hand on the back of his neck. He shudders, shakes his head clear, and gives the box he's been fighting with one last shove. The rumble of Martok's singing follows him out the door as he goes to fetch another.

CHAPTER SIX

"Good news!" Martok announces over breakfast the next morning. "We've hardly begun to put this place in order, and already we are set to receive our first client!"

The three of them are in the great room that takes up much of the first floor of the house, seated at a thick cherrywood table big enough for a dozen grays. Above the table, a brass light fixture hanging from the ceiling pushes back gamely against the still-dark winter morning, but the dark-stained walls drink up the light. Martok is perched delicately on a sturdy-looking wooden chair that seems to be holding up well enough under his bulk despite the occasional squeal of protesting joints when he shifts his weight or leans into the backrest. John and Six have to kneel on their chairs to reach their plates, and as he picks at his salted meat and gruel, John can't help but wonder how someone who could sit comfortably at this table might measure up to Martok.

"A client?" Six says around a mouthful of food. "Are you serious?"

Martok grins and takes off half a protein brick in one massive bite. "Oh, entirely," he says, and drains what's left of the flagon of ale he's poured himself for breakfast while John chases a particularly salty bit of gristle with a sip of lukewarm water. "Not half an hour ago I received a message to that effect from my new friend, the good Chairman Sinta."

"The one who gave you the trundlecar?" Six asks.

"The very same! The good Chairman is in fact the grandest of grandees in Lake Town's society, nearly equal in stature here to Chief Administrator Tund himself. His word holds sway over all of the Western Province, more or less. If you recall, he told me at that time that the car should be thought of as both a gift and as a down payment of sorts. It seems now that he could not bring himself to wait even a day to collect! You see, John? Since the moment I first told you about this opportunity, you have doubted me. Why, if you can believe it, at times you almost made me doubt myself! Here, though, we have proof of the soundness of my concept, do we not? All we need to do is make sure that this fellow that the good Chairman sends to us has a deeply moving and spiritual experience here in our little refuge from the mundanity of frontier life, and your note is as good as paid!"

"A deeply moving spiritual experience?" Six says. "How do you plan to provide that? Are we building a temple? Or, like, an altar? Because I have to warn you, I don't know jack about carpentry."

John winces at that, but Martok seems in too good a mood to take offense at her tone.

"No," Martok says. "No temples. No altars. No sacrifices to the gods of either my people or of yours. We have the lake here, and we have the trees. We have the birds and the fish and the crawling things in the forest. And, let us not forget, we have this magnificent monument to the things that your people were once capable of. It is a flaw of my kind that we seldom leave our little enclaves. Please trust me when I say that after a day or two of relaxation in this place, our guests will find themselves transformed." He finishes the last of his breakfast in one great bite, chews and swallows and pushes to his feet as his chair groans in complaint. "Why, I've been here less than a day, and already I feel myself changing. Don't you, my friends?"

With that, he lumbers across the room and into the hallway, humming to himself in a register so low that John feels it deep in his chest, tugging at his heart and leaving him struggling for breath.

"So," Six says as they're carrying the breakfast dishes to the kitchen. "Martok is crazy, right? That's the deal here? I got picked up by a lunatic?"

John shoots her a look, but doesn't answer.

"Oh, don't get me wrong," she says as she climbs up onto a stool in front of the sink and starts running the water. "I'm not complaining. I definitely had a date with the underside of some nursemaid's foot in my future when he pulled me out of that crèche. I am kind of wondering, though, whether that date might have just gotten delayed."

"I've been with Martok for a long time," John says as he climbs up beside her. "I know he seems a little . . ."

"Delusional?"

"Enthusiastic. I was going to say enthusiastic. He gets worked up about things, and maybe doesn't think them all the way through before he acts. It gets him into trouble sometimes. It gets *us* into trouble sometimes." He takes the first clean plate from Six and wipes it dry while she washes the next. "The thing is, though . . . look, you're fresh out of the crèche. You haven't seen the way some grays treat their employees. Martok never—"

"I'm not stupid," Six says, and hands him the second plate. "I may not have been out in the world much yet, but I keep my eyes open. When they put us on display, I always knew they weren't there for me, but I paid attention anyway. I saw the same grays come back to the crèche again and again. Martok's new best friend, Sinta? He took at least a dozen of us over the past couple of years. Why do you suppose he came all the way from Lake Town to find bondsmen? I'm guessing it was because whatever he was doing with them was gross enough that even the other grays would have disapproved. It definitely wasn't because he's putting together a big, happy human family."

"Right," John says. "That's exactly what I mean. Martok isn't like that. If I'm hungry, it's because he's hungry. If I'm cold, it's because he's cold. If I'm—"

"Grays don't get cold, John."

He flicks his towel at her, but she blocks it with the third plate and then hands it to him to dry.

"You know what I mean. And the big thing is, Martok doesn't use physical discipline—or at least he never has with me. I only know what I've seen in the markets and boardinghouses, but I don't get the impression that many grays can say that." He sets the last plate aside, wipes his hands on the wet towel, and steps down to the floor. "What's gonna happen when some Ice River bigwig shows up here expecting us to . . . I don't know . . . give him a foot rub or something? Your guess is as good as mine. Whatever disaster follows, though, I can promise you this: Martok won't take it out on us."

Six dries her own hands, then hops down and looks up at him. "And what happens in two months when he can't pay your note?"

John looks at her for a long moment, eyes blank and jaw set, before saying, "Well, I guess then he'll be your problem, won't he?"

Then he walks out of the room without waiting for a response.

Later, as he's sitting on the porch watching two squirrels chase one another up and down the trunk of one of the trees in the yard, John finds himself pondering the question of how honest his defense of Martok actually was. It's true enough that Martok has never abused him, and from the impressions he's gained from the few other humans he's been able to interact with over the years, that seems to be a rarity. Still, though, he can't help but wonder if he might have been better off in the employ of a Greatfoot administrator or one of the merchants in the markets. Would that have meant the occasional beating? Probably. Would he have been killed by now in some offhand way, like the children Chairman Sinta took from Six's crèche? Possibly. Either way, though, he wouldn't be where he is now, staring down the probability of dying in an unusually unpleasant way at the hands of an unusually unpleasant gray.

It's a moot point, of course. The merchants and administrators were never interested in taking on John's bond. His alternative to leaving the crèche with Martok was aging out and ending in a garbage midden with a crushed skull. It seems that was Six's next option as well. All in all, they'd probably both do well to think about practicing gratitude rather than moaning about Martok's eccentricities.

John, in particular, would probably do well to do everything he can to make sure that Martok's half-assed plans for this place come to some semblance of fruition. Martok expects his guests to have a spiritual experience here, a first communion with nature for people who have literally never left their little cities. It occurs to John that maybe with the time he has now he should do a bit of exploring in the nature that surrounds them, to see if there's anything worth communing with.

A light snow is falling, fat white flakes drifting down through the still air in ones and twos, then vanishing when they touch the not-quite-freezing ground. John gets to his feet and steps down off the porch and into the yard. Tufts of brown grass poke up through the ankle-deep drifts of dead leaves near the house, but as he walks deeper into the trees, the ground is increasingly nothing but rotted leaves and bare soil.

It occurs to John now that he's never been in a real forest before. There's a wooded park on the outskirts of Farhome where Martok used to take him walking from time to time—they even spent several cold, wet nights sleeping there at one point when Martok found himself in between boarding rooms—but as he runs his hand down along the scaly bark of a massive sugar maple here, John realizes that that place, which he thought at the time was entirely and terrifyingly wild, was to these woods as he and Six are to the long-gone humans who must have built their new home. The trees in the park were mostly flowering cherries, magnolias, and dogwoods. They were planted in neat rows, with paved paths running through them. The trees here are haphazardly placed, sprouting up wherever they can find a bit of soil and sun and then fighting one another for space in the canopy. The losers stand bare and rotting or lean drunkenly on their healthier neighbors, massive root balls torn half-out of the ground.

John walks on, winding his way through the sparse underbrush, hands shoved deep into his jacket pockets. He's following what seems to be a path of sorts, although at times he thinks he might be imagining that. It leads him eventually to a house-sized rock jutting up out of the ground. From there the path dips into a narrow, shadowed walkway between the rock and a dense thicket of thornbushes. It looks dangerous down there, and despite the warmth of his coat and hat John feels a shiver run down his spine. He turns to look back at the house . . .

The house isn't there.

John's heart lurches into a faster rhythm. How long has he been walking? It couldn't have been more than a few minutes. He just needs to follow the path back the way he came. He takes two hesitant steps away from the boulder. He came past that oak, didn't he? Or did he? He remembers seeing the rock, but from what direction, exactly? He stops, takes a deep breath, and turns a full circle, looking for some hint of the path he followed here.

There is none, of course. No human has walked through these woods in a hundred years. Why would there be a path?

"Oh," he says aloud. "Oh. This isn't good."

He closes his eyes and takes a deep breath in, holds it, and then lets it out slowly. When he opens them again, it's as if he's looking at these woods for the first time. He hasn't the slightest idea which way leads back to the house, and which leads deeper and deeper into the forest where he will presumably starve or freeze to death or be eaten by a bear. He puts his back to the rock, cups his hands to his mouth, and calls out, *"Six! Hello? Martok? Can you hear me?"*

He waits then, holding his breath. Nothing. He breathes out and in to try again when he hears an unfamiliar voice, close behind him.

"Well. What do we have here?"

John freezes, feeling suddenly like a mouse under the eyes of a hawk. He hears the soft crunch of boots on rock.

"Looks like our friend is back," says a different, deeper voice.

John turns slowly, hands open and held out to his sides. He looks up to see a man and a woman crouched on the top of the rock, looking down at him. They're wearing clothes like none he's seen before, all rough brown leather and lined with fur. Their skin is a few shades darker than his, their hair near-identical masses of thick black curls pulled back from their faces with thin leather bands.

The woman is huge. Even from here John can see that she's at least half a meter taller than he is, and probably more. The man is even bigger.

They're both carrying bows with arrows nocked. The woman stands and glares down at him. "What about it, little man? Are you Daro's new pet? Didn't he tell you what happened to the last one?"

"I don't know what you're talking about," John says, being careful to keep his hands open and visible. "I don't know anyone named Daro."

The woman grins, but the look in her eyes makes it more like a baring of teeth. "Are you sure? My understanding was that he's an important person. Third nephew to the Chief Administrator?" She draws her bow back and takes careful aim at John's forehead. "Is this ringing any bells?"

He's already drawn breath to say that no, it's not ringing any bells, and also to beg this woman to please not skewer him, when he realizes with a start that he has, in fact, heard the name Daro before. Daro Lia née Greatfoot. Third nephew to the Chief Administrator? Maybe. Martok didn't mention that part. In one great rush, everything that's happened to upend John's life over the past few days suddenly becomes clear—and no sooner have the thoughts formed in his head than they come gushing out of his mouth.

"Oh. Oh gods. You're *ferals*. That's why Daro sold Martok this property for a promise and a bond. I knew Martok was the fool in this somehow, but I didn't think . . . I mean, you're not . . . how are you . . . how . . ."

"Oh, for shit's sake," the man says. "He's gonna start crying."

"Oy," the woman says as she lowers her bow and releases the tension on the string. "Have a little dignity, huh?"

John drops his hands to his sides and glowers up at them. "I'm not crying. I'm just confused. I mean, you're not supposed to be here. You're supposed to be *extinct*."

The woman barks out a short, humorless laugh, then crouches and hops down off the rock, drops what seems to John to be an alarming distance, and lands in a feline crouch before straightening. "Is that what they teach you in the breeding pens? That we're gone?"

"Wishful thinking," the man says. He sits, his impossibly long legs dangling off the edge of the rock, and grins down at them. "They think if they repeat it to themselves often enough, it'll be true."

"Daro knew you were here," John says. "He must have . . . did you meet him? Did you talk to him?"

"We're still alive, and so is he," the man says. "Does that answer your question?"

"I'm pretty sure he at least suspected we were here," the woman says. She pulls a long knife from her belt and slings her bow across her shoulders. "After a few things disappeared from the house while he was away last winter, he sent his pets out hunting for us." She points the tip of the knife at John. "Is that what you're doing now, little man? Hunting us?"

"I'm not armed," John says, and shows her his open hands. "Also, I have a name. It's John."

He'd had a vague idea that giving her his name would establish some sort of bond between them—not enough to get him invited to her molt-day party, maybe, but with any luck enough to keep her from gutting him on the spot. Her response doesn't give him much confidence that he was right about that. She does something with her hand, too quick for John's eye to follow, that causes the knife to spin around and then snap back into place with the point even closer to his nose than it'd been before.

"John, huh? Well tell me, *John*. What the fuck are you doing in my woods?"

John stammers, his eyes fixed on the tip of the knife, until the man on the rock bursts out laughing and says, "Come on, Dana. Look at him. He's no hunter."

The woman—Dana, apparently—glances back at him, then visibly relaxes. She spins the knife around again, fingers dancing across the hilt, and slams it back into its sheath at her waist. "Fair enough. Could still be a scout, though, or a spy. He wouldn't be here if there weren't a gray in the lake house again, and there's no way of looking that's gonna make that good."

The man puts his hands on the rock beside him, gives himself a shove, and drops down beside her. Now that they're on the same level, John can see that while this man—this *human*—lacks Martok's bulk, they're nearly of a height. The man drops to one knee in front of John. "What my friend just said there? That's some true facts, John. Old Daro made things ugly for us when he was in the lake house, and we made them uglier for him. You can see how us finding another gray's pet wandering around in our woods might set us a bit on edge, yeah?"

"I'm not a *pet*," John says, while at the same time remembering that Six had called him that as well. "I am a bonded employee of Martok Barden née Black Hand. He recently purchased this property from Daro Lia née Greatfoot." He folds his arms across his chest and sets his jaw. "Which is to say, *you* are in *his* woods, not the other way around."

Dana grins at that. "Look at that, Tanner. He's got a little fire in him after all." She draws the knife again, tosses it into the air, and catches it by the hilt. "We're killing him now, right?"

CHAPTER SEVEN

John was eleven years old the first time someone threatened to kill him. One of the nursemaids, an ancient, withered gray named Rema Ba née Green Hills, had taken John and three other boys in his cohort to the market. They were there nominally to select a special treat for the next day's breakfast, which was to celebrate the arrival of three new babies to the crèche, but in truth they were mostly there to carry Rema's bags and parcels. She could barely manage to drag her own bulk around town by that point, and carrying any sort of burden was for her more or less out of the question.

John, being the smallest of Rema's four helpers, was naturally given the bulkiest parcel to carry—a wooden crate of protein bricks that was big enough that he could barely get his arms around it, and heavy enough that his back was screaming at him almost as soon as he'd picked it up. More importantly, the side of his face was pressed against the wood of the crate as he carried it, and he wasn't able to see where he was going. He tried to protest, but Rema was near-deaf even by gray standards and didn't seem to hear him, while the other boys clearly found his struggles hilarious.

This went on for five minutes or so, with Rema shuffling ahead of him through the market, occasionally rumbling for the boys to keep up, keep up, while John staggered along behind her, and the other three followed after, carrying their own packages slung over their shoulders and shouting out laughing directions to John, telling him to look out for that tent pole here or watch the step-down there. It ended in the worst possible way, with John walking the sharp corner at the front of the crate directly into the rear-end of a gray who was busy arguing with a human vendor over the price of a new handheld.

What happened next might have been funny under different circumstances. The gray bellowed like a gored ox, arched his back, and flailed his arms so wildly that he brought down one of the supports of the vendor's stand. The vendor shrieked and jumped back as his display collapsed, John dropped his crate and looked up in horror at the gray's affronted anus, and his three companions burst out in laughter and scattered.

The gray spun around then to see what had violated him. He reared back and kicked the crate, which exploded in a shower of splintered wood and shattered protein bricks. That accomplished, he turned his attention to John, who was crouched on the sidewalk with his arms protecting his head.

"You!" he rumbled. "You did this?"

John looked up at him, opened his mouth to stammer out an apology, but before he could work out what to say, Rema was there, stomping her feet in impotent fury.

"Ho, there, young fellow! You've destroyed my parcel!"

The gray turned to face her, the look on his face a mix of confusion and anger. "Did I? Well, perhaps I did, old crone. Your parcel near destroyed my asshole!"

A crowd was gathering now, grays and bondsmen alike. All of them were taking care to keep their distance, though. When one gray became *absent*, it was all too easy for others nearby to be sucked down with them like flotsam following a sinking ship. An argument could easily turn into a riot, and a riot could just as quickly turn into a bloodbath.

"Your asshole is none of my concern," Rema said. "You'll pay for that parcel, though, or fetch me a new one. I've business to attend to, and no time for your nonsense."

The other gray's crest darkened and his shoulders swelled, blood rushing into his muscles and away from his brain. "I'll do neither, crone. I'll—"

"It wasn't her fault, nor yours," another gray said, and stepped out of the ring of bodies that now surrounded them. This one was bigger than the one John had hit, and he towered over Rema. He wore the blue sash of a constable. "It was him that injured you. I saw it happen." He gestured toward John. "Settle, now, both of you. If there's any violence to be done, it'll be done to him."

Rema peered up at the constable with squinted eyes, as if she'd never seen such a person before. The other gray took three deep, huffing breaths, visibly calming himself, then said, "Fair enough, Constable. I'll stomp him flat, and we'll consider it done."

The constable tilted his head in agreement, then turned to John and said, "Head on the ground, boy. Let's make this quick."

John looked up at him, eyes wide and mouth gaping. Thirty seconds ago he'd been worried about dropping the crate and earning a scolding from Rema. Was it really possible he was going to *die* now? He wanted to say . . . something . . . but his mouth was a desert and his mind was a howling void. The constable bared his tusks and said, "Come, now, boy. Don't make this harder on yourself than it needs to be." The other gray stepped over the wreckage of the crate and raised his foot.

"Now, just one moment," Rema said. "There is still the matter of my parcel."

The gray hesitated, then turned to face her. "Your what?"

"My parcel," she said, "which you destroyed." She turned to the constable. "This parcel, sir, was my property. My *asset*, if you will, and this oaf has utterly destroyed it. This boy is also my asset, or at any rate that of my crèche, as we hope to bond him out for a good fee someday soon. Now, I will concede that the oaf has also suffered damage to a valued asset." She looked to the other gray, then back to the constable. "I'm referring to his asshole. You see?"

"Yes," the constable said. "I see. Do you have a point, madam?"

"I do," Rema said. "At this moment, both he and I have suffered a loss. It seems to me, then, that we are evenly matched. If he destroys this boy, however, and robs my crèche of his future value, then I will have come out the worse for it. I shan't stand for this, you see?"

The constable ran his hands back over his crest, then said, "What do you propose, then? I can't leave a citizen with a grievance here."

"Well," she said, after considering, "if the oaf were to fetch me a new crate of protein bricks, paid for with his own credit, and then carry it back to the crèche for me, I suppose I would consider that just recompense. In that case, I should certainly withdraw my objection to his flattening the boy."

The constable looked to the other gray. "Is this acceptable to you, citizen?"

The gray looked back and forth between them. "How far is your crèche?"

"Oh," Rema said, "it's quite a ways."

The other gray's eyes went from her to the constable, then down to John, where they stayed for what felt like an impossibly long while before he said, "Bah. I have better things to do." He took one last kick at the remnants of the protein bricks, scattering what was left of them to powder, and then turned and stalked away.

Rema waited until he was gone, then said, "Gather yourself, boy. We still have errands to run."

John can't help but remember that afternoon as Dana and Tanner try to decide whether to kill him here and now, take him back to the hole, wherever or whatever that is, and kill him there, or turn him loose, possibly after removing his tongue so that he won't be able to tell Martok that there are feral humans in his woods. He thinks at first that Tanner might be playing the role of Rema, feigning indifference to his death in order to work Dana around to thinking it was her own idea to let him live. It quickly becomes apparent, though, that Tanner really is indifferent to John's death, and that his only points of hesitation about killing him revolve around his own convenience, and secondarily the remote possibility that Martok might for some reason decide to avenge him.

"Look," Dana says, "we killed three of Daro's pets—"

"Four," Tanner says. "Don't forget the one I drowned in the creek."

Dana rolls the knife across the backs of her fingers, catches it by the hilt, and brings it around to point at Tanner. "You're making my point for me. We killed *four* of his, and what did he do? Packed up and ran, that's what. If we make this gory enough, maybe we can get this new gray to bail after one."

"If we make it gory enough," Tanner says, "maybe we convince him to bring in the spiders."

A cloud crosses Dana's face at that last word, and John can almost imagine that he sees a shudder run down Tanner's spine as well. He doesn't actually think there's any possibility that Martok would do what they're saying, but the ferals' fear that he might is a branch he can grasp to pull himself out of the current. All he knows of the spiders are the things that everyone knows—that they're the things the grays used to seize this planet from the remnants of humanity after The Fall, that they're almost as much of a horror to the grays themselves as they are to their victims, and that an infestation is not something to be undertaken lightly or without immense expense. To that list now, though, he adds the following: They're his best hope of getting out of this alive.

"If I could," John says, "you should know—"

"Quiet!" Dana says, and snaps the knife back around in an arc that ends a finger's-width from the tip of John's nose. "Grown-ups are talking here."

"Oh, let him speak," Tanner says, and pushes the blade down and away with one hand. "Maybe he's got something useful to say."

John swallows hard, and his eyes flicker from Tanner to Dana and back. Neither of them looks remotely sympathetic, and he has no illusions that any sort of appeal to their common humanity is likely to help him here. So, what does that leave him?

Once again, it looks like it's time to bluff.

"Thank you, sir. As I was saying, you should know that my relationship with Martok Barden née Black Hand is not remotely like whatever relationship this Daro may have had with his employees. I know how most grays treat us—like disposable commodities, easily lost and easily replaced—and I can understand why you might think Martok might write my death off as a business cost and maybe decide to cut his losses. The thing you have to understand, though, is that Martok and I have been together, just the two of us, for more than twelve years. He's said many times that I'm not an employee to him. I'm his family. On this world, I'm his *only* family. If you kill me, he *will* seek vengeance."

Dana rolls her eyes and opens her mouth to speak, and John realizes that he probably has seconds at most to save himself.

"And," he says, the words tumbling out of him now, "*and* he has the means and more to make good on his desire. Martok is an enforcer. Do you know what that means?" He hurries on without waiting for a response. "It means he's one of the very few who can kill another gray without becoming *absent*. It means he has wealth, and power, and access to weapons. And yes, it means he has access to spiders, and that he won't hesitate to call on them if you drive him to it."

The two of them stare at him now, Tanner with his arms crossed and head tilted to one side, Dana with the hilt of her knife spinning first one way and then the other across the backs of her fingers in a way that seems impossible to John but that apparently doesn't even require conscious attention from her. After a span of time that feels like an eternity to John but is probably closer to five or ten seconds, Dana says, "I think he's full of shit."

"Hmm," Tanner says. "Maybe. What if he's not, though?"

"I assure you," John says, "I am not—" He cuts off abruptly as the knife snaps around and the flat of the blade raps against the side of his head.

"Enough," Dana says. "You said your piece. We don't need to hear anything more from you."

Tanner sighs. "You don't need to be a dick about this, Dana. None of this is his fault. If we have to kill him, we have to kill him, but in the meantime it doesn't hurt to be nice."

"Thank you," John says, "I just wanted—"

"I didn't mean you should start talking again. I just meant Dana didn't need to smack you around." Tanner turns back to Dana. "Like I said, I don't disagree that he's probably lying. Convincing us that his owner gives two shits if he lives or dies is the only way he's getting out of this in one piece. He knows that as well as we do. On the other hand, though, we've got a pretty heavy downside risk here, don't we? You've never seen the spiders. You don't know what they can do. We had a bigger, stronger community at Owasco than we've got here, and I'm the only one who got out when they came through. You really want to take a chance on bringing those things down on us?"

Dana opens her mouth to reply, then bites her lower lip and looks down at John, knife blade tapping absently against her thigh. "Okay," she says finally. "So what do you propose? If we kill him now and make it gross, maybe his owner gets spooked and runs, or maybe his owner gets spooked and calls in the monsters. If we let him go, maybe he keeps his mouth shut and everything is fine, or maybe he blabs and his owner gets spooked and calls in the monsters. If we disappear him, maybe his owner doesn't give a shit and everything is fine, or maybe he really does care about him and he comes looking, finds the hole, and calls in the monsters. Tell me, Tanner, what's the option that keeps us safe here?"

"Please," John says into the silence that follows. "Can I speak?"

Dana glances over at Tanner, then grimaces and says, "Sure, John. Give us your best pitch."

"Okay," John says. "Okay. Look. First, as I said, Martok is dangerous. You don't want to be on his bad side. On the other hand, though, he's also a decent person, and he's not intending to expand his presence here. Daro, from what I understand, thought he could build a gray settlement around the lake. That's why he sent his employees after you. Martok, though? He just wants to run a guesthouse. He doesn't have any interest in building more or spreading out into your land. As long as you keep your distance, there's no reason he'd ever find out that you're here. So maybe we could just . . . I don't know . . . be neighbors?"

"A guesthouse?" Tanner asks, one eyebrow raised.

"That's great," Dana says without waiting for John to answer. "That presupposes, though, that we trust you not to *tell* him that we're here. That's the bridge I'm having a whole lot of trouble crossing."

As she says this, the knife slides back into its sheath, and for the first time since she originally suggested killing him, John feels a tiny trickle of hope. "Why would I tell him? Until a few minutes ago I didn't know that you . . . that people like you . . . I thought you were all gone. Wiped out. And for all I know right now, you might be the last ones left. You think I want to end that? You think I *like* feeling like we're barely tolerated guests on our own world? If you weren't talking about chopping me up, this would be the greatest moment of my life."

Tanner looks at him with narrowed eyes for a long moment, then turns to Dana and says, "Are you buying this?"

She shakes her head, but the knife stays where it is. "Not really. I wonder, though . . ." She trails off, then drops to one knee in front of John and says, "Hey. Little man. John. Believe it or not, I don't actually want to kill you. None of what's happening here is your fault, and of all the fucked-up things the grays have done to this planet over the last hundred years, what they did to you people is probably the worst. The thing is, though, I've got real, actual humans who are depending on me. Little kids. Old people. A *community*. Just like you said, maybe the very last *human* community left on this planet. You understand? I can't let anything happen to them, and if killing you and mutilating your body is what I have to do to make sure they stay safe, then that's what I'll do. I need you to convince me that letting you live is the safest path. Can you do that?"

John nods. He opens his mouth to respond, but then finds that he's run out of words. She's right there, a half-head shorter than him on one knee, waiting for him to give her something to let them both walk away from this place, and he can't. He simply can't. The truth is, if he were in her place, he'd probably already have used the knife. After ten seconds of silence, Dana sighs and gets to her feet. She turns to Tanner, arms folded across her chest.

"Look. Are we doing this?"

Tanner looks down at John. "Anything else to say, little man?"

John shakes his head. He can already feel the blade dragging across his throat.

Tanner looks back to Dana and shrugs. "Your call, homie."

The wind has kicked up now, and it's started snowing in earnest. A shiver runs from the top of John's head to the base of his spine. Dana's fingers drum on the knife's hilt as she stares down at him. John stares back, unblinking, until finally she scowls and says, "You know what? Fuck it." She pulls her hood up, turns on her heel, and stalks away. Tanner watches her go, then looks down at John, winks, and follows her. It's only a few seconds before they're both lost in the snow, and John finds himself alone once again.

CHAPTER EIGHT

"John? Where the hell have you been all day? Martok has been looking for you."

John scowls at Six as he closes the door behind him. She's standing in the middle of the hallway leading to the kitchen, arms folded across her chest and eyes narrowed to slits. It's well into the afternoon now, and John is red-faced and chilled to the bone after spending hours trying to find his way back from the rock where he met Dana and Tanner. In the end, he was embarrassed to see that he'd never been more than four or five hundred meters away, but the trees and the thick falling snow were disorienting in a way he'd never experienced before, and in nearly equal measure he's grateful to have found his way home at all.

"I was in the woods," he says. "I thought I'd take a little walk, just to see what I could see, and I got lost. I've been wandering around out there forever. For a while, I thought I'd be walking in circles in the snow until I froze to death."

"Yeah, well, when Martok gets done with you, you might wish that you had. Our guest is supposed to be arriving sometime in the next couple of days, and Martok is frantic to have this place looking appealingly rustic or whatever before he gets here. He's been storming around like a lunatic, yelling at me to *fetch this* and *pick up that* and *by the way where is John? Have you seen John? Please go find John*. I tried to explain to him that I am not your nursemaid and that I had no idea where you had gotten yourself to, but he didn't seem to buy it. So, I would suggest that you go find him now, explain that you're an idiot and that this is in no way my fault, and beg him not to kill you, because I'm guessing that's about where he is by now."

John pulls off his hat, shakes the snow off of it to melt on the shiny-clean hardwood floor of the foyer, and stuffs it into the pocket of his jacket. "Martok isn't going to kill me, because—and I get that this is probably a foreign concept to you—Martok likes me. Do you know where he is right now?"

"Upstairs, trying to get one of the rooms ready to host a gray. Good luck. I think you might be in for a surprise, as far as how much he likes you goes."

With that, she turns away and stalks back into the kitchen. John watches her go, rubs his face with both hands, sighs, and starts up the stairs.

JOHN FOLLOWS THE rumble of Martok's tuneless humming to the bedroom at the far end of the upstairs hallway. He opens the door to find Martok inside, staring down at the bent and twisted remains of a black metal bed frame. The mattress and box springs are leaned against the wall next to the only window, which looks out over the porch and into the woods beyond. John waits a beat to see if Martok has noticed his arrival, then knocks on the open door.

"Ah, John!" Martok says, and spreads his arms in welcome. "Six and I have been wondering where you've been today. She seemed to believe that you were shirking, but I assured her that you would never, and that you must be hard at work, just as we have been. Tell me, what have you accomplished?"

"Oh," John says as he steps into the room. "Absolutely. I've been . . . um . . . outside, and . . . what do you have going on here, Martok? Problems with the bed?"

Martok curses in rumble-speak, then says, "It seems so. The chairs in this place have proven to possess the fortitude to support me, and the bed in the largest room was brought here by our friend Daro Lia née Greatfoot. Those in our guest rooms, however, appear to be made of weaker stuff. I thought to test this one against my weight, and you can see the outcome. The arrival of our first guest is imminent. If we wish to have a second, we cannot have this one sleeping on the floor."

"No," John says. "No, we definitely can't." He edges past Martok and crouches down next to the ruined frame. "I think . . ." He lifts one side rail, and sees immediately where the problem lies. "I think we just need to put some wooden blocks under the crossbars. You see? They're just held together in the middle with a couple of rivets. That's what gave way. If we put some support under the weak point it should hold up fine."

Martok squats down next to him and squints as John points out the break point. The grays all have terrible eyesight by human standards, and Martok's is poor even for a gray. "I will confess that I fail to see what you mean, but I trust your judgment, John. Tell me, though—where would we find such supports?"

"I could cut a few rounds from one of the downed trees out in the yard, for the moment. They'll be under the bed, so our guest isn't going to see them. If we want something nicer later, I guess we can pick up some hardwood blocks in Lake Town."

"Ha!" Martok says, and claps John's back hard enough that he has to catch himself with one hand against the floor to keep from falling face-first into the bed frame. "You see? We must make a success of this venture, John, because I clearly could not live a day without you. Make enough supports for all of the beds in the guest rooms. Take Six with you if you think she might help. I shall continue to tidy up here, and when you've finished your work we will gather downstairs for a late supper." He gets to his feet, and then pulls John up as well. "Brilliant! Absolutely brilliant!"

"BRILLIANT," SIX SAYS. "Just fucking brilliant."

She and John are out in the yard in the cold and gathering darkness with a pair of handsaws. Six has the brand-new one that Martok bought on his shopping spree in Lake Town. John has a rusted one that someone—Daro? Or maybe even the ones who built this place?—left hanging from a peg driven into the basement wall. There's a thick-boled ash tree lying on its side just a few dozen meters into the woods. They've been trying to cut rounds from its trunk, but making the cuts clean and parallel is proving to be quite a bit more difficult than John had anticipated.

"You're crooked," she says. "You know that, right? Stop cutting. We're gonna have to trash this one and start over."

"We can't keep doing this," John says, but he stops cutting and yanks his saw free. "We need at least twelve of these. At some point we're gonna have to just say they don't need to be one hundred percent straight."

"If they're not straight, they won't work, right? If we put a wedge under those bed frames instead of a block, we're just gonna have a broken bed with a wedge stuck under it."

John scowls down at her. "I didn't say to make a wedge. There's a lot of space between a wedge and a perfect cylinder."

"Yeah, well, so far I've got two perfect cylinders, and you've got three half-assed wastes of perfectly good trunk."

John raises both hands in surrender. "You know what? You're right. You're really much better at this than I am. You should definitely cut the rest of them yourself. I'll just watch and try to learn from you."

Six scoops up a handful of snow and flings it at him. It mostly breaks up in the air, but enough hits his face to leave him sputtering.

"Not a chance," she says as he wipes his eyes clear. "This shit was your idea, remember? I'm out here helping you because I was tired of having Martok hovering over my shoulder and telling me that I wasn't cleaning right, but I'm not your servant."

That said, she leans into her saw and starts working to clean up the end of the trunk that John has just mangled. As she works, her saw moving quickly and cleanly through the wood, it occurs to John that the issue he's having might have more to do with his equipment than any difference in skill between them. He looks down at the saw in his hands. In addition to the thick coat of rust, it has at least a dozen missing or worn-down teeth, and the blade is subtly bent in two different directions.

"You can start the next cut while I'm working on this one," Six says.

John shakes his head. "I think I'll wait until you're done. We can trade off using the good saw."

She stops cutting and looks up at him. "Come on, John. We're gonna be out here forever."

"We'll be out here forever if I screw up every round by trying to cut with a busted saw."

Her eyes narrow, but then she sighs and starts sawing again. "Whatever."

He watches in silence as she finishes her cut, then straightens and holds the saw out for him.

"I left you a nice clean end there," she says. "Don't screw it up, okay?"

John rolls his eyes, lines the blade up as carefully as he can, and starts cutting. His first reaction is astonishment at just how much easier this is. The old saw was constantly twisting in his hand, blade catching in the cut, and he had to apply a shoulder-cracking amount of pressure to get it to grab at the wood. This one, though?

"Keep it straight," Six says. "You're letting the blade tilt."

John stops cutting and glares at her. "Really?"

"Really," Six says. "I'm serious about not wanting to be out here all night, but I'm not about to let you get away with pretending to be completely incompetent so that I'll do all the work. If you keep this up, we're gonna wind up working our way through this entire trunk."

John looks down at his work.

She's right, actually.

He backs the blade out a bit, straightens it, and starts again.

"So," Six says when he's finished the cut and handed the saw back to her. "Are you gonna tell me what you were really doing out in the woods all day today?"

John lets that hang between them for a moment, then says, "I already told you. I went for a walk, and I got lost. It took me a while to find my way back."

Six stops cutting to look up at him, then shakes her head and returns to her work. "Okay. You think I'm an idiot. I don't know exactly when you left, but you were gone for a couple of hours at minimum. There's no way even you could get lost enough in this little stand of trees to be gone for that long just wandering around. Also, not for nothing, you've been acting weird since you got back." She stops again, halfway through the trunk now, stands, and folds her arms across her chest, leaving the saw stuck in the cut. "You're up to something, John. You did something in the woods, or you met someone, or you went somewhere. If it hadn't been snowing and blowing all day, I'd just follow your tracks back to wherever you were, but since it has been, I'm gonna have to figure this out the hard way." She hops up onto the log, then steps down in front of him. "Spill. Now."

John looks down at her, mouth hanging slightly open, then says, "Are you . . . is this some kind of threat?"

She folds her arms across her chest and steps closer, until her elbows actually bump into his belly. "Maybe."

John bursts out laughing.

Six punches him in the gut, hard enough to double him over.

"Hey!" John says when he's recovered enough to speak. He's backed away now, and as he straightens he holds one hand out to keep her away from him. "What the hell, Six? That hurt!"

"Yeah, well," she says, and manages to look at least slightly abashed. "You kind of forced me to do it. I don't like being laughed at."

John straightens fully, takes a deep breath in, and lets it out slowly. "Okay. Well, here's the thing. You were acting like a thug, and it was funny. If you don't want me to laugh at you, maybe try not being ridiculous."

"Now you're just being a jerk."

"Me? You just . . . No. No, you know what? I'm not doing this right now. It's getting dark, and I'm freezing, and I'd really like to just finish what we're doing here and get back inside where it's warm. Is that okay with you?"

Six glares up at him, then looks away and says, "Fine. Be that way." She hops back over the log and reaches for the saw. "I'm gonna figure this out, though. I'll be keeping my eye on you, and if it turns out you're doing something shady, I'm telling Martok."

She leans back into the work. John watches her, eyes narrowed, as the snow swirls silently around them.

John is underneath the last of the guest beds, struggling to get a slightly mis-measured round of ash trunk wedged beneath the center crossbar, when he hears the groan of the floorboards straining under Martok's weight as he steps into the room. John finishes what he's doing, gives the crossbar a tug to make sure it's set securely and that the frame is stable, and then slides out to see Martok standing in the doorway.

"Ah," he says. "Here you are. The work is done?"

"I think so. I guess we won't know for sure until you test them out and we see if my idea holds up."

"Oh, fear not. I have checked each of the other beds thoroughly." Martok crosses the room, steps past John as he gets to his feet, and sits down on the edge of the bed. The frame creaks, but holds. He lies back, and then swings his feet up onto the bed and stretches out. "Yes. Just as the others, this now appears to be a functional bed, if a bit small and not particularly comfortable." He sits up again and swings his feet back to the floor. "I suppose we shall have to sell these minor miseries as a part of the rustic experience, no?"

"Sure," John says. "If you say so."

Martok sits in silence then, watching him. John meets his gaze for a long moment, then looks away. "If there's nothing else—"

"John," Martok says, and pats the bed beside him. "Please. Sit with me for a moment."

John hesitates, then climbs up onto the bed and sits, hands knotted in his lap and eyes on the floor.

"I have begun to worry about you," Martok says after an awkward silence. "Since we left Farhome, you have not seemed yourself. From the day we met, you have been nothing but a boon companion to me. You have celebrated our triumphs with me, and you have helped raise my spirits after our most crushing defeats. Do you remember our encounter with Numu Garok née Singing Trees, John? Do you remember that terrible night in the park?"

Of course he remembers. This would have been seven years ago. Or maybe eight? Long enough after his bond for John to understand what he'd gotten into with Martok, but not long enough for the memories of what Martok had saved him from to have dulled. Numu was a food vendor in the Farhome markets. Singing Trees was no better represented on Earth than Black Hand, and Numu had probably had nearly as difficult a time making a life for himself here as Martok had. The experience had affected him differently, though. Whereas Martok seemed to have some alchemical process for converting misfortune into manic good cheer, Numu's response to his circumstances had been to curdle every setback into black, bitter bile.

They first encountered one another in a lumber stall in the markets, where Numu was scowling at a pile of rough-cut boards and Martok was trolling for work. Numu was looking to expand his own stall. Martok presented himself as a master craftsman. They agreed on a price, enough to keep Martok and John housed and fed for a month if they were frugal. Martok spent every bit of credit he had on hand, and a bit more, on tools and supplies, and the two of them set to work.

As his evening with Six just demonstrated, John is no carpenter, and Martok is little better. When Numu saw their finished work, he refused to pay. Martok summoned a constable, who took one look at the lopsided display table and sagging roof and sided with Numu. They were already behind on their payments to the master of the boardinghouse where they'd been staying. Martok tried to trade the tools he'd just bought for another week's lodging. The landlord took them, let Martok know that these barely covered his arrears, and threw them in the street.

"I nearly surrendered that night," Martok says. "We'd had a string of misfortunes, and when that miserable Singing Trees vagrant cheated us of our fairly agreed wages—when his criminality was then supported by a duly sworn constable, whom he'd no doubt bribed for the purpose—well, I will confess now, it was more than I could bear. We wandered into the park, because we had nowhere else to go. We had no food, no credit, no prospects . . . I have never told you this, John, but I thought to die that night. I thought to take you in my arms and walk into the pond and be done with this world, once and for all."

John lets that sit between them. Finally, he says, "Why didn't you?"

Martok puts one heavy hand on John's shoulder and squeezes gently. "Because of you, my friend. We walked to the edge of the pond. Do you remember? The sun had set, and we sat down beneath a tree. I had actually begun my death-chant when you leaned against my side and said, 'Today was bad, but it doesn't matter. Tomorrow will be better. I can feel it.' You believed in me, John. Even when I had lost all belief in myself, you believed in me. And so, I did not walk into the pond. I did not surrender. We slept there under the tree, your back resting against mine, and the next day was better, just as you said."

Martok gets to his feet then, turns, and offers John a hand

up. "I need for you to believe in me now, John. If you can bring yourself to do this, I know we will succeed. If you cannot . . ."

John waits for him to go on, but it seems there's no more to say. After a long silence, Martok pats John's shoulder once more, then turns and walks out of the room. The rumble of his humming follows him down the stairs.

CHAPTER NINE

"Good news, friends! I have just this moment received a communiqué from the Chairman. Our first guest is confirmed and will be arriving today!"

John and Six have just sat down to breakfast at the big table in the dining room—hard bread and dried fruit for John, a bowl of cold oats for Six. Martok is pacing back and forth across the room, protein brick in one hand and stein of ale in the other, too excited to sit.

"The missive was admittedly a bit cryptic," Martok says around a mouthful of food. "The Chairman said this guest will not require 'the full treatment,' but only 'a minor corrective.' I can only assume that this is his acknowledgment that we have not yet had time to bring our little resort fully up to the standards of service that we aspire to. Still, we must do our utmost to meet and exceed our guest's expectations. From the Chairman's description, this worthy may be suffering from nervous exhaustion or something similar. It seems he will be with us only for a single day and night, but we must make this time the most relaxing of his life!" He swallows, gags briefly, and then drains the stein so hastily that he's left with a trail of ale dripping down his chin and into his already ragged-looking sash. "In any case," he says as he crams the last of the protein brick into his mouth, "we have far too much to do in the next few hours to spend them lallygagging at the breakfast table. Finish up, friends. Our future begins today!"

Six waits until Martok has dropped his empty stein in the kitchen and bustled up the stairs to say, "Okay, John. What the hell?"

John, who's just shoved the last bit of bread into his mouth, takes his time chewing and swallowing before saying, "What do you mean? I didn't say anything."

Six scowls, then shakes her head and says, "Look, John. I'm sitting right here, okay? I'm looking at you. I can see your face, and unlike Martok, I know how human faces work. Your eyes practically bugged out of your head when he said that thing about *full treatment* or whatever, and right now, while I'm talking to you, you are desperately trying not to shit yourself with fear. Will you please tell me what's going on? Because I do not for one second believe that this is just you worrying that we're not quite ready to give some minor Ice River grandee a super-fun evening."

John stares her down for a long moment. He could tell her, couldn't he? *Chairman Sinta thinks Martok is an enforcer. This guest he's sending us? Sinta is expecting Martok to hurt him. Someday he may send us another for the* full treatment. *Have you ever killed a gray, Six? Do you even know* how *to kill a gray? Because I don't.* He's beginning to suspect that she may actually be significantly smarter than he is. Maybe she'd have some sort of idea for how this can end with all three of them still alive.

If it turns out you're doing something shady, I'm telling Martok.

No, he can't tell her.

"Nothing's going on," he says finally. "Not sure I've mentioned this, but my continued survival hangs on us being able to make this place generate enough revenue to pay off the note that Martok owes to Daro Lia née Greatfoot. If this guest has a bad time, we won't get another, and a few weeks from now Daro will come to collect on his debt. If our guest has a good time, on the other hand, there's a chance that I get to live out the winter. I get that the worst thing you're facing is having to go back to Farhome and take my place as Martok's partner in poverty, but can you understand why maybe I'd be a little bit nervous right now?"

Six watches him, eyes narrowed, then sighs, scrapes the last bit of oatmeal out of her bowl with one finger, and gets to her feet.

"Right. Well, in that case, I guess you'd better get moving, huh? Don't want our guest to find himself in an unmade bed, do we?"

An hour later, and John finds himself out in the woods again. He won't get lost this time, anyway. The day is bright, cold, and clear, with just a hint of a breeze coming down from the north, and the low morning sun glinting off the calf-deep snow makes the yard into a field of diamonds. His prints are the only ones out here, stretching out behind him, a clear trail all the way back to the porch.

He's not entirely sure what he's doing out here, other than avoiding Six and Martok. Contrary to what Martok said over breakfast, there really isn't much of anything to do in the house. The gray's manic energy is too much for John to handle at the moment, though, and he doesn't like the way Six has been watching him. He knows she's not a mind reader, but he's never really had to deal with anyone who could interpret human body language before, and her ability to read his emotions is unnerving.

The wind picks up a bit as he nears the rock—not enough to make him worry that it'll obscure his trail, but enough to make him duck his head and push his hands deeper into the pockets of his coat. His mind is turning over slowly, walking circles around his problem without making any actual progress toward a solution. In just a few hours, their guest will arrive. If he's alone, things will be a little simpler, at least in the short run. He won't have any idea what Sinta intends for him here. All they have to do is give him a comfortable, boring evening, and presumably he'll head home in the morning, with nobody any worse for wear.

What then, though? Sinta will expect him to arrive home chastened at the least, and possibly injured as well. What happens when the Chairman asks their guest how his stay was and hears that he spent a boring evening with an obsequiously manic gray and two frightened bondsmen?

John honestly doesn't know the answer to that question, but he strongly suspects that it's nothing good.

Even worse, what happens if their guest arrives with company, drugged or bound or otherwise prepared for what Sinta thinks Martok is going to do to him? It's not clear to John how far normal grays are able to go with one another before their instincts and taboos against intraspecies violence kick in. Trickery and subterfuge seem to be in the green zone, but can they go beyond that without *absenting*?

Seems likely the next few weeks are going to teach him more about the topic than he wants to know.

He's almost to the rock, eyes slitted against the wind and watering as he contemplates that unhappy thought, when Dana's voice comes down on him from above like the heart-stopping tribune of a vengeful goddess.

"Well, hello, there, John. Didn't we agree that you were gonna stay out of my woods from now on?"

John spins a full circle before looking up to see her crouched on a wooden platform three or four meters up the trunk of a maple tree, just off the path.

"These aren't your woods," he says when he's confident that he can speak without his voice breaking. "They're Martok's. I'm not here to bother you, but I can walk in them if I want to."

Dana grins down at him, bow held loosely in her left hand. "Doesn't matter if you're here to bother me or not, little man. You *are* bothering me. I've got people to feed today, and you're scaring away the deer." She makes a point of looking him over, then adds, "I guess I could take you back, but after I'd gotten done gutting you I doubt there'd be enough meat left on you to make it worth the trouble."

"No," John says. "Probably not."

He looks up at her. She looks down at him. After an inordinately long while she says, "So . . ."

And now, in a sudden flash of self-awareness, John realizes why he came out here, and simultaneously why something deep in his mind hid his purpose from him until this moment.

"Do you . . . do you think you could kill a gray with that bow?"

That stops her. It stops John, too. He didn't pause to think about the words before speaking them. Now that they've had time to register, a gut-churning horror at what he's just said descends on him, and he has to fight against the urge to turn and run.

"Never really thought about it," Dana says, her voice slow and wary. "Killing grays is generally a pretty bad idea, wouldn't you say? They tolerate us as long as we mostly keep to ourselves and they can pretend that we don't exist, but I feel like that's the sort of thing that might convince somebody to call in the spiders."

"Killing a gray would be a terrible idea," John says. "Unthinkable, really. The grays are our protectors. They saved us after The Fall." He looks down at his feet, then back up at her, eyes slitted against the sun. No way out now but forward, right? "Hypothetically, though. Do you think you could?"

"Hypothetically?" She looks down at John, then at the bow in her hand. "Well. This thing has a thirty-five-kilo draw. I killed a full-grown black bear with it once. Now, a gray's a lot bigger than a black bear, but he's also slower, and I doubt his hide's any tougher. It might take more than one arrow, and I'd need to think a bit about where, exactly, to sink them. Speaking purely hypothetically, though—yeah, I think I probably could."

"Would you eat him afterward?"

Dana lets that hang between them for a long moment, then slings her bow across her shoulders, picks up her quiver from the platform beside her, and scrambles down the trunk to the ground.

"Okay," she says. "I'm not gonna lie, little man. You're kind of weirding me out right now. You want to tell me what the hell's going on?"

And so, he tells her, the words pouring out of him in a barely coherent rush. He tells her about his run-in with the Ice River roustabouts in the Lake Town station, and the unthinkable lies, and Martok's ridiculous plans, and the gray who's coming today, and the ones who are likely to follow. He tells her about the note, and the fact that he's in acute danger of being hunted for sport someday soon by Daro Lia née Greatfoot.

He tells her about the crèche.

By the time he's wound down, Dana is on one knee in front of him, her face a mask of concern bordering on alarm.

"Wow, little man. You've really gotten yourself into quite a pickle, haven't you?"

"I need your help," John says. "I'm not . . . I don't know what else to do."

"You need something," Dana says, and stands in one fluid motion. "Not sure why you think I'm the person to give it to you, though. I was the one who wanted to put an arrow through you the last time we met, remember? It was Tanner who was feeling sorry for you, but I'm telling you right now that you wouldn't get anywhere pushing this shit on him either. We're still here a hundred and eighteen years after those fuckers took our planet from us for one reason, and one reason only, and that's because it's easier and cheaper for the grays to pretend we don't exist than it is for them to hunt the last of us down. Believe me, I'd like nothing better than to take them all out, one by one, but that's not how this would go, is it?" She turns away and starts walking. "Now you've probably screwed this stand for me today, and as I said, I've got people to feed. I'd run along home if I were you."

"I'll tell Martok about you."

Dana stops walking. She sighs, then turns back to him and pulls an arrow from the quiver at her hip. "Okay, little man. Have it your way." She's already nocked and drawn when John says, "I already told Six about you. If I'm not back in an hour, she'll tell Martok. He'll tell the Ice Rivers, and they'll call in the spiders."

She stares him down along the length of the shaft for what feels like a long while—long enough, at any rate, for John to imagine what it would feel like to have her arrow punch through his eye and out the back of his skull. It doesn't happen, though, and eventually Dana releases the tension on the string and lowers her bow.

"You said you wouldn't tell on us, John. You promised. Remember that? You said bringing the spiders down on what might be the last actual human community on this godforsaken planet was just the absolute last thing in the world that you'd ever want to do. That's the only reason you're still alive. I hate to ask this, but . . . was that a lie? Are you a liar, John?"

John's voice carries a quaver when he answers that belies his narrowed eyes and jutting chin. "I said I wouldn't tell Martok, and I didn't. I told Six because I didn't want you to be able to kill me and walk away. Seems like that was the right call, doesn't it?"

Dana mutters something John doesn't quite catch, then slams the arrow back into her quiver and says, "We have a community here, John. Just like you said before, a *human* community. We have old people. We have children. We're the last ones left in this area for sure, and for all I know, we really could be the last ones left in the *world*. I'm sorry your dipshit owner and your own stupid mouth got you into trouble, but do you really expect me to risk all of that to get you back out of it?"

"Nothing has to happen to them," John says. "Nothing has to happen to you. I just need you to help me, and—"

"By killing grays, John! That's what you need, right? How the *fuck* do you expect that to end well for us?"

"I told you," John says. "They're grays that Sinta *wants* to have killed. Why would he care who's actually doing the killing, as long as it gets done? Anyway, I don't even know for sure that he'll ask that. The one coming today just needs to be scared a little. Maybe that's all it'll ever be? And, and . . . I'll pay you. You need food? I can give it to you. Metal, too. We have lots of things you could use. You'll see, Dana. This can be good for both of us."

She stares down at him, her jaw muscles working, her grip on the bow so tight that he wonders if the wood might crack.

"Come to the house tonight," he says. "Come after midnight. Bring Tanner with you. You'll be in and out in an hour, no problem."

He can see clearly that she's fighting the urge to kill him now, consequences be damned. Nothing for it, though, and nothing she could do to him would be worse than what Daro or Sinta or even Martok might do to him if this all falls apart. After what feels like an hour but is actually probably more like five seconds, she turns without a word and stalks off into the snow.

"Don't forget!" John calls after her. Then, absurdly, "I'll see you tonight!"

THE TRUNDLECAR BEARING their first guest arrives at the house just before sunset. Martok, who has been alternating between manically cheerful and morosely terrified all afternoon, sends John and Six, dressed in matching blue smocks and pants purchased just for the occasion, out to provide a welcome while he waits in the foyer, mug of ale in hand.

John breathes a small, silent sigh of relief when he sees the gray step out of the car alone. His plans, such as they are, would have been entirely impossible if their mark had arrived bound or drugged and been dragged up to the porch by Sinta's minions. John is still unsure whether such a thing might actually be possible, but either way it's not something he needs to worry about today.

The gray stands in the snow of the yard staring at them, the door of his car still open behind him, before giving an angry huff and saying, "I am Min Hara née Ice River. I was told, though I should be clear that I did not for a second believe, that I would have a pleasant evening in this place. Is it truly possible that I have been put entirely at the mercy of a pair of witless dullards?"

"No, sir," Six says, after shooting John a glance that says clearly that she expected him to take the lead here. "The master of this house, Martok Barden née Black Hand, has sent us, his humble servants, to greet you, while he waits inside with a more proper welcome. Please rest assured that your stay here will be a rewarding one."

Min huffs again, then shuffles across the yard and up the stairs to the porch. It's not easy to guess the age of a gray, but from the way he moves and the sagging flesh around his chest and belly John can see that Min is old—not as old as Rema was, probably, but far past the bulk and strength of his youth.

Better and better.

"Welcome," John says as he pulls the door open for him with a bow. "Please, sir, do enjoy your stay."

CHAPTER TEN

"Disaster, John! Disaster is upon us!"

John looks up from the sink full of dinner dishes that he's just set to work on to see Martok hovering in the doorway to the parlor, one hand on the lintel and the other pressed to his chest over his gleaming new sash.

"Our guest has been here for two hours. How could this be a disaster already?"

Martok steps through into the kitchen and lets the door swing closed behind him. When he speaks again, his voice is a hoarse whisper. "How could it be? He did not care for the roast beast, John! My family recipe, passed down through generations of the Black Hand clan, and he called it inedible! How was I to know that our first guest would be a wretched old skeleton, with rotten tusks and teeth too feeble even for such a delicacy? I should have blended the meat, and served it to him with a straw!"

"Oh well," John says, and turns back to his washing. "It looks like he finished the first course, and the third."

"Oh, he did, but not without complaint. The first he called

overcooked, and the third practically raw. Both were done perfectly, John! Why, I myself have not eaten so well in months!"

John thinks to point out that Martok's diet for the past several months has consisted entirely of boardinghouse slop and the cheapest available protein bricks, but Martok is clearly on a knife's edge, and John has no interest in pushing him over.

"I'm sure it's fine, Martok. Some people enjoy complaining, even when there's nothing to complain about. We'll fill him with ale this evening, and you'll regale him with stories of your vagabond youth. He'll have a restful night's sleep, a fine breakfast, and then maybe a peaceful walk in the forest tomorrow before heading home, where he'll tell all his friends that this was the best day of his life."

Martok closes his eyes and takes several deep, calming breaths as his crest returns from a dark flush to a dull, quiet gray. When he's fully settled himself, he says, "You see, John? I truly could not function without you. Here am I, nearly in a panic, and you, who in the end have far more to lose in this venture than I, stand ready to give comfort and remind me of my courage." He gives John's arm a too-hard squeeze, then straightens, squares his shoulders, and says, "I am a charming rogue, am I not? All I need to do now is go back out to our guest and be what I am."

The door has just closed behind him when Six says, "Wow. That was quite a performance."

John's head snaps around. Six is standing in the door to the walk-in pantry, gnawing on a strip of dried apple.

"Shouldn't you be working right now?"

She grins. "I am. Right now I'm working on finishing this apple. When I'm done with that, I'm planning to start in on a sack of walnuts." She lets the pantry door close behind her. "The fact is, I was busting my ass all day yesterday and most of today, while you were hiding out in the woods doing whatever shit you were doing. Handling all the cleanup tonight is the least you can do to thank me for not ratting you out to Martok."

John is well aware that she did, in fact, rat him out to Martok while he was busy convincing Dana and Tanner not to summarily execute him, but after a moment's consideration, he decides that there's no real point in pushing the matter.

"Fine. I'll do the dishes, and I'll clean up the sitting room after the two of them have drunk themselves stupid and stumbled off to bed. Fair enough?"

She looks at him, chewing thoughtfully, then swallows and says, "Something's going on with you, John. What did you find in the woods yesterday?"

John sets aside the plate he's been scrubbing, heart rate spiking, and turns to face her. "I told you, I didn't find anything. I got lost. That's all. So far as I know, there's nothing out there but trees and snow."

"And that's why you went back out there again today?"

John glances at the closed door, then lowers his voice. "I'm under a lot of stress right now, remember? The woods are calming."

Six laughs. "Calming? You're talking about the woods that you got lost and almost froze to death in yesterday? Those woods?" She waits through five seconds of silence, then sighs and says, "You're a really terrible liar, John. Are you this bad with Martok?"

"I've never lied to Martok," John says. He folds his arms across his chest and glares at her. "You know how you can tell that? I'm still alive."

Six snorts out another laugh. "That's how I can tell he hasn't caught you yet—which is amazing, because, like I just said, you are a terrible liar." She pops the last bite of apple into her mouth, chews and swallows, then says, "How many of them are there?"

John's eyebrows come together over the bridge of his nose. "How many of what are there?"

"Humans," Six says. "Ferals. How many of them are out there?"

John startles, gut twisting, then stammers, "How . . . how did you know . . ."

"I didn't," Six says with a wicked grin. "I do now, though. Gods, you're so easy."

That's enough to snap John almost instantly from terror to fury.

"Look, Six, I don't know who you think you are or what you think you're doing right now, but—"

"I spent five years living with a bunch of ferals near Owasco, up by the lakeshore. Did you know that?" John stares at her, open-mouthed. Her grin widens. "I guess not, huh? To be honest, I don't remember that much about them. I was only seven when the spiders came through and wiped them all out. The one thing I do remember for sure, though, is that they were a hell of a lot nicer to me than the grays ever were."

"I don't . . . does that mean that you're . . ."

"A feral? You've seen ferals now, John. Do I look like a feral?"

"I mean—"

"If I were, I wouldn't be here right now, would I? I told you, the spiders got the group I was with. So far as I know, the only ones who survived the raid were me and one other crèche-born kid they had with them. I guess the spiders could tell the difference between us and the real humans somehow? Anyway, I was always kind of afraid that the ones I was with, the ones the spiders killed, were the last ones there were left in the wild. Not gonna lie, I'm pretty happy to find out that there's more of them out there. So, like I said in the first place, how many of them are there?"

John stares at her. He has soooooo many questions.

This is not the time for any of them, though. This is a time for begging.

"You can't tell Martok, Six. He'll go off the deep end if he finds out. He'll call in the spiders. You said you're happy there are more of them out there, right? If you tell him anything, there won't be anymore."

"Martok doesn't have two credits to rub together. Do you have any idea what it costs to lease out an infestation of spiders?"

Until yesterday, John hadn't known anything at all about the spiders beyond the better-be-good stories that the nursemaids whispered to children up too late in the crèche. He still doesn't know what they are, beyond the vague idea that they're something terrible that grays use to kill humans. He doesn't say that, though. Instead, he just shakes his head mutely.

"Well," Six says. "Neither do I, actually. I bet it's a lot, though. The grays are mercenary shits. They don't do anything for free, even when it would help them all. You're right that Martok would probably go absolutely bonkers if he found out that his woods are full of ferals, though." She leans back against the doorframe, crosses her arms over her chest, and gives him a thoughtful look. "Now that I think about it, that might be fun to watch. What do you think?"

"Six, please—"

"Oh, don't panic, you big baby. I'm not gonna tell Martok. I'm pretty sure he couldn't afford a bondsman hunting party, let alone a pack of spiders, but there's a fair chance he'd try to make us do something about them, and I remember enough about the ones I lived with to know that wouldn't end well for us."

John briefly pictures Dana rolling her knife across the backs of her fingers as if it were a part of her. Six isn't wrong on that point.

"Okay," he says. "So what now?"

"Now?" Six says. "Now we get honest, John. Now you tell me everything."

Martok keeps his guest up drinking late into the night, late enough that John begins to worry that they might still be awake when his friends arrive. John can't follow most of the grays' rumble-speak, but as the evening wears on Min seems to loosen up, relaxing into his almost-too-small armchair in the parlor and laughing loudly and often. It seems Martok really can be charming when he wants to. Who knew?

Eventually, though, Min rises unsteadily and announces that it is far too late for one of his advanced years to be up and about, and that he must be off to bed. Martok rises to help him, but has to steady himself against the back of his own chair before he regains his balance. Alcohol has similar effects on both grays and humans, and they drink it habitually for similar reasons. It takes an enormously greater quantity of alcohol to debilitate a gray, obviously, but Martok and Min between them have put away enough this evening to kill John a dozen times over.

"John," Martok says as the pair make their shuffling way toward the stairs, "would you please be so kind as to straighten up the parlor and secure the house for the evening? Our guest and I will now retire."

"Of course, Martok. Sleep well, Min Hara née Ice River."

Min pauses at the sound of his name. He turns to look at John, the expression on his face clearly conveying that he'd forgotten entirely about John's existence.

"Yes," he rumbles eventually, and turns his attention back to the stairs. "I am certain that I will."

It takes a half hour for the shuffling and scraping and

thumping on the floor above them to settle down, long enough for John to clear and wash the steins that Martok and Min left in the parlor and to get the kitchen and the dining room back into reasonable order. After another twenty minutes, Martok's snoring echoes down the stairs.

Six, who's been sitting cross-legged in Martok's chair in the parlor while all this went on, gestures toward the ceiling and says, "Is he always like this?"

John shrugs. "Not so bad most nights, but when he drinks? Yeah, pretty much."

"Huh. I'm starting to see why you think you can pull this off."

To be clear, John actually has very little confidence that the rest of the night is going to go as planned. He's happy that Tanner and Dana didn't wander in while the grays were still carousing, but now he worries that they might not come at all. He remembers being reasonably sure in the moment that Dana had swallowed his bluff, but now he's having trouble recalling exactly why.

"So?" Six says. "When do your friends show up? I can't wait to meet them. I remember the ones I lived with being tall as trees and strong as bears, fast and fierce and fearless. I remember wondering how people like that ever let the grays take their world away from them. I know that's probably just my kid brain screwing with me, but I'm curious to see what they actually look like."

"Well, I don't know about bears, but they're definitely big, and the two I met seemed pretty fierce. I'm not sure what you mean by taking their world away from them, though. The grays didn't take this world. Humans lost it. The Fall is what wiped them out. The grays just came through and cleaned up the wreckage."

Six rolls her eyes. "Come on, John. You can't possibly believe that, can you? I mean, I know you spent half your life in a crèche having gray propaganda shoveled into your head, but you've got eyes, right? And at least a little bit of a brain?"

John's eyes narrow and he folds his arms across his chest. "Yeah, Six. I've got eyes. I can see that after a hundred-plus years here, the grays occupy one city and a few smaller towns in one tiny patch of the planet. How many are there here, total? A couple of million? And how many were there when they first showed up here? A tenth of that, maybe? If you're so smart and well-informed, explain to me how a few hundred thousand grays took on a whole planet full of your fast, fierce, gigantic humans, and won. And while you're at it, explain why there haven't been armies of ferals coming in to take their revenge from the ninety-nine percent of the planet that the grays *don't* occupy. Whatever the spiders are, the first grays to arrive here couldn't possibly have had enough of them to scour the entire world, could they? And by the way, didn't you learn pretty much everything you know in a crèche too? Come to think of it, didn't we literally just pull you out of a crèche a couple of days ago? You're really good at pulling this world-weary attitude, Six, but the truth is that you're no smarter or better educated than me, and you've seen *way* less of the world than I have."

"Did I not just mention that I was raised by ferals?"

"Until you were *seven*! Are you really trying to tell me that you were getting history lessons from those guys while you were wandering around in the woods looking for roots and berries and trying to remember not to pee yourself?"

Six's voice drops to a sullen growl. "They taught me plenty."

"I bet they did. So? You teach me now. How did they do it? How did the grays instigate The Fall, defeat the survivors, and then steal our world from us?"

Six glares back at him, then shrugs and says, "I don't know how they did it, John. I don't think the people I lived with knew either. The Fall was a long time ago, and the survivors have had bigger things to worry about than history lessons. Maybe the grays bombed us from orbit? Maybe they seeded the planet with a new virus or bacteria or something that the human system couldn't deal with? They're crazy good with bio-science, you know. The spiders aren't natural things. They're monsters the grays cooked up in a lab somewhere. If they can do that with entire animals, imagine what they could do with a disease. As far as I'm concerned, though, it doesn't matter *how* they did it. It only matters *that* they did it."

"Okay. So how do you know *that* they did it? You're right that they told us in the crèche that the grays found a dying world and just managed to nurture this one little patch of it back to health. They told us that we're the descendants of the tiny number of sick, starving survivors that they fished out of the wreckage, and that if they hadn't come along, humans would be extinct. So I'm using my eyes, and my little bit of a brain, and I'm looking around, and that explanation pretty much lines up with the world we've got, doesn't it? It even explains how there are still a few bands of ferals running around, because those first gray colonists didn't have the resources to find and help all the survivors."

"Help? *Help?* I'm not even gonna *touch* the idea that breeding us into *this* was some kind of favor—and sure, the grays came up with a sort-of-plausible explanation for what they did to us. What I see is this, though: For thousands of years, maybe *millions* of years, there were no grays, and humans covered every square inch of this planet. Then, within just a few years, the grays showed up, and the humans were gone. Could that have just been a wild, crazy coincidence? Like, could some random disaster have just happened to strike right before the gray colony ships got here? Sure, I guess so. Weird coincidences happen.

They don't happen very often, though. That's why we call them *weird*. Seems to me like the obvious explanation is that whatever happened to this planet, it was the grays that did it."

John's education in the crèche mostly revolved around practical matters—buying and selling in the markets, how to cook and clean to a gray's satisfaction, memorizing the many, many offenses that might prompt one of them to kill him. He's not ever been acquainted with the distinction between correlation and causation—or with Occam's razor, for that matter. Still, though, something about Six's argument seems unconvincing to him.

Mostly, he thinks, it's exactly the bewilderment that Six mentioned earlier. After meeting Tanner and Dana, after mentally sizing them up against Martok or Min or Chairman Sinta, he can't manage to convince himself that a gray invasion of a planet populated by millions or billions of humans like them wouldn't have ended promptly and decisively with a few hundred thousand gray corpses piled up in a field somewhere.

"Anyway," Six says, "it doesn't make a shit's worth of difference at this point, does it? This used to be our world, and now it's not. However it happened, it happened, and it doesn't look like it's going to un-happen anytime soon."

Fair enough. John has just opened his mouth to say something about the fact that it was never *their* world, because John and Six are very much not the sort of humans who built this house and ruled this world, when the creak of a loose floorboard on the porch bending under a heavy tread stops him short.

"I guess we can finish this later," Six says, and a manic grin spreads across her face. "It sounds like your friends are here."

CHAPTER ELEVEN

"Huh," Dana says. "I like what you've done with the place."

John squints up at her as she peels off her fur-lined coat and Tanner closes the door behind himself and brushes snow from his shoulders. "You've been here before?"

"This is a fully functional house right in the middle of our hunting grounds, little man. Of course we've been here before. Who do you think was maintaining the building before Daro showed up? I mean, we didn't *live* here or anything—permanent dwellings tend to draw the grays' attention—but we used it as a hospital from time to time, and as a hunting lodge when the weather got too bad." Her eyes drift around the room, then settle on Six, who's staring at her with wide-eyed adoration, before shifting back to John. "Who's your little friend?"

"I'm Six." Her voice is practically bubbling. "I was raised by humans like you. I'm very happy to meet you."

"Ah," Dana says. "Six. This is your insurance policy, right? This is the one you told about us? The one who's going to tell Martok if anything ever happens to you?"

John's pulse spikes abruptly as Dana's hand drifts to the knife at her waist. "She's not my only insurance. I've also . . . I've got . . ."

"I know you," Tanner says.

John turns to look at him, but the big man's eyes are on Six.

"Me?" Six says, her eyes wide as dinner plates.

"Yeah," he says. "You're bigger now, but your face is the same. Your name wasn't Six when I knew you, though. It was Ani. You were Ariane's girl."

She stares at him, mouth half-open, then says, "You were at Owasco?"

John had had it in his head that Six might have been lying about being raised by ferals earlier.

Apparently not.

Tanner nods. "I was away when the spiders came—obviously, right? I didn't think anyone else survived."

"It was only me and Sasha, I think."

"Right. The other little one."

Six looks away. "The other bondsman."

"Okay," John says into the awkward silence that follows. "If we could just . . . as I was saying—"

Dana laughs. "Oh, relax, little man. I'm not gonna kill you, even though I totally could right now. I wasn't going to before, and I'm definitely not after this little reunion. Tanner gets sentimental, you know? Don't get me wrong, though. I thought about it. I was still thinking about it on the walk over here, actually. I was thinking about maybe catching you and Six together, dragging you out into the snow, and making it look like a murder-suicide or something. So much for your insurance policy then, right? Tanner, though . . . you really ought to do something nice for him, John. Like, you ought to make him a fruit basket. He convinced me that the upside of this little arrangement might actually be worth the risk. You said you could pay me. You remember that? Said something about food and metal?"

John nods, then cuts his eyes over to Six, who is looking substantially less enraptured now. "Martok and Min left half their dinner uneaten tonight. We could wrap the leftovers in paper and—"

"I'm not interested gray table scraps, John. You're Martok's dog, not me. Right now what we need is medicine—antibiotics and painkillers, to be specific. We've got a sick kid. We've already lost one this year, and we can't afford to lose another. Also, this one happens to be mine, which ups the stakes for you considerably. So, you're gonna give us both of those things, as much as you have."

"I don't—"

"We've got painkillers," Six says. "No antibiotics, though."

"Okay," Dana says. "We'll take the painkillers now. Go get them. I'll give you a pass on the antibiotics for the moment, but you'll need to get them tomorrow at the outside if you want us to cooperate—by which I mean, if you want to keep your blood and organs on the insides of your bodies, obviously."

"Done."

John shoots Six a look. She shrugs and turns for the kitchen, where Martok stowed what few meds they brought with them in a high cabinet over the sink. Maybe she actually has an idea for how to do what she's promised? If not, he suspects she's just doomed them both. Doesn't matter, though. Tanner's coat is off now, and John sees that he's brought a long wooden club along with him. Time to get to work.

"Ugh," Tanner says. "I've never seen one up close before. Have you?"

Dana shakes her head. "How the hell does something that ugly not just wake up in the morning and kill itself?"

They're standing over Min's bed while John hangs back by the closed door. It's interesting in a detached way to hear them talk about the gray in the bed. John has spent his whole life around grays. They don't look like anything but themselves to him. He's certainly never thought of them as ugly. He can't help but wonder what Martok would look like to him if he were seeing him for the first time.

This isn't the time to worry about that, of course. Gotta focus.

Six is in the hallway watching and listening for any movement from Martok's room, despite the fact that John has no idea what Dana and Tanner plan to do if the master of the house does rouse himself.

No, that's a lie. He knows exactly what they plan to do. He just can't bring himself to acknowledge it.

The only light in Min's room comes from the full moon outside the window. Min is sprawled face down on the bed, arms stretched out and hanging down from either side and head turned away from them on the thin pillow. The two humans are speaking in hushed tones, but Min's snoring rivals Martok's, and John suspects they could probably shout without rousing him.

Dana looks back at John. "You sure this isn't gonna bring ol' Martok charging in on us?"

"Pretty sure. Gray ears are terrible on a good day, and Martok drank even more than Min did tonight."

"Okay, then." She turns back to Tanner. "You think you can hold him?"

"If I can get him into an arm bar before he figures out what's happening? Yeah, for sure. If not, you'll probably need to kill him."

"You can't kill him," John says. "I told you, Sinta just wants this one taught a lesson."

"That's at least four hundred kilos on the bed there," Tanner says. "If he gets loose, you bet your ass we're killing him. You ready, Dana?"

Dana hefts the club, moves to the foot of the bed, and nods.

"Okay, little man. Do your thing."

John crosses the room to stand by Min's head. He has a spare pillowcase in his hand. He looks up at Tanner. The big man nods. John leans across the bed and pulls the pillowcase down over Min's head. At the same moment, Tanner grabs the gray's closer wrist in one hand, leaps up to straddle the gray's back, grabs Min's other arm, and pulls them both high, elbows locked and wrists nearly touching. Min starts to thrash, but Tanner grimaces and squeezes his arms even closer.

"Silence," John says, his mouth nearly touching Min's upturned ear through the pillowcase. "Shout and my master will break your shoulders. Shout again and he will kill you."

"You . . ." Min manages in rumble-speak, his voice barely audible. "You . . ."

"You have just understood that my master, Martok Barden née Black Hand, is not an innkeeper, and that this is not an inn. You have realized that he is, in fact, an enforcer, and that he holds you pinioned now. It must also be dawning on you that Chairman Sinta is aware of what you have done, and that he has consigned you to Martok's care so that you may be taught a lesson. His intent is not that you should be killed at this time, but he has made clear to my master that if you are killed, he will not be overly sad. Do you understand?"

Min growls, a subterranean rumble that John feels more than hears. John glances up at Tanner, who presses even harder, until the backs of Min's wrists actually brush against one another.

The gray groans. John drops his voice an octave. "I said, do you understand?"

"Yes!" Min gasps out in a hoarse whisper. "Yes! I understand!"

"Good. Your punishment is to be twenty lashes. Control yourself, and this will be over quickly."

John looks to Dana now, who winds up and slams the club into the bare soles of Min's feet where they jut off the end of the bed. Min quivers, but holds his silence.

It occurs to John after the tenth or eleventh blow that Min must be wondering right now how Martok could be simultaneously holding his arms and beating his feet. Nothing to do about it now, though, except to hope that the gray is too terrified to worry about it.

After twenty blows, Dana steps back and lowers the club. She wears a savage grin.

"You see?" John says to Min, whose entire body is quivering now. "Not so bad. Chairman Sinta now considers your account with him to be fully paid, and my master will release you in a moment. When he does, you will remain perfectly still. If you move in any way, my master will kill you. Do you understand?" He waits a beat, then says again, "Do you understand, Min Hara née Ice River?"

"Yes," Min says. "I understand."

Tanner releases pressure on Min's arms and carefully steps over him and back to the floor. Min's arms drop to the bed beside him, and he shudders with relief. Tanner waits a beat to be sure that Min will stay still, then silently crosses the room, opens the door, and steps out into the hallway. Dana follows a moment later, and pulls the door closed behind her. John takes his hands from the pillowcase and steps back as well.

"Sleep well, Min Hara. In the morning, we will be sure to

have a fine breakfast waiting for you to send you on your way." He starts to open the door, then turns back to say, "Oh, one other thing. Chairman Sinta wishes for us to remind you that when you return to Lake Town, you will say nothing to anyone about what happened here. If you cannot abide by this request, my master will be forced to visit you in your own home—and in that case, he will be far less merciful. There may be others, after all, who require my master's services."

"Wow," Dana says. "You were pretty good at that."

They're back on the porch now. Dana has packed up most of the dinner's leftovers after all, as well as their entire supply of painkillers. She's buttoning her coat against the cold now, while Tanner waits for her at the bottom of the steps.

"Seriously," she says. "You were creepy as fuck, little man. I wouldn't have thought you had it in you."

"Yeah, well," John says. "You'd be surprised what I have in me."

She gives him an appraising look, then says, "Huh. Maybe so." She steps down into the yard, making a point to use the club to obscure her footprints in the snow. As she and Tanner start back into the woods, she looks back to say, "Don't forget about the antibiotics, little man. Sunset at the big rock. If you're not there, our deal is off and we'll kill you the next time we see you. Got it?"

"Yeah," John says. "Got it. Have a good night, Dana."

She grins back at him as she turns to go. "You too, John. You too."

"So," Six says, "what do you think our friend upstairs is doing right now?"

John shrugs. It's late enough now that the insides of his eyelids feel like sandpaper and a headache is working its way from the back of his neck to the front of his eyes, but both he and Six are far too wired for sleeping. Instead, they're sharing a pilfered stein of ale in the parlor while they let the adrenaline slowly leach out of their systems.

"Hopefully, he's lying in bed, scared out of his mind, trying desperately not to soil the sheets."

That gets a giggle from Six. She lifts the stein in both hands, takes a long drink that leaves a bit of ale dribbling down her chin, then says, "Gods, that was such a rush! Do you know how many times I've dreamed of being able to hurt a gray? I honestly can't believe we pulled it off."

John takes his turn with the stein. He has some doubts about whether they're actually in the clear now, but this isn't the time to voice them. Instead he says, "It really was something. Those two ferals . . . Tanner probably isn't quite as strong as a gray, but you were right about the fast and fearless part. And Dana? She was brutal. I wouldn't be surprised if Min has trouble walking tomorrow."

Six shakes her head. "I wish I could have seen it. Next time, you're standing watch in the hallway."

"You think there's gonna be a next time?"

Six takes another drink. "Why wouldn't there be? Enforcers are something special, right? Everybody wants a piece of them. Whatever Sinta is paying Martok for this shit, we're giving him his credit's worth." She grins. "The good Chairman is probably telling all his scummy underworld friends about us right now. Martok's Torture Palace is open for business and accepting new clients! Call now, before all slots are filled!"

"Great," John says. "And what happens when one of Sinta's

friends contacts Martok and straight-up asks him to kill someone?"

She shakes her head. "They won't. They can't. Grays can't even say that kind of thing without losing their shit. We've both got some psychological conditioning stuff in our heads around thinking about killing grays, but for them it's hardwired into their brains. Sinta and his friends will hem and haw and hint around what they actually want, and Martok will pretend not to know what they're talking about, which will be really easy for him, because he really, truly won't know what they're talking about. They'll send their victims down here to have a nice time wandering around in the magical forest, and we'll send them home with a lesson learned. Or we'll kill them and bury them in the woods somewhere, and then tell Martok they had to head out early for a big business meeting or something. Everyone wins!"

John takes another long pull at the stein. He's starting to feel the alcohol, starting to feel the sharp edge of anxiety dull a bit as his eyelids begin to droop. He'd been worried about how Six would react to all this. He'd been afraid that she'd go straight to Martok, just as she threatened to do yesterday. The idea that she'd be just a little *too* enthusiastic about the whole project hadn't occurred to him.

After a long silence in which they work their way through most of the remaining ale, John says, "What about the drugs?"

Six lifts her face out of the stein. "The what, now?"

"The drugs. The antibiotics. You promised Dana you'd have them before sunset tomorrow. That's like sixteen hours from now. How do you plan on getting them?"

"Oh, don't you worry your pretty little head about that," Six says. Her eyes are unfocused now and the words come out a little slurred, and it occurs to John that she's probably even drunker than he is. "Nope. No worries there at all. I've got a plan."

JOHN WAKES TO a rough shake and the weight of Martok's hand on his back.

"Come, John! The day is well along, and a great adventure awaits you!"

John groans, rolls over, and sits up. Martok's bulk fills half the windowless converted storage room that John has taken as a bedroom. The gray shakes his head ponderously and says, "One might almost think that *you* had been the one up drinking late into the night rather than me. Come. You must be up and dressed, or you will miss any chance at breakfast."

"I don't understand." John rubs his face with both hands, then groans and gets to his feet. His eyes are less irritated than when he went to bed, but his head is pounding and his mouth feels as if someone has slipped tiny fuzzy socks onto each of his teeth. "What time is it? Is Min awake already?"

"It is early yet," Martok rumbles, "but our guest was up well before the sun, and he has been behaving very strangely. I thought we had established a rapport over the course of the evening, but that seems to have vanished with the dawn. When I saw that he was awake I suggested a refreshing walk in the woods together, but he reacted with what almost seemed like horror. I can only assume the poor creature has never been outside of a town, and that he has a terror of the wilderness." He shakes his head again. "I do hope he doesn't permit this irrational fear to color his memory of his stay here. As our first customer, his opinion will carry a great deal of weight in determining the future of our little venture."

"I'm sure he won't," John says. "Is he planning to leave early, then?"

"He is indeed. I could barely convince him to wait for you."

That stops John midway through pulling on his shirt.

"Um . . . wait for me?"

"Yes. There is another fly in the honey of this beautiful day. It seems that Six has developed an infection of some sort. The poor girl is flushed and febrile and can barely speak. It's most distressing. My only real experience with caring for a human has been you, John, and I have never seen you nearly so ill. Fortunately, however, whatever Min's opinion, we appear to still be in the good graces of our benefactor, Chairman Sinta. I have spoken with him already this morning, and he has graciously arranged to have the necessary medications ready for your retrieval, and even to provide you transport back from Lake Town."

"*Back* from Lake Town? So how do I . . ."

Oh.

"Yes, John. This is why you must hurry. Min has agreed to take you, but as I mentioned, he seems to be in a terrible rush. Come along! I shall pack you something for the ride."

"Is it okay if I eat my breakfast back here?"

John waits through ten seconds of silence broken only by the rumble of the trundlecar's wheels on cracked pavement, both hands grasping a half-unwrapped hard biscuit. In the front, Min sits stonily, his withered hands clutching the steering wheel and his eyes fixed straight ahead.

"You were there," Min says finally. "I remember your voice. It was you who spoke to me."

John hesitates, then says, "That was business, Min. I don't know what you did to anger Chairman Sinta, but I assume that you do. Whatever it was, that was the cause of what happened last night. I had no more choice about it than you did."

Min growls, and the sudden juddering in his chest tells John that the gray is cursing in rumble-speak.

"What of your master?" Min says when he's wound down. "What of this Martok Barden née Black Hand? Did *he* have a choice in the matter?"

"Martok . . . Martok is a tool—an instrument of justice, if you will. He does what his clients pay him to do. You must have run into enforcers before, right?"

"Oh, indeed I have—though I have never been subject to one's ministrations before, and I had hoped at my advanced age that I might escape this world without ever experiencing such a thing. I must laugh, however, when you call your master an *instrument of justice*. If you knew what I did to draw the attention of Sinta, and more than that, what he has done to prompt me to it, you would think twice before saying such things."

John takes a huge bite of the biscuit, chews, and swallows. It's crunchy and sweet, and after a second bite the foulness of whatever grew in his mouth overnight begins to dissipate. "Anyway," he says as he washes the biscuit down with a swig from his water bottle, "it was surprisingly decent of you to agree to bring me to Lake Town, given our circumstances. So, thank you for that."

Min laughs, but in a way that makes it clear that what John said isn't funny in the least. "Decent, am I? You miserable, wretched . . . I would have as soon crushed your skull in my hands as carry you to Lake Town today." He pauses then, and John can see his hands flexing rhythmically on the wheel. "And really, why should I not? Yes, I'm sure your master would make an end of me in turn, but what is that to me? Time and infirmity will do that soon enough in any case, and with any luck, whatever your master might do to me would at least be speedy."

Well. This isn't good.

"I don't mean to disagree, sir," John says, while simultaneously wondering whether he could outrun the old gray if he managed to get out of the car, "but if you were to hurt or kill me, what my master would do to you would not be quick. Please understand—I am not simply property to Martok. He and I share a special bond. We have lived and worked together for twelve years now. I can promise you that any hurt done to me would be repaid to you with interest."

"Yes, well," Min growls, "that your relationship with this Martok is . . . unusual is clear enough, in any case. In all my long years, never have I heard of an enforcer allowing a bondsman to witness his work, let alone participate in it. Why, the sheer obscenity of it, the humiliation . . . your master is monstrously cruel, even for one of his twice-damned kind." He falls silent for a beat, then mutters, "I don't doubt that if I were to harm you, he would spit me mouth to anus and roast me alive."

He falls back into rumble-speak after that, but his level of agitation seems to be falling, so John takes the opportunity to finish his breakfast. Outside the window, the broken highway rolls past. On the ride down to the lake house with Martok and Six, John remembers wondering at the sheer immensity of it in an idle way. Now, though, after meeting Dana and Tanner? He can't help seeing it as a reminder of whose world this really ought to be.

CHAPTER TWELVE

"These are powerful drugs, little fellow. You understand this? Strong medicine."

John nods up at the chemist, a kindly-seeming old female who wears a tattered Greatfoot sash.

"Good," she says. "When you get back home, you make sure to tell Chairman Sinta that I don't like him sending you bondsmen down here to pick up things like this. These pills come with side effects, and he needs to know what they are before he goes shoving them down the throats of his employees." She shakes her head, then lowers her voice and adds, "If you ask me, I'd say that if he wants to keep them healthy, he might want to think about not being so rough on them to begin with. I always say it's easier to prevent an injury than to fix one, you know."

She leans forward, plants her elbows onto the counter, and rests her chin in her hands. "I saw one of his bondsmen after a hunt once. The Chairman brought her here himself, that one. A frail little thing she was, and just torn to shreds from tip to tail. I told him he needed painkillers, antibiotics, and nanos if he wanted her to live, but when he heard how much all that would run him, he just put her down right there in the street. Made a terrible mess, he did, and didn't even clean up after himself . . ." She trails off there, then looks down at John as if she'd forgotten he was there, or to whom she was talking. "In any case," she says as she straightens and turns away, "next time, you tell him to send a *person* to do his pickups. You hear?"

Huh. John revises his estimate of her kindliness down by eighty percent. He glances around the shop. It's all dark wood and high shelves and thick glass bottles, labeled in a script he can't make out. He'd had the idea when Min dropped him off that he might be able to steal something to use in future negotiations with Dana, but the painful truth is that even if he could reach any of the bottles, which he definitely cannot, he wouldn't have the slightest idea what to steal.

Also, of course, if he was caught, the chemist would be perfectly justified in killing him. Can't forget that.

"You can tell me what the side effects are," John says as she funnels pills into a jar. "I'll let the Chairman know."

The chemist rumbles with laughter. "Now, now. Don't you worry yourself about such things. I'll talk to Sinta myself, once we're finished here. You just run home with this, and don't even *think* about opening up the package."

John has to struggle for a moment to keep his face from twisting into a scowl before getting it to settle back into what he imagines to be a placid smile.

"Oh, don't worry. I wouldn't dream of opening the package. Can you imagine? The Chairman would skin me alive! He did specifically ask me, though, to find out the dosage and side effects. I know I won't understand what you say, but I've got a gift for mimicry, and I promise I'll repeat it back to the Chairman word for word."

The chemist pauses what she's doing long enough to give

him a dubious look, then bobs her head and says, "Very well. I wouldn't want the Chairman to punish you just because he was fool enough to trust a bondsman to think."

She tips the jar and spills a few pills into the palm of her hand, then comes out from behind the polished oak counter and crouches down in front of John. She shows him the pills and says, "You see these? These are cut for a bondsman about your size, more or less. If you were the sick one, you'd take one of these, twice a day, for two weeks. You can't stop taking them when you feel better. You have to finish out the whole course. Understand?" John nods. "Now. You see the little crease in the middle of each pill?" John nods again. "For a little one, you'd snap the pills in half. For a big fellow, say one of the bondsmen who do Sinta's construction work for him, you might take two at a time, but only until your tummy started to hurt. That's the main thing you watch out for with these pills, is bellyache. If you get that, you could try dropping the dose, but you might also drink a little milk with the pills. You take 'em too long, or too many times, and you might find you're having trouble keeping your balance. That happens? You can't take these anymore, ever again. Next time you're sick, we'd need to give you something else."

She gets slowly back to her feet, groaning as she does so, then makes her way back around the counter and drops the pills back into the jar. She caps the jar, seals it with a strip of tape, and then turns back to John.

"Now, little fellow—repeat that all back to me."

John stares at her blankly for a moment, then says, "What?"

"You've a gift for mimicry, yes? That's what you told me. So? Repeat it back."

John sighs, then closes his eyes and says, "One pill, twice a day for two weeks. Half pill for a little one. Two pills for a fatso. Finish out the course. Watch for bellyache. Really watch for dizziness." He opens his eyes again and looks up at her. "Close enough?"

She stares down at him for long enough that he begins to wonder if the time has come to run, but then her body quivers with laughter and she says, "Yes, little fellow. Close enough." She leans over the counter and holds the jar out to John. He takes it in both hands. "Now run along back home. And don't forget to tell Sinta what I said. Next time, send a person!"

SEND A PERSON.

John has time to ponder that directive while he waits on the curb outside the chemist's shop for Sinta's driver to come for him, jacket pulled tight around him and chin ducked to his chest against the cold. Isn't he, in fact, a person? Martok has always treated him as one, hasn't he?

Or has he?

Would you put a person's life up as bond against a business loan?

Martok cares for him. John doesn't doubt that. He said this morning that he'd never seen John as sick as Six is pretending to be (thinking of which, John needs to ask her how she managed to convincingly fake a fever), but the truth is that three winters ago John picked up a virus that was circulating among the bondsman population of Farhome that left him bedbound, gasping for air like a fish in a boat, and unable to keep down anything solid. For three days, Martok hovered over him, clumsily checking his temperature and his pulse, fussing over his blankets, bringing him broth, and wiping down his face with cool, damp cloths. Martok's fear was palpable, to the point that John began to worry that he actually was dying and that Martok knew it. When he woke on the morning of the fourth day, drenched in sweat from the broken fever and starving, Martok snatched him up into a hug, almost before he'd managed to climb out of bed, and clung to him, nearly weeping with relief.

Martok's fear during John's illness was real. John has to admit to himself now, though, that it's possible that Martok's fear was that of losing a prized possession rather than a friend.

John is contemplating that thought when a garish blue-and-white-striped trundlecar stops in the road in front of him without pulling to the curb. A window slides down, and the gray inside says, "Ho, there, little fellow. The Chairman sent me. You're the one I'm to transport?"

John gets to his feet and nods.

The window closes again, and John hears the click of the lock on the rear door disengaging. After a moment's hesitation, he yanks the door open and climbs in.

THEY'RE WELL OUT of Lake Town, most of the way down the cracked, ancient highway, before the driver speaks again.

"You know, I don't believe I've ever driven for a bondsman before."

John's head snaps up. He'd been dozing, arms wrapped around the pill jar, half dreaming about his first encounter with Dana, of watching that knife dance in her fingers and imagining what it would feel like to have it plunged into his chest. He blinks twice as his brain engages and processes what the gray in the front seat just said.

"Yes," John says finally. "I guess that's probably right. We don't get driven around much."

The driver laughs at that. He's a younger male, huge and smooth-skinned, his crest nearly brushing the roof of the car. "I'd allow that's true. I would indeed. Most times, a bondsman's traveling with the boss. Don't see you fellows out on your own much—and when I do, you're walking."

John doesn't respond to that. After a minute or two of silence, the driver says, "I've been thinking to myself while we've been riding along. *Say, Toran,* I've been thinking, *what's the rumble here? What's so special about this particular bondsman that he's got Chairman Sinta sending his personal driver to bring him halfway out to nowhere?*"

"That's your name?" John says. "Toran?"

"It is. Toran Gil née Ice River."

"I'm happy to meet you, Toran. I'm John."

"John, eh? Just John? The sort of bondsman who gets this kind of service, I thought he might have a full name, yeah? John Whatsis née Greatfoot or some such." The driver laughs again at that, and after a moment John joins him. It's ridiculous, isn't it? A human, with a full clan name?

Ridiculous.

"For true, though," Toran says. "I would dearly love to know how you managed to come to the personal attention of the Chairman, John Whatsis. Most times, if he notices a bondsman at all it's because the poor fellow has slipped up somehow, and those sorts of things don't end with a nice chauffeured ride in a trundlecar, if you take my meaning."

John has a quick, visceral vision of Sinta's wrinkly foot coming down on a human skull.

Best not to think of that now.

"The truth is," he says, "I haven't come to the attention of the Chairman at all. That would be ridiculous, wouldn't it? This ride is a favor to my employer, not to me. I'm just an errand boy, sent to fetch a supply of medicines from the chemist on his behalf."

"Ah. Well, now, that does make more sense. And who's your

master, then? He must be some Greatfoot grandee, I suppose? Oh! You're not one of that Daro Lia's, I hope?"

John has opened his mouth to say, *Master? Don't you mean my employer?* Before he does, though, the last thing that Toran said registers.

"Daro Lia née Greatfoot?" John says, trying and failing to keep his tone casual. "Why, um . . . why do you ask about him, specifically?"

"Oh," Toran says after a moment's hesitation. "Oh, never you mind, John Whatsis. I certainly don't mean to offend if he *is* your master. As they say, a Greatfoot's business is his own, and it's not for the likes of me to judge."

"I'm not offended," John says, "and he's not my master. I'm just curious, and making conversation. What do you know about Daro? Something juicy?"

"Well . . ." Toran says. "Well, since you asked, and only since you asked, Daro Lia née Greatfoot has a place down this way, or did, at any rate. That's what made me think of him. He wasn't here for all that long, but he got himself a . . . a bit of a reputation, if you see what I mean."

"I'm not sure I do," John says. "What kind of reputation?"

Toran mutters something in rumble-speak, too low for John to catch, then says, "Well, not a good one, I'll say that much—particularly around the topic of bondsmen. Ran through them like water, he did. Why, for a while there we thought he might empty out every crèche in Lake Town! Now, I don't know for sure what he might have been doing with all those fellows, but I can tell you that there were . . . rumors."

John is beginning to regret pursuing this particular line of questioning, but he doesn't have it in him to stop now.

"Rumors? What, ah . . . what sort of rumors?"

"Oh, I don't want to say, John Whatsis. Not wise to speak

ill of your betters, is it? I can tell you, though, they were dark. Old Daro Lia, he's said to have . . . strange tastes, if you get my meaning." Toran runs one thick hand back over his crest, then says, "I've said too much, though. Probably best if you just forget all that, if you wouldn't mind too much."

He'd like to keep pushing, but they still have a long way to go and John doesn't want to wind up walking the next thirty klicks. So, after a moment's hesitation, he says, "Consider it forgotten. My master doesn't have any connections to any of the Greatfoots, let alone this Daro Lia. Whatever he did or does is no business of mine."

"Oh. Well, then. Your master must be one of ours after all, I suppose?"

"No, he's not an Ice River either. His full name is Martok Barden née Black Hand."

That gets him a surprised exclamation in rumble-speak, then, "Black Hand, you say? Why, I didn't even know they had a holding here. I'd wager they must be big in Farhome?"

"Not exactly. So far as I know, they've got no holdings on this world at all. Truthfully, Martok is the only Black Hand I've ever met."

Toran laughs again. "Oh, you're having a game with me, little fellow! I've known the Chairman all my life, and I've never known him to be solicitous of a clanless rogue. Why, the only way I could imagine such a thing would be if your master were a . . ."

John lets the silence hang between them. He can almost see the thought turning itself over in Toran's head. "Well, then," the gray says finally. "You were dozing before I woke you, weren't you? I suppose you'd prefer a quiet ride."

There is zero chance that this ends well, John thinks as they pull off of the highway and onto the snowy, cracked pavement of the secondary roads. *In the meantime, though, I think I could get used to it.*

John wastes much of the rest of the ride back to the house wondering how he and Six are going to manage to fool Martok into thinking they still have the antibiotics after they've turned them over to Dana. It takes him less than a minute after Toran Gil née Ice River backs down onto the road and trundles away to realize that he shouldn't have worried.

"John!" Martok says as he pulls the front door shut behind him, sets the pill jar on the floor, and shrugs out of his jacket. "You've arrived just in time. Our friend Six has been fading throughout the day. She is now unable to rise from her bed, and has required almost constant attention. Did the good Chairman's chemist give you instructions for the use of these medicines?"

"Yes," John says as he picks the jar up again. "She said—"

"No, John, there is no need to explain to me. I have a great deal of work to do, work which my attention to Six has delayed unacceptably. I must entrust her care to you, my friend. I have no doubt that you will bring her back to good health in short order. Go, now. She needs you."

With that, Martok bustles into the kitchen, leaving John slack-jawed, standing in a puddle of snowmelt.

"Hey," Six says. "Nice to see you. How was the trip?"

John closes her bedroom door behind him. Unlike John, Six has been given a real room, with a big bed and a window. She had been lying on her back with a thick woven blanket pulled up over her chin, but she sits up now, fluffs a pillow against the headboard, and leans back with a grin.

"It was fine," John says, and sets the pill jar down on the bedside table. "I thought Min might kill me, and the chemist acted as if she thought I had brain damage, but the driver who brought me back here was nice enough."

"Glad to hear it. I've been keeping things together here."

"Yeah, I can see that. Honestly, I don't know how you managed."

"Hey," Six says, as her grin morphs into a smirk, "this job wasn't so easy, you know. I had to walk a line between keeping Martok convinced that I was really sick and making him so worried that he actually tried to take me to a doctor."

"Do they even have any bondsman medicos in Lake Town?"

"Maybe not. Doesn't matter, though, because my performance was perfectly tuned. I kept Martok right on the border between worried and frantic for half the day—and now that you're here, I can start my slow, painful recovery, helped along by plenty of good food and bed rest."

"I don't think so," John says, and shakes his head. "The chemist told me these are miracle drugs. You're gonna be up and around and ready to work in no time at all."

"Come on, John," Six pouts. "We've got to make this believable. As sick as I've been? I'm pretty sure that even with your miracle drugs I'll be laid up for a week."

John folds his arms across his chest. "I'll give you till tomorrow morning."

"Four days."

"Two."

"Three, and I'll share the extra food Martok gives me with you."

John stares her down. She grins up at him.

"Fine. But today counts as day one."

"Done."

She holds out her hand. John hesitates, then shakes it.

"So," she says, "how do you plan to get the pills back out of the house without Martok seeing? Dana will be expecting you in a couple of hours, and she doesn't seem like the sort that you want to keep waiting."

John opens his mouth, hesitates, then closes it again.

He hadn't thought of getting the pills back out.

"I guess . . ."

"Let's assume you figure that out. Martok's gonna expect to see them sitting here by my bedside. What happens when he comes in to check in on me and they're gone?"

"I didn't think—"

"Sure, maybe he won't notice . . . but maybe he will. You need to think about this kind of stuff, John. You're a conspirator now. Slacking off on details is gonna get you caught, and you getting caught is gonna get me caught, and I can't have that. I'm too young to get my head crushed."

John opens his mouth to answer, but her smug smirk stops him. He scowls and says, "Okay, you've obviously got all this figured out, so just tell me and get it over with."

She gives him a seated half bow. "I'm glad to see that you're starting to appreciate my talents, John. Here's what's gonna happen now. You're going to leave the pill jar here with me while you go down to the kitchen and get a sack of dried white beans. There's a pile of them on one of the bottom shelves in the pantry. You're going to bring the beans up here, empty them out onto the nightstand, and then pour the pills into the sack. Then you're going to put the beans into the jar, which you will leave here with me when you take the sack of pills out into the woods and hopefully don't get killed by Dana. Finally, just to be sure, I'm going to chuck a handful of beans out the window every day until the jar is empty, just in case Martok happens to check up on whether I'm taking my pills."

"The pills don't look anything like white beans."

"Please, John. Martok's eyes are terrible. We could fill the jar with milk if it weren't for the fact that it'd spoil and start to stink."

And he'd like to argue, if only to wipe that expression off of her face, but . . .

Well, she's not wrong, is she?

"Okay," he says finally. "You've actually thought this through, huh?"

She shrugs. "In all fairness, I've been lying here with nothing to do all day but thrash and moan and do isometrics under the blanket to keep my temperature up. I've had plenty of time to think."

"Yeah, well. Thanks, I guess. Might as well go get the beans now."

"Sure, but watch out for Martok while you're down there. There are enough of them that he won't notice one sack is missing, but if he actually sees you pinching them you're gonna have some explaining to do."

"Right. I'll keep an eye out."

He's already turned to open the door when Six says, "Hey, John?"

He looks back over his shoulder. "Yeah?"

"We make a pretty good team, don't you think?"

Is she making fun of him? He contemplates throwing something sarcastic back at her, but the combination of her tone and expression are almost enough to make him believe she's being sincere. In the end, he grins back and says, "You know what, Six? Maybe we do."

CHAPTER THIRTEEN

John finds Dana waiting by the big rock, standing with her back against a tree. Her knife is out in her hand. As he watches, she spins the handle once across the backs of her fingers, then tosses the knife into the air and catches it by the blade in her other hand. She looks up at his approach, flips the knife around so that she's holding it by the handle again, and points it at his chest.

"You're cutting it close, little man. Sunset was four minutes ago."

"Yeah, well," John says. "This was a big ask, you know? I kind of thought you'd be impressed that I managed to pull it off at all."

Dana sheathes her knife and pushes away from the tree. A clot of snow drops from a branch above her to burst on her shoulder, but she doesn't seem to notice. "You've got the pills?"

John pulls the bean sack out of his jacket pocket and holds it out to her. He's tied the open end off to keep the pills from spilling out. Dana takes the sack from his hands and peers at it dubiously.

"These are antibiotics, right? Not magic beans?"

"Yeah, they're antibiotics. I had to use the bag to sneak them out of the house."

"Did they come with directions?"

"No, but the chemist told me how to use them. How big is the sick kid?"

Dana squints down at him for a moment, then says, "About your size? Or maybe a little smaller?"

"Okay. So one pill, morning and night, for two weeks. Watch for bellyache. Give her some milk with the pills if you see it. Watch for dizziness. Stop the pills if you see that. I think that's it."

"Huh. You're sure about this?"

"I'm just repeating what the chemist told me."

"Okay." Dana pockets the pills and turns to go. "If Miri comes around, we'll call it square for last night."

That doesn't sound very reassuring. "What if she doesn't?"

"You'd better hope she does," Dana says without looking back.

"Hey," John calls after her. "How do I get in touch when we need you again?"

"You don't," Dana says. "You wait until I get in touch because I need something from you."

"That's not fair! I went all the way to Lake Town to . . ."

He trails off as it becomes clear that he's only talking to himself. The woods are getting dark now, and he hasn't brought a light. He sighs, pulls his jacket tighter around himself, and goes.

THE NEXT MORNING finds Martok in an ebullient mood, bordering on manic.

"Friends!" he fairly bellows from the upper floor as Six and John are sitting down to breakfast. "Friends! A wonderful thing has happened!"

Six looks up from her bowl as Martok thunders down the stairs and into the foyer. John glances over at her to make sure that she's looking sufficiently wretched, then says, "If you mean that Six is up and around again, I should tell you that while she's feeling better, the chemist said it would be another couple of days before she's fully recovered."

Martok, who's come to a skidding stop in the entrance to the great room, looks momentarily confused before saying, "Six? Oh, I never doubted she would be well. Our medical science is entirely wondrous, you know. It's one of the many gifts that we've brought to this world. It was quite the scientific tour de force to be able to adapt the many and various medical advances that we have devised for ourselves over the past centuries to the benefit of wholly alien creatures such as yourselves, and even more so to successfully combat the microorganisms of this world, which I must say are a tenacious and devious bunch. Why, I've often thought that if we had arrived here just a little while earlier than we did, we may have been able to prevent the disaster that overcame your ancestors entirely."

Six barks out a short, sharp laugh at that, which seems to confuse Martok even more.

"Why do you laugh, Six? You cannot possibly doubt the potency of our science now. Why, only yesterday you appeared on the brink of death, and now look at you!" He peers at her, eyes squinted, then says, "What is that you're eating?"

"Boiled white beans," Six says.

"Is that a normal thing for you to eat for breakfast?" He turns to John. "Is this something humans crave? Should I have been providing you with breakfast beans all these years? I am terribly sorry if I've neglected your needs, but you never requested such a thing."

"No," John says. "Boiled beans are not a normal thing to eat for breakfast, and you don't need to provide any for me, thanks."

"I'm sick," Six says. "My body needs protein to rebuild itself, but I'm too weak to even think about eating leftover beast. So, beans are my next best option. I'll probably be eating them for the next couple of weeks or so—you know, just until I'm one hundred percent recovered."

Martok looks from John to Six, then back to John. He seems about to say something more on the matter when he abruptly remembers what he'd been doing before allowing himself to be sidetracked. "Ah, it matters not at all. From this day forward, you may have all the beans you want, my friends. As I have been trying to tell you, a wonderful thing has happened!"

John has a long and unpleasant history with Martok's announcements of wonderful news. He half expects to hear that Martok has decided to take out a second note on his contract, this one for a jar of tusk polish, or perhaps an extended warranty on the trundlecar. He's about to ask what this wondrous news could be, but before he can figure out a way to phrase the question in a sufficiently diplomatic way, the words begin tumbling out of Martok in a rushed, bubbly jumble.

"You both know, of course, that I had severe reservations about our recently departed guest's state of mind yesterday morning. Oh, severe indeed! Why, from his demeanor, I might have thought that he hated us! More than that, he appeared to have developed a pronounced limp during the night, and I felt sure he would blame the quality of the bed we had provided him. As I have said, the opinions of the first few customers carry a far outsized weight in determining the success of a fledgling venture like our own. This would be true if we had opened up a stall selling protein bricks in the market. How much more so, then, with a business as unique as ours?

"Most of our people would never have heard of the sorts of services we provide, and might have trouble picturing what a glorious addition they can make to one's life. Given that, the report brought back to the fine people of Lake Town by our friend Min Hara née Ice River had the potential to either make or break our prospects. It was a fine omen that he agreed to take you back to Lake Town with him, of course, but I will admit to a certain amount of trepidation as you climbed into the car with him. Not that I thought he would kill you, of course. Perish the thought! I did think it possible, though, that he might throw you out into the snow somewhere between here and Lake Town and leave you to your own devices to find your way home. Of course, I had full confidence that you would find a way to do so. You are a most resourceful person, as I have always said."

He pauses there, and looks from John to Six and back again as if he expects some kind of response. When it's clear he's not going to continue without one, John says, "Martok?"

"Yes, John?"

"You were going to tell us about the wonderful thing that's happened."

Martok's face lights up again. "Ah! Yes, of course! As I was saying, I was quite concerned when our friend Min Hara née Ice River drove away with you—not for your safety, as I was just explaining, but for the reports he might bring back to his fellows in Lake Town and beyond. I had hung all of my hopes on the idea that our first guest would return with a glowing impression of the services we had provided, and it seemed to me to be tragically possible that those hopes had been dashed entirely."

"Oh," John says. "Well. That does seem . . . possible, doesn't it? Min Hara did appear to be in a bit of a mood when he dropped me at the chemist's."

"Oh, he did. However, it seems that it may well be that what we took for dissatisfaction was simply Min's manner. Perhaps he has a congenital dislike for early mornings? He is frightfully old, you know. It is possible—likely, even—that his joints pain him when he wakes, and that his apparent mood had nothing to do with his feelings toward us or the business we are trying to build here."

"Okay," John says. "That's a hopeful interpretation. Do you have any evidence that it's true?"

Martok bares his tusks in a manic grin. "Oh, I do, my friend. Indeed, I do. I have just this moment checked my accounts. Chairman Sinta, blessings be upon him, has paid for Min's lodgings here, as promised. Would you care to guess, John, how *much* he has paid?"

John fights back the urge to roll his eyes. "I don't know how much you asked for, Martok."

"It would do you no good if you did, my friend, because the good Chairman paid *five times* our asking price! *Five times!* He followed this with a personal note to me, in which he stated that our services were 'entirely satisfactory' and that both he and Min himself are most grateful for the 'corrective' that we provided to him. Just as I predicted, our people, who are so accustomed to spending all their time huddled together, find this wilderness experience to be a soul-soothing tonic. Why, this single fee gives me enough to repay all the merchants in Lake Town for the credit they granted us when we set out from there, with nearly enough left over to pay the first installment on your note. Another such, and we will have funds sufficient to keep this place maintained and supplied, and more importantly, to keep you from the clutches of Daro Lia née Greatfoot, for the better part of a year!"

"Oh," John says. "Oh. Well, that, uh . . . that is good news."

"It is indeed. It beggars belief, does it not, to know that I have better news yet in store?"

John glances over at Six. She shrugs. He looks back to Martok, who seems about to burst waiting for John to ask.

"Okay, I'll bite. What news could possibly be better than that?"

"Only this, John. I said before that another fee would secure our future for the better part of a year. Chairman Sinta has told me, however, that we cannot expect another such fee."

John stares at him, waiting for the punch line, then says, "I don't—"

"We cannot expect another such fee, because our next fee will be *double again* what we have just received! Apparently word must have spread, because the good Chairman tells me he already has another client in mind for us—and for this one, my friends, he expects us to deliver the *full treatment*."

"So," Six says. "Are we doing a murder?"

They're back in her room now, Six tucked into bed, John sitting in a too-large chair next to the door with his elbows on his knees and his head in his hands. He looks up at the word *murder*, his gut clenching, then shakes his head and says, "No, we're not doing a murder. Why would you think that?"

"Really? Because I'm pretty sure we are. Why is that, you ask? Well, mostly because you had a run-in with a couple of low-status Ice River nobodies while Martok and I were out shopping, and the only way you could think of to get out of it was to tell them that our gentle, dopey patron is actually a soulless killing machine. Those two passed the word to Sinta, who now believes that this little hostel is a cover for Martok's Torture Palace. We gave our friend Min a pretty good beating the other night, but that apparently wasn't the *full treatment*. So? What's next on the ladder of escalation? Seems pretty obvious, doesn't it?"

John stares at her blankly, then drops his head back into his hands and says, "I can't . . . I don't understand you. How can you just talk like that?"

"Probably because I missed out on my first seven years of brainwashing in the crèche. I can think about hurting a gray—killing one, even—without going fetal and puking my guts out. That's part of the reason why nobody wanted to bond me out, and also probably why I was a week away from winding up in a refuse bin with a crushed skull when you and Martok came for me." She tilts her head to one side, considering him. "You must have a few defects in your noggin too, right? Most crèche-born wouldn't have been able to do what you did with Min, you know—and even if you're not exactly admitting it to yourself, you're definitely thinking about how we're about to kill this next visitor. Honestly, just sitting here listening to me ought to be making you wet yourself. Maybe instead of wondering what's up with me, you should be thinking about yourself a little more, huh?"

That sits between them until John says, "I don't actually know how to . . . kill . . . a gray. I don't even know where their vital organs are. Do you?"

"Nope. That topic wasn't exactly covered in the crèche. The ferals I was with might have known a bit more on the subject, but if they did, they never talked about it in front of me. If you think about it, though, there are a few things that will kill pretty much anything, right? Beheading. Bleeding out. Immolation. Any of that sound good to you?"

John swallows bile, then shakes his head and says, "I don't think you and I could manage to do any of those things even to a geezer like Min, and our next visitor could be a bull in his prime for all we know. Anyway, we can't have Martok realizing what's going on, and I'm pretty sure even he would pick up on the fact that we'd beheaded his guest." He leans back in his chair and rubs his face with both hands. He can feel his heart hammering in his chest and a light sweat has broken out on his forehead, but all in all he's a little surprised at how well he's still functioning. "What about poison? Maybe we could slip something into his food—something that would make it look like he'd died naturally?"

"Okay. Do you know anything that would do that to a gray?"

John hesitates, then shakes his head.

"Neither do I, and I don't think Martok is likely to let us borrow his handheld and run a search on easy homemade poisons. So where does that leave us?"

John knows where it leaves them, of course. It leaves them exactly where they were before: at the mercy of Dana and Tanner.

"I'm not sure the ferals will help us this time. After I gave Dana the pills, she didn't seem too interested in talking to me anymore."

"Meh. They need things that we have. Those antibiotics definitely aren't the only medicines they could use. What about metal? The ferals I was with were using stone arrowheads. They would have loved to get their hands on a few knife blades. The clothes we've got are warmer and more comfortable than leather and furs, I bet. And what about food? We've got vegetables and fruits. What do they have between now and spring? Venison sandwiches on dried venison bread probably gets old after a while, wouldn't you think?"

John drops his head into his hands again. "Maybe. I mean, I'm sure there's a lot of stuff they'd like to have. They'd have to want it pretty badly to murder a gray for it, though. That's the kind of thing that brings the spiders in, isn't it?"

"Maybe," Six says. "If the gray who gets murdered is one that the boss grays want to get murdered, though, who knows?"

The afternoon finds John out in the woods with an oversized shovel, laboriously clearing a pathway through the knee-deep snow. Martok has been unbearable for much of the day, putting him to one pointless task after another without giving him enough time to finish any of them. An hour or so after lunch, Martok decided that the *full treatment* must of course include a leisurely nature walk, in order to give their guest the opportunity to fully appreciate the subtle beauty of a forest in winter. Such a walk must obviously be clearly demarcated and free of inconveniences like piles of ice and snow. In order to make this possible, John must therefore break his back moving several tons of the stuff with a tool found abandoned in the basement of the house, one which was clearly built for someone twice his size.

If he's being honest with himself, John doesn't actually mind the work that much. Sore back and all, it's far better to be out in the cold, crisp, silent woods than scampering from one thing to another in the house, always with Martok's voice chasing after him. *Make haste, John! Our fortune is finally within our grasp, if only we have the courage to reach for it! Fetch a bucket, John! I've clogged the toilet again!*

Ugh.

As he works, John finds his mind tiptoeing carefully around the ideas that he and Six discussed after breakfast. He can't picture himself doing direct violence to a gray. He was able to participate in what they did to Min, he sees now, only because he imagined himself to be a passive observer, watching while Tanner and Dana did the actual damage. When he tries to think of himself using a knife or a bow or a rifle on their next guest, his hands shake so badly at the thought that he has to conclude that if he actually attempted such a thing, he'd be far more likely to kill himself than the gray.

Not that he imagines he'd be able to carry out the deed in any case. He learned how to shoot in the crèche—many of the more fashionable grays have a taste for game, and it's not unusual for bondsmen to be employed as hunters—but he doubts the weapons they used there had the power to even punch through a gray's hide, let alone do any real damage. Dana seemed to think her bow might do the job, but John has never handled a bow, and, if he understood what she said about her weapon's draw weight properly, he wouldn't have the strength to use it even if he knew how.

What about a blade? John drifts briefly into a half-hysterical giggle at the thought of himself flailing away at their next guest's leg with a kitchen knife while the gray looks down at him in confusion, unsure whether this is part of the entertainment.

So where does that leave him?

That question is answered almost immediately by Dana's voice, low and menacing, almost close enough behind for him to feel her breath on his ear.

"Nice to see you, John. I've got a bone to pick with you."

CHAPTER FOURTEEN

Midway through his second winter with Martok, John had a run-in with a wolf.

It was late evening. The sun only spent a few wan hours per day above the horizon at that time of year, and the sky was a clear, moonless, star-speckled black. Martok had just managed to secure them a week's lodging with the wages from an inexpert but enthusiastic repair job on an elderly Greatfoot's leaky roof, and he'd sent John off to the night market to fetch a few protein bricks and a jug of ale.

There was a reason that they'd been able to afford the room Martok had found for them. It was located in an outlying district, far from anything other than dingy clusters of similarly run-down dwellings interspersed with the occasional gambling den or dream hall, and the expanse of the park stood directly between them and the nearest respectable businesses. Ordinarily John would have been cautious about traversing the park alone. It wasn't unheard-of for young bulls to waylay stray bondsmen in lonely places like that and kill them just for the sport of it. On this night, though? It was dark, and it was cold, and he thought the probability of running into roustabout grays was low enough when weighed against the extra hour or more of walking that going around would require to justify the risk.

The risk wasn't zero, though, so John was wary. He kept his head on a swivel and his footsteps soft on the dirt pathways. Even so, the first hint he had that he wasn't alone was a low, angry, bowel-loosening growl coming out of the even darker shadows under the trees to the right of the trail, no more than a half-dozen meters away.

John froze then, heart pounding, and turned his head to see the shadow of something shaggy and long-legged and lean standing motionless as well, looking back at him. Thinking back now, he remembers gleaming teeth and yellow eyes, but that can't be right, can it? Truthfully, he can't have seen more than a silhouette in the darkness. What was it doing there, in the middle of Farhome? Come in search of food, probably, or a safe place to overwinter.

In that moment, John was acutely aware of the fact that from the wolf's perspective, he himself was made almost entirely of food.

What to do, then? Fight or flight? In John's rising panic, neither seemed possible. If he ran, he had no doubt the wolf would be on him in moments. He had nothing with him that could conceivably be used as a weapon, and the wolf was nearly as big as he was and, John assumed, much more accustomed to violence.

What to do? Nothing. There was nothing to be done.

John closed his eyes.

After what felt like an eternity of waiting for those jaws to close around his throat, but was probably more like twenty or thirty seconds, John opened his eyes again to find himself entirely alone.

"DANA," JOHN SAYS. "I need to talk to you."

"No," Dana says. "You need to listen. Those pills you gave me? They're shit. Miri isn't getting better."

That stops John briefly. He remembers what Dana said when he asked what would happen if the pills didn't work.

"It's only been a day," he says, hating the frightened squeak in his voice. "Those were antibiotics, not miracle pills. You need to give them time to work."

Dana shakes her head. "Even if I were sure that you hadn't screwed me over here and given me a sack of aspirin or some fucking thing, which I am totally not, we don't have time to let this play out. I told you, we can't lose her." Her face twists momentarily, and her voice cracks when she says, "*I* can't lose her. Twenty-four hours is long enough to break a fever, and it's not happening. That could mean that you gave me junk. I'm not killing you right now, though, because it could also mean what she's got is some kind of virus and antibiotics are the wrong thing. I can't tell which is which, and every minute that we wait to see how it goes makes it more likely she ends up in the ground, and I tell you truly, John, I will not have that. We need a medico—someone who actually knows what the fuck he's doing, and who doesn't carry his meds around in old plastic bags."

John glances around quickly. He's only a few hundred meters from the house, but the snow-covered trees are thick enough that he's completely out of sight. "I don't . . . it was hard enough getting those pills. We took a huge risk, tricking Martok, and there aren't many human docs out there, you know. Most grays don't care that much if their bondsmen get sick and die. Getting one to come out here on short notice would be insanely expensive, if it was even possible. I guess Six could pretend to take a turn for the worse, but it's hard to fake being on the brink of death."

Dana looks down at him, chewing her lower lip. "Hmmm . . . you're probably right. Even if Six pretends to get sicker, Martok could always just wait to see if she gets better, couldn't he? There's no way she could fake the way Miri is feeling right now, and we don't have time to wait. Anyway, you're the one he has this special bond with, right?" She bends down to take his left hand in hers. "Sorry, little man. Faking isn't gonna cut it this time. What we need here is a real emergency."

It's not until she grabs his elbow with her other hand that John realizes what she's about to do. His eyes go wide and he nearly dislocates his shoulder trying to pull away, but her grip is like iron and she barely seems to notice his struggles. She drops down in front of him, raises his forearm up in both hands, and slams it down against her knee.

The pain is exquisite.

During his time in the crèche, John mostly avoided the nursemaids' more elaborate punishments. He saw an older boy's hand crushed to a bloody pulp for stealing food from the pantry. He saw a girl no more than five or six lifted by one foot and slammed face down onto a table hard enough to shatter her nose and crack half her ribs for crimes unknown. He heard the wailing of a boy who'd been given up on as unbondable as he was carried out to the refuse bin. The worst pain he'd ever personally endured, though, was a badly sprained ankle suffered during a game of chase in the backyard near the end of his thirteenth summer.

He remembers that injury clearly, even now. He remembers the abrupt loss of balance, the *snap* of his ligaments giving way, the bewilderment as he fell, the sense of *betrayal* as he looked down to see his left foot suddenly pointing in the wrong direction to support him. And then, when he'd hit the ground and had time to draw breath, he remembers the searing shock of pain radiating all the way up to his knee, so fierce that his entire body trembled under the force of it.

This is worse. This is much, much worse.

He drops to his knees and stares down at his arm. The thick sleeve of his jacket hides the worst of it, but there's a new joint now where there shouldn't be, midway between his wrist and his elbow. His nerves are jangling, so overloaded with pain that they can't seem to settle on exactly where the damage is. As he cradles his broken arm against his belly, pain pulsing along with the beat of his heart and breath coming in ragged gasps, a thin trickle of blood runs out of his sleeve and begins dripping into the snow in front of him.

"You slipped," Dana says, and gets back to her feet. "You slipped and fell on a patch of ice, and you broke the shit out of your arm. That's a compound fracture of the radius and the ulna right there. Can't just splint that up. If you ever want to use that arm again—hell, if you want to *keep* that arm—you're gonna need to see someone who knows what he's about, medicine-wise. He's gonna need to set that, stitch you up, cast it, pump you full of all kinds of drugs to make sure it doesn't get infected. While all that's going on, you and Six are gonna figure out some reason to get him out of the house without any grays around. I'll take it from there." She takes two steps back and folds her arms across her chest. "Now get your shit together and get on your feet, little man. You need to get back to the house before you go into shock."

JOHN EXPERIENCES THE next hour through a haze of pain so thick that at times he feels almost as if he's drifting away from his body, watching himself dispassionately as he staggers home through the snow with his broken arm cradled against his belly.

Twice he falls, and despite his best efforts to twist around so that his right shoulder and arm absorb the impact, the jolt that travels up his arm, through his shoulder, and directly into his brain is so absurdly bad that the second time he bursts out into hysterical laughter, curled up there on the ground at the base of a tree, just at the edge of the woods where they crowd in around the house.

That's where Martok finds him, an unknown time later. John, who had been slowly relaxing as the cold ate into him and dulled the pain, hears the door slam open and closed again, and then Martok's voice pitched somewhere in the indeterminate space between anger and concern.

"John? What are you doing there, lying in the snow? We have work to do! Get up right now, and get into the house!"

John has no interest in doing either of those things, and so he squeezes his eyes closed and breathes in tight, shallow gasps as Martok thumps down the steps and starts toward him.

"John! Are you hurt? Answer me!" He's starting to say something else, the first syllable already pushing its way out of his throat, when John rolls half-over to show him his blood-soaked sleeve and his hand pointed in a direction that it has no business pointing in. A beat of silence follows, broken only by his own harsh breathing and a low gurgling sound from Martok that John has never heard before, and then John is swept up in Martok's arms, his bones grinding agonizingly against one another, and they're pounding back across the yard, up the steps, and into the house.

"Oh, John," Martok moans as he carries him up the stairs. "What have you done? What have you done?"

"I fell," he tries to say. "I slipped and fell and broke my arm." He's coherent enough to tell, though, that all that comes out is a low, slurred mush of syllables, and he has a moment to wonder whether Dana might have overestimated his constitution or underestimated the amount of damage she'd actually done before Martok lays him out in his bed and drapes a blanket over him, with the broken arm carefully laid across his chest.

"Rest here," Martok says. "Gather your strength, if you can. Help will come soon."

"SLIPPED AND FELL, huh?"

John opens his eyes to see Six silhouetted against the light coming in from the hallway through the half-open door. She's pulled a chair up next to his bed and is sitting with her legs crossed and her arms folded across her chest.

"Unnh," John says, then blinks, swallows, and tries again. "Uh, yeah. Something like that."

"A doc is on the way—a bondsman doc, real high-status. Apparently they actually let him travel alone, if you can believe that. Martok called him as soon as he got you settled in, moaning about the outrageous expense the entire time. I guess we know who actually rates around here now, huh?"

John tries to sit up, groans at the jolt of agony that shoots up his arm at even that tiny motion, and settles for turning his head to face her. "I mean, you were faking. I'm actually dying here."

She rolls her eyes. "One, I was *acting*, not *faking*, and two, you're not dying. You've got a broken arm. Granted, it looks nasty as shit, but I saw the nursemaids do worse to kids in the crèche for stealing snacks from the kitchen."

"Did they die?"

She shrugs. "Sometimes."

John closes his eyes and breathes through a surge of pain, then says, "I didn't fall, you know. Dana did this to me."

"Really? This is my shocked face."

John doesn't open his eyes to see what, exactly, that means. He can imagine.

"When the doctor gets here," he says, "you need to figure out a way to get him out into the woods."

Her chair creaks as Six leans forward. "Really? Now, that's interesting. Why would I want to do that?"

"The kid we got the drugs for isn't doing well. Dana wants a doc to look her over."

"I see. So what you're saying is that Dana absolutely shattered your arm—like, really just broke the hell out of it—just to lure a medico here to give her kid a look-see. Is that right?"

John opens his eyes. She's giving him a quizzical look, eyebrows knitted and one finger tapping her chin.

"Yeah. Yeah, that sounds about right."

"And you want to give aid and comfort to this psychotic bitch because . . ."

"Because we need her help, and this is the only way to get her to give it."

"For the murder, you mean."

John hisses through clenched teeth. "Yeah, for that."

Six grins. "Look at you, talking about murdering a gray without getting all weepy. I'm proud of you." She pauses then, and her smile fades. "What you're asking for isn't as easy as you're making it sound, though. Martok is going to want to be hovering over the two of you every minute that the doctor's here. You may not quite get this, but he's absolutely frantic about you right now. Either he really does love you, or he's a hell of an actor. I'm definitely not going to be able to waylay this guy before he fixes you up."

John's eyes sag closed again. "Take him for a walk after he's done with me. Tell him he absolutely has to see the magic of the woods in winter or something. I cleared out a little path that goes a hundred meters or so back into the trees. I'm guessing Dana will be waiting somewhere around there."

"Do we have a guarantee of safe passage?"

John hesitates, then shakes his head. "It wasn't discussed."

"It should have been. If I take him out there and then don't bring him back, Martok is going to have to answer to his employer, and it's not gonna end well for any of us. The bond payout on someone with those kinds of skills has got to be crazy high."

John's breath hisses in and out. "Sorry, Six. Next time I'm out in the middle of the woods having my arm broken I'll try to remember to do a better job of negotiating terms."

"Well," she says. "No need to be snotty about it. On the off chance I'm actually able to get him out from under Martok's nose and into Dana's hands, I'll try to impress on her that killing him would be an excellent way to bring the spiders."

"Think she'll listen?"

She pushes her chair back and stands. "You know her better than I do, my friend. I guess we just have to hope she doesn't get it into her head to break his arm too."

OVER THE COURSE of the next few hours, John learns the contours of his pain. At its best, when he's perfectly still and breathing easily, it's a dull thrum, pulses of just-tolerable ache timed to the beat of his heart. Any movement, though, brings sharper jolts that seem to come in an unlimited array of forms. The worst comes when he tries to shift some of his weight away from his right shoulder, which has begun to issue its own complaints against being pinned half-underneath him. An inadvertent flexion of his left bicep drags the broken ends of his bones against one another, and the electric flood of pain that induces flashes up his arm and back down again, bouncing back and forth like a wave trapped in a bathtub. His reaction to that produces more movement, and then a second cascading series of jolts, until finally he masters himself, grits his teeth, and breathes through the pain until it subsides back to something nearly bearable.

Other than that, he's having a lovely afternoon.

He's nearly dozing, pulled back from sleep over and over by the stabbing pain of movement each time he starts to relax, when the door bangs open and Martok bustles in, followed closely by what would have been the tallest human he'd ever seen until his run-in with Dana and Tanner. The newcomer is thin and bald, with deep-set wrinkles around his mouth and at the corners of his eyes. He wears a knee-length black leather coat and carries a massive canvas bag slung over one shoulder.

"Here he is," Martok says, and steps to the side so that the newcomer can approach John's bedside. "This is Alph, John. I am told he is the finest practitioner of the healing arts that there is to be found so far from the comforts of Farhome."

"Or anywhere else," Alph says. "Leave us, please."

That earns him a moment of stunned silence before Martok says, "I will stay, thank you. I will not interfere with your work, but I—"

"Your presence is a distraction, both to me and to my patient," Alph says without looking away from John. "Parts of what I must do here will be distressing to you. I cannot have your emotional reactions pulling my attention from my work."

Martok hesitates another beat, his mouth hanging slightly open, then mutters something in rumble-speak and backs out of the room, closing the door behind him.

"So," Alph says after waiting to hear the thump of Martok's footsteps descending the stairs. "John, is it? Let's see what you've done to yourself, shall we?"

CHAPTER FIFTEEN

"This was no fall," Alph says, and shakes his head as he gently prods John's shattered arm. He's cut the sleeve of John's jacket and shirt away from the break, and as John watches through slitted eyes he peels the bloodied strips back like the skin of an orange to expose the mess underneath. It looks even worse than John imagined, with a ragged point of bone protruding from the flesh of his forearm and purple-black bruising spreading from his elbow to his wrist.

"It was," John says. "I was shoveling a path through the woods, and—"

"At your height and weight, a simple fall would be highly unlikely to break a bone. At worst you might have a sprained wrist if you'd tried to catch yourself against the ground and landed particularly badly. A break of this sort can only be the result of substantial force applied at the midpoint of the arm, with countervailing force at one or both ends. I've seen such injuries occasionally in factory workers whose limbs got caught up in their equipment. More often, though, they are the result of an employer imprudently disciplining his bondsman." He makes a show then of peering around the room. "I see no heavy machinery here, John. So, what am I to conclude?"

They stare each other down then in silence. When Alph speaks again, his voice is gentler.

"I've come here to help you, John. I can only do that if you are honest with me. This is why I sent your employer away. Now tell me—he did this to you, did he not?"

"No," John says. "Honestly. Martok isn't that sort. He's never hurt me, or anyone else that I'm aware of."

"Hmm," Alph says. "Min Hara née Ice River might dispute that assertion."

In the stunned silence that follows that, Alph grasps John's wrist and elbow and *pulls*. In that moment, John realizes that what he'd thought was pain before was barely an annoyance in the greater scheme of things. His vision grays and his throat locks up so that he isn't even able to scream as someone plays a blowtorch over the raw meat of his arm. When he comes back to himself a minute or so later, he's surprised to see that his bones are back inside of him where they belong, and his forearm, though still grossly swollen and discolored, is more or less straight again.

"There," Alph says. "Now hold still, please. I need to make sure the limb is fully immobilized. I'd honestly prefer to get you into an operating theater and drop a few screws into the bone to make sure it holds, but with the proper bracing here I think we can make do."

He pulls a sheet of something thick and white and pliable from his bag, wraps it carefully around the arm from wrist to elbow, and then pulls out a handheld and taps something on the screen. The wrap swells then, takes on the contours of John's arm, and applies a light, almost-painful pressure to the region of the break.

"How does that feel?" Alph asks. "Tolerable?"

"Uh," John says. "I guess so?"

"Excellent." Alph taps his screen again, and the wrap goes fully rigid, locking John's forearm in place, but leaving room for his elbow to bend. "The wrap will produce synthetic osteoblasts. With luck, these should cut your full healing time from eight weeks to two. In the meantime, the brace will allow you to function normally. Feel free to undertake any activities that your pain tolerance permits. You will of course need antibiotics and anti-inflammatories while these tools do their work. My understanding is that you have an adequate supply of the former, so—"

"No," John says. "I don't. You'll need to leave me a supply of both."

After another long silence, Alph reaches into his bag, pulls out two bottles, and places them on the table next to John's bed.

"Two of each, morning and night, until they're gone. Understood?"

John nods. He expects Alph to pack up his things and go now, but instead the medico sits silently, seeming to study him. After what feels like an unreasonably, uncomfortably long time, John says, "What is it? Am I dying?"

Alph waits another beat, then says, "You must be the bondsman who participated in the torment of Min Hara, no?"

John doesn't answer, but he can feel his pulse throbbing in his arm, and he's sure his face tells Alph all he needs to know.

"Please don't be frightened," Alph says. "I haven't come here to take vengeance on Min's behalf or anything of that sort—though I will admit with some chagrin that for most patients I would have applied a nerve block before setting a compound fracture. I understand that you have little choice in what happens here, and that you had none at all when an enforcer came to claim you from the crèche. However, I cannot help but wonder whether you might have given any thought at all as to what Min Hara may have done to anger Chairman Sinta sufficiently to provoke him to contract for your services?"

John opens his mouth to deny everything, but the expression on Alph's face stops him. He hesitates, then says, "No, I never considered it."

Alph sighs. "I will admit to some disappointment, but not to surprise. In future, however, you may wish to spare a moment for these sorts of questions." He glances over his shoulder at the still-closed door, then says, "Have you wondered at the fact that I came here alone, without any minder or handler? I am permitted my own trundlecar. Did you know that? I drove it here myself from Lake Town. This is unusual for a bondsman, is it not?"

"I . . . that wasn't top of mind for me, honestly, but now that you mention it . . ."

"It may interest you to know that Min Hara was sent to you for speaking out in a meeting of senior Ice River administrators. Min is no radical, no rabble-rouser, but in this instance his conscience got the better of him, and he took it upon himself to offer some mild chastisement to Chairman Sinta. That worthy, who presumably paid for Min Hara's abuse, has of late made a habit of amusing himself by forcing his bondsmen to fight one another while he and his cronies place wagers on the outcomes. These fights are not nominally to the death, but . . . well, things happen. I'm sure you understand.

"In addition to his distaste for this sort of sport, Min Hara has been known to support the idea, advanced recently in several anonymously posted screeds in the Lake Town opinion feeds, that bondsmen like ourselves are in fact fully sentient creatures, and that therefore we should perhaps be granted the same rights and considerations given to any other citizen. A ludicrous idea, no?

"Min Hara may have seemed a ridiculous figure to you. He

is old, and he can be cantankerous. However, he is the leader of the largest family grouping in the Ice River clan. If it were not for Sinta's ability to use his wealth to buy influence, Lake Town would likely fall to Min's faction. You can see, therefore, why Sinta found it necessary to put him in his place."

Alph stands now, closes and latches his bag, and slings it over his shoulder. "Chairman Sinta has been working diligently to determine the source of these foolish ideas about bondsmen's rights for some time now. There are rumors that he may have finally succeeded." He turns to go, then pauses with his hand on the doorknob. "You may wish to consider that fact when your next client arrives."

John closes his eyes. He hears the door open and then close again, and then the soft tread of the medico descending the stairs.

"WELL. THAT WAS fun."

John opens his eyes as Six flips the light switch on and closes the door behind her. He runs his tongue across his cracked lips as she comes over to take the chair that Alph left next to his bedside, then says, "What time is it?"

"Late," Six says. "We should have had dinner hours ago, but Martok was waiting for me to get back from my walk in the woods with the good doctor, and for you to wake up. He's heating up some soup for us now."

"Your . . . you managed to get Alph out into the woods? Did you find Dana?"

"That wasn't a problem. She was waiting just past the tree line. She's like a ghost, that one. Popped out from behind a tree, almost close enough to touch us. No lie, John—I almost crapped myself."

"Yeah, she has that effect on people. How did Alph take it?"

"Honestly? He didn't even seem surprised. You didn't tip him off or anything, did you?"

John shakes his head. "Not a word."

Six shrugs. "Maybe he saw her before I did. Maybe he's just got ice water for blood. Either way, Dana took him away with her and left me standing there alone in the woods, freezing my ass off, for almost four hours."

"She didn't take you with her?"

"Nope. Apparently she doesn't want us to know where her little village is. Anyway, she finally did come back, and she brought Alph along with her, so I guess we don't have to worry about telling his employer that we lost him."

"Was he able to help her kid?"

"No idea. He got back into his car and drove away without so much as a goodbye, and the only thing Dana said to me was, 'Tell John he's got one credit in the bank now.'"

"Huh. That sounds positive, right? If he wasn't able to help, I guess she would have said something more like, *Tell John I'm gonna break his other arm the next time I see him*, right?"

Six grins. "Yeah, that's probably right. So, I guess we're on track for the whole murder thing, huh?"

When John doesn't respond, her smile fades and she says, "Hey, you okay? You're not going wobbly on me again, are you? Crèche conditioning kicking in or something?"

John hesitates another moment, then says, "Did Alph say anything to you about Min Hara?"

Her face twists in confusion. "What? No. Did he say something to *you* about him?"

"He knows what we did to him. He doesn't know the ferals were involved—he thinks it was Martok who did the beating—but he knows that I was there."

"Did he . . . was he trying to blackmail you or something?"

"No. I don't think so, anyway. He told me why Sinta had us punish Min Hara."

Six scowls. "Why would we care what one Ice River grandee did to piss off another one?"

"Because the thing that Min Hara did was to advocate for bondsmen to have basic rights, and for Sinta to stop forcing his employees to fight each other while his friends wager on the outcomes."

That gets him a moment of stunned silence before Six says, "Oh."

"Yeah, oh. Alph didn't know about our next client—I mean, I don't think he did—but he implied that Sinta had figured out who the real rabble-rouser was, and that he was planning to do something about it."

They sit in silence then for the better part of a minute before Six says, "This whole murder thing just got a lot less fun, didn't it?"

Martok brings John his dinner, helps him sit up and get his soup and bread situated on the nightstand, and then stays to make sure he finishes it.

"Growing new bones is hard work," he says. "You mustn't deny yourself the energy needed for the task."

"I'm not denying myself," John says. "It's just hard to have an appetite after a day like this one."

Out in the hallway, John hears Six padding past his door toward the bathroom, then the sound of running water. As Martok stares down at him, his face a mask of concern, John leans across his injured arm to spoon up a bit of soup. All but a carrot slice and a fatty hunk of meat spills onto his sheets before he gets it to his mouth.

"This doctor," Martok says as John manages a few bites of broth-soaked bread. "He was a strange one, don't you think? I do not believe I've ever been spoken to in such a way by a bondsman. And he was so tall! Have you ever seen a human quite so large?"

John has a moment to wonder what Martok would make of Tanner before, almost in spite of himself, he finds himself imagining the two of them fighting, Tanner wrestling Martok to the ground as the gray flails helplessly, Tanner locking his arms around Martok's neck and squeezing . . . An instant later his gut heaves, and he nearly vomits up what little dinner he's managed to eat.

"Oh!" Martok says, and rubs John's back with one hand while easing him back onto the pillows with the other. "John, are you ill? Must I summon the doctor again?"

"No," John says when he can speak again. "No, I'm fine. I just . . . I think I need to rest a little. It's been a hard day."

"Yes," Martok says. "Yes, of course. Your dinner will keep until you are ready for it." He smooths John's hair back from his forehead and helps him settle in, then pulls the sheets up to his chin. "Shall I sit with you for a while?"

"I don't think that's—"

"I would like to, John."

John opens his mouth to protest, but when he sees the expression on Martok's face, he closes it again. Instead he sighs, then says, "That would be nice. Thank you."

After a minute or so of silence, Martok says, "It occurs to me—it must have occurred to you long ago—that I may perhaps have been pushing you overly hard since we came to this place."

John chuckles. "Ah, it hasn't been so bad. You've done the hardest work. Six and I—"

"No, John. Even in your weakened state you try to comfort

me, but I know this to be true. I am familiar with the nature of the work of the frontier, but you? You have never been accustomed to hard labor. This injury should not have happened. I should never have had you out in the cold and the snow, working with a tool almost too big for you to carry. This was work that I could have done far more easily and safely than you, and I should have done so. It's only . . . you must understand—the thought of losing you haunts me, day and night. At times, I even regret the bargain with Daro Lia née Greatfoot that brought us here. Our circumstances were far from ideal in Farhome. You know this. We were safe, though—or as safe as two vagabonds can be in this world, at any rate. This is why I press so hard to make everything perfect. This is why I pick at everything you and Six have done. I have risked more than you can understand on this venture, and if it fails . . . if it fails, I do not know that I will survive it."

The obvious answer—*That's funny. I know damn well that* I *won't*—is halfway out of John's mouth before he bites it back. Martok is deep in his feelings now, and it wouldn't be kind to poke him for it.

"It's okay," John says, and closes his eyes. "I want us to succeed here too, you know. I don't mind you pushing a little, and what happened to my arm was my own stupid fault, not yours."

"You are kind, my friend. I wish I could absolve myself as easily as you absolve me."

After another long silence, John feels Martok's heavy hand resting briefly on his chest through the sheet. A moment later he hears the chair creak as Martok rises, the door opening and closing, and then Martok's feet on the stairs. The ache in his arm is duller now, oscillating above and below the line of tolerability along with his heartbeat. John sighs again, shifts his weight in the bed as much as he can with his cast laid across his chest, and tries to sleep.

John dreams of the crèche.

This shouldn't be a surprise. Suffering always brings memories of the crèche to the fore.

When John was very small—five years old, or maybe six—he woke one night in the dark, cold hour after midnight with a gnawing hunger in the pit of his stomach. Dinner that night had been vegetable mash served over boiled grains, a dish they'd been having with increasing regularity that winter, and John had stubbornly refused to eat it. He'd felt righteous and well-justified in the moment, but the nursemaid in charge of the meal had simply taken his bowl away without comment while the other children grimaced and forced the stuff down their throats and then sent him to bed when the meal was over. Now here he was, five hours later, wide awake and starving, with seven long hours to go until breakfast.

He knew better than to do what he did next, but hunger is a powerful motivator, and six-year-olds aren't known for iron self-discipline.

He slid out of bed, itself a punishable offense at this hour, crept out of the bunk room and into the hallway, and from there made his way silently downstairs, and then down the long hallway to the kitchen.

He was young enough then to have never seen a nursemaid truly angry. If that hadn't been the case, he might have stayed in bed and gritted out the night. Still, though, he knew enough to be cautious, and to at least try to cover his tracks. He took a single stick of dried meat from a half-full bin in the back of the pantry—surely they didn't keep count of how many of those things they had on hand?—and an apple from a bowl on the counter by the sink. He ate them both on the spot, even gnawing his way through the apple's core.

If he'd left it at that and gone back to bed, he probably wouldn't have thought much about it later.

He didn't, though. Sitting next to the apples was an unopened tin of sweet bean paste that one of the nursemaids must have pulled out and then neglected to put away.

Any kind of sweetness was a rare treat in the crèche. John couldn't resist. He wrestled the tin open, dug two fingers into the paste, and then licked them clean. Then, realizing what he'd done, he screwed the lid back onto the tin in a panic, climbed down off the counter, and shoved the tin into the cupboard under the sink, as far back as he could get it.

As far as he's ever known, John's crime that night was never discovered, but he spent much of the next year in a constant state of terror, sure that at any moment the opened tin of bean paste would be discovered and somehow linked back to him. It's that terror that comes back to him now. In his dream, a nursemaid comes into the bunk room and wakes him in the early morning half light, opened tin in one three-fingered hand. John tries to run, tries to scream, but dream-paralysis holds him as the nursemaid reaches down with her other hand, wraps her thick fingers around John's head, and squeezes.

John wakes with a headache so intense that for a long moment he can't separate the real pain from the dream pain. His room is dark, but a shaft of light cuts across the floor from the half-open doorway.

"Wake up, John," Six whispers. "We need to talk."

CHAPTER SIXTEEN

"Martok knows about the ferals."

John squints up at her. His heart is still juddering in his chest from the terror of the dream, and for a moment he wonders if he's still asleep.

"What . . ." He blinks. Nope, she's still standing there. Seems like maybe this is real? "What the hell are you talking about?"

She closes the door, and the room returns to absolute darkness.

"You heard me," she says. He hears her footsteps crossing the room, and then the scrape of the chair against the floor as she sits. "I heard him talking with someone through the door of his room. He was trying to be quiet, but you know what that means for a gray."

"Okay." The pain in John's head is a little less now, but he decides to try sitting up a bit anyway, hoping to take some of the pressure off of the back of his neck. He braces himself, then rises and scoots himself back with his good arm. Much to his surprise, the broken arm doesn't seem to mind, with the pain there continuing at a steady, dull throb. "What did he say, exactly?"

"Well," she says, and John can hear in her voice that she's already starting to backpedal. "It was all in rumble-speak, so I don't have all the details. I've got a good ear for that stuff, though, and I'm pretty sure I got the gist—or most of it, anyway."

John rolls his eyes. Most of rumble-speak occurs below the range of human hearing, so no matter how good Six thinks she is at interpreting it, the truth is that whatever she's about to tell him is definitely at least half conjecture.

"He was talking about you at first," Six says. "He said your name a couple of times, and then *hurt* and *danger.* He was quiet for a while after that, but then he said *no* twice, and his voice got louder, and I'm pretty sure he said *humans.*"

She falls silent then. John waits for her to go on, but after ten seconds of silence he concludes that that's all she's got.

She woke him up for this?

"Look," he says, "I think you might be getting a little paranoid. Ordinarily I wouldn't blame you, but right now there's enough shit coming down on us without making stuff up out of thin air. Martok was in with me earlier, before I fell asleep." He puts a little extra emphasis on that last bit, just in case she's missing his point. "We talked for a while, and he never hinted that he thought my arm was anything but an accident. If he knew there were ferals around here, don't you think he would at least have asked about what happened? And anyway, what does it matter that he said *humans*? You said he was talking about me, right? I hate to break this to you, but I'm a human."

"You're not," Six says. "I told you that before, remember?"

John closes his eyes, then opens them again. It doesn't make a difference. She's still sitting there. "Well, you'll have to take that up with Martok, because he calls me human all the time."

"Sure he does. In English. What does he call you in rumble-speak?"

That stops him for a moment. "Martok doesn't talk to me in rumble-speak. Why would he?"

"The word the grays use for us when they're talking to each other means *bondsman*, not *human*. I guess you wouldn't ever have had a chance to hear the word they use for actual humans, but I have. I heard it when I was a kid, when the grays came to do cleanup after the spiders had wiped out all the adults in our clan and they were trying to decide which I was, a *human* or a *bondsman*." Her voice drops now to a rough whisper. "I heard it when they were trying to decide whether to kill me with the rest of the ferals—with my family and friends. Trust me. I remember that word, and I know what it means."

That sits between them for a while. Finally, John says, "Okay. Suppose you're right. Suppose there is a word just for ferals, and suppose Martok used it tonight. What does that actually tell us? You don't know whom he was talking to, or what he was talking about. It could have been anything."

"He was talking about you, about your injury, and then he was talking about humans. It doesn't take a huge leap of logic to put this together, does it?"

Doesn't it? John's brain is turning over more slowly than usual, but still . . .

"I'm sorry," he says. "I don't know where you're going with this. What do you think we should do?"

"I don't know," Six says after a moment of silence. "Something, but . . . we haven't actually lied to him yet, have we? If we did and he caught us, do you think he'd actually kill us? Martok doesn't seem like the type, but all grays are sticklers for their laws, you know?"

Of course not, John starts to say, but the words die in his mouth. Martok has always been good to him, more or less . . . but then, John has always been a good boy, hasn't he?

"I don't know," John says finally. "I don't think so, but . . . I don't know."

"Yeah," Six says. "Me neither. Just in case, though, I'm gonna start thinking about ways to get out in front of this."

John hears the scrape of the chair legs against the floor as she stands, then her footsteps crossing the floor.

"We'll be okay," he says as she opens the door. "Don't do anything drastic right now, Six. Everything will be okay."

She looks back at him for a moment, silhouetted against the light from the hallway. Then she shakes her head, says, "Uh-huh," and pulls the door closed behind her.

No matter how minor his troubles might be at the time, John has always found that there's something about being awake in the silent, cold blackness of the wee hours that magnifies them until they seem apocalyptic.

This is even more true when they actually are apocalyptic, he's now realizing.

As he lies there on his back, trying desperately to ignore the not-quite-painful but hideously unnatural *squirming* sensation in his broken arm, which his rational mind tells him is probably whatever gray magic Alph set loose in him doing its work, but which his lizard brain insists is definitely an infestation of parasitic worms that must have gotten inside of him sometime between when Dana opened his arm and when Alph closed it back up again, he finds himself running through a million permutations of Martok confronting him with the absolutely unrecoverable mess he's made of their lives.

Scenario 1

MARTOK: John, it has come to my attention that you may have told a number of individuals, among them our honored guest Min Hara née Ice River, that far from being a simple innkeeper, I am in fact an *enforcer*. Is this true?

JOHN: Um . . .

MARTOK: *(crushes John's head like a grape)*

Scenario 2

MARTOK: I have just received a call from our recent honored guest, Min Hara née Ice River. He claims that the reason he declined our offer of a nature walk on the morning of his departure was not in fact that he was feeling unwell and needed to return to Lake Town, but rather that he had been brutally beaten during the night. Would you care to explain this, my friend?

JOHN: Um . . .

MARTOK: *(crushes John's head like a grape)*

Scenario 3

MARTOK: Were you aware that these woods are full of feral humans, John?

JOHN: Um . . .

MARTOK: *(breaks John's other arm, then crushes his head like a grape)*

John's brain continues down this path for an unreasonably long time. When he finally sleeps, he falls back into his dream of the crèche. For once, the only feeling this brings him is a sense of relief.

John wakes late, to the sound of Martok's thick fingers tapping against the half-open door.

"Breakfast is ready, my friend. Are you able to rise?"

That's a good question. Is he? John raises his head, then sits half-up and uses his good arm to scoot back against the headboard. He looks down at the broken one, now lying across his lap. Green and purple bruising shows on his wrist where it emerges from the wrap and his fingers are stiff and puffy, but the pain of the break is a tiny fraction of what it was yesterday. Cautiously, he flexes his fingers, then bends his elbow and raises his arm.

Nothing.

The dull ache is still there, deep inside the arm, but moving doesn't seem to present a problem at all anymore. He's not interested in putting any stress on the joint, but . . .

At that moment, it comes to him in a surprised jolt exactly how hungry he is. He hasn't eaten more than a few bites of soup and bread in almost twenty-four hours, and his body has been working overtime in the meanwhile. As Martok said, growing new bones is hard work, synthetic osteo-whatevers or no.

"Yes," he says. "I'll be down in a minute. Thanks."

"Of course," Martok says. "Six has already begun, but I shall await your arrival."

When Martok is gone, John swings his legs around to hang off the edge of the bed, then carefully slides off and drops to the floor. His head spins briefly before settling in, which mostly leads him to realize that last night's headache is gone. Gone as well are John's midnight fears of discovery and punishment. Martok has never, in all the time John has known him, taken any effort to hide his feelings about literally anything, and John honestly doubts if he would know how to do it even if he wanted to. If he knew anything about what John and Six have been up to, he wouldn't have been able to cheerfully invite John down for breakfast. More likely he would have stormed through the door, *absented*, and stomped John into jelly. And yet, here John stands, entirely unstomped.

Seems like everything is coming up John this morning.

As he pulls off his mangled shirt and bloodstained pants and then struggles into a set of clean clothes, John finds himself running back through his midnight conversation with Six. Martok clearly doesn't know anything about their involvement with the ferals, but could she actually have been right that he knows they exist?

It seems impossible.

As John has just learned, and as Martok must know, feral humans are dangerous. They're certainly not the sorts of things you want hanging around your cozy wilderness guesthouse. If Martok knew they were there, he would at least *try* to do something about it, wouldn't he? Daro Lia née Greatfoot apparently did, much good though it did him.

That thought leads him to picture Martok putting a rifle in his hands and sending him out to hunt ferals. He giggles, then briefly wonders what Six might know about shooting. John did as little target practice as he could get away with in the crèche, and he was never particularly good at it—but for all he knows, Six might be a sharpshooter.

That's a question for another time.

He's gingerly working his broken arm into the sleeve of a clean shirt when a different question pops into his head: What if the issue is that John actually has a completely incorrect idea about who and what Martok is? They've known each other for the entirety of John's adult life, so this also seems impossible, but almost despite himself he finds his mind turning over items that he's ignored to date, like a tongue probing at a sore spot on a tooth. For example: Martok has two bondsmen now, both basically pulled out from under the feet of the nursemaids. Why? If John is being totally honest with himself, he's really never contributed anything in particular to Martok's material well-being, and material well-being is something that Martok has never had an abundance of. And now, after years of sharing what little he had with John, Martok has acquired Six in the same way, just at the moment when his finances were at their most precarious.

He could argue that Six was brought on because they needed the extra hands to get their little business off the ground. John almost has himself believing that, until he flashes back to his conversation with Martok from the night before, to Martok telling him that he could have done the job he'd tasked to John both faster and more safely.

That's true for pretty much everything, isn't it? This world isn't built for John, and accomplishing anything physical is always going to be a struggle for him. Seen from this perspective, Martok's constant hectoring starts to seem more understandable. It's not that he's being an unreasonable perfectionist. It's that he's frustrated by the fact that he's handed tasks to John and Six that he could have easily done himself in a fraction of the time, and he's constantly frustrated at how slowly and incompetently they're handling them.

John also can't help but consider now that Martok either didn't notice or didn't care that Alph disappeared into the woods for over four hours after finishing up with John yesterday. That's an awfully long time for a nature walk through knee-deep snow, isn't it? He would have expected at least a question from Martok as to what, exactly, was going on there, but as far as he knows, Martok just ignored the entire situation.

So, where does all this leave him? What does it mean for John's future prospects if Martok has plans and motivations that John isn't privy to?

It leaves him with a resurgent headache, that's where. With a sigh, he pulls on a pair of thick, warm socks one-handed, flexes the swollen fingers at the end of his broken arm, and heads down to breakfast.

"We've had quite the time of it for the last few days, have we not, my friends?" Martok looks back and forth between John and Six, then returns his attention to the platter of dried meat and hard cheese in front of him. "Between Six's frail constitution and John's clumsiness, I worry that I may soon find myself entirely alone here."

Six narrows her eyes, then scrapes up the last of the jam from her nearly empty plate with one finger. "Even if you lost us both," she says as she licks her finger clean, "you wouldn't be *entirely* alone, would you?"

John shoots her an alarmed glance, but Martok just rolls his shoulders in a ponderous shrug and says, "I suppose I might still have our guests from time to time, but how would I manage them without the two of you to help me?"

"Oh," Six says, "I'm sure you'd figure it out."

This isn't the conversation John was hoping to have over breakfast. He takes a bite of jam-smeared bread and says, "My arm's feeling much better, actually. I don't think I can lift anything with it yet, but I should be able to help out with any one-handed jobs today."

"Are there a lot of those?" Six asks. "One-handed jobs, I mean."

"There is actually little that needs to be accomplished today," Martok says around a mouthful of cheese. "Our next guest arrives in two days' time, but I believe that most of what must be done to accommodate him has already been done. I can finish clearing the walking path that John began yesterday. Six can ensure that a room is prepared, and that we have the makings of several proper meals on hand. I think your time would be best spent resting and healing, my friend. I know you wish to contribute to the general welfare of the enterprise, but in my opinion you can best accomplish that by doing what you can to ensure that when we do need you, you will be available and ready to work."

There doesn't seem to be any answer required, so John just nods and returns his attention to his breakfast. He's already eaten more than he usually would and he can feel his stomach starting to bloat, but his appetite seems to be untouched. He takes another piece of cheese from the platter in the center of the table, then a strip of dried meat. Six raises one eyebrow. "Planning on leaving anything for us to prepare for our guest?"

John gives her side-eye as he bites into the cheese. He's about to say something about how he's just basically fasted for twenty-four hours and anyway it's not really any business of hers how much he eats when she grins and says, "Oh, it's okay. I doubt he'll be too hungry, now that I think of it."

John freezes, the remainder of the cheese halfway from his mouth to his plate. Six is watching Martok, her expression unreadable. Is this her way of trying to get out in front of things? If so, is he dooming himself by staying silent?

Martok seems not to have heard her at first. His eyes are on his plate, and he's chewing the last of his breakfast, one hand wrapped around a mug of ale. He swallows, drains the ale, and wipes his mouth with the back of his arm, then sets the mug down and turns his gaze to Six. The three of them hold that tableaux for a full ten seconds before Martok says, "Yes. As to that. I have given this some thought, my friends. I know this is not in our best financial interests—but despite that, and despite the wishes of the good Chairman . . . when our next guest arrives, I would like to humbly request that you refrain from killing him."

CHAPTER SEVENTEEN

"How long have you known?" Six asks, and John feels a flutter of terror in his belly that threatens to bring up everything he's just eaten.

Martok looks down at his hands on the table in front of him, then up again at Six. His lips are pulled back from his tusks in an expression John has never seen on him before.

That can't be good. John's pretty sure he's seen all of Martok's happy expressions.

"The answer to that question depends on what is meant by *known*. Before I hazard an answer, perhaps it would be best if you were to tell me all the things I *should* have known—" He turns to John. "All the things I would have thought my two closest friends in this world would have confided in me immediately but apparently did not, I mean to say. Tell me these things, and I will then tell you which ones I was already aware of, and when I became aware of each. Does this seem reasonable?"

Six shoots John a quick side-eyed glance. John shrugs. They're in uncharted territory now, and he has no idea whether Martok is really interested in an open and honest discussion, or if he's five seconds from going *absent* and crushing them both into puddles of bone shards and goo.

"Well—" Six begins, but John hurriedly cuts her off.

"Chairman Sinta thinks you're an enforcer. It's my fault. I'm sorry. There were these roustabout grays back in Lake Town and I didn't *tell* them that's what you were but I kind of *implied* it and I thought they were going to take our stuff and I couldn't think of any other way to stop them but I never actually lied, I swear it. Things just kind of happened, and when I realized what they'd done, that they'd gone straight to Sinta, I didn't know how to make it right. I'm sorry, Martok. I'm so, so sorry."

Six is watching him now, a look of distaste on her face. Martok looks down again, and when he speaks his voice is uncharacteristically subdued.

"Oh, John. After all of our years together, after all the hardships and the joy we have shared, after all the times I have called you not just *friend*, but *family*, can you really have thought that I would punish you for such a bizarre misunderstanding? You did the best you could in this terrible situation—a situation that *I* put you in by leaving you alone with our possessions when I should have known that the underbelly of Lake Town would see that as an invitation to thievery. I tell you truly, the fear I see in your face now cuts me as deeply as anything I can remember."

"As long as we're clearing the air," Six says, "there are humans—feral humans—in the woods. It was one of them that broke John's arm, and they took the drugs John got for me—I was never sick, by the way, I was just pretending to be so that we'd have an excuse to fetch some antibiotics. That jar next to my bed is full of white beans, not pills. Oh, and they helped us beat Min Hara when he stayed with us. That's why he was so upset the morning that he left. We beat him and told him it was you—and we were planning to have them help us kill our next guest. I guess we won't do that now that you know, but we should probably figure out what we *are* going to do, about him and about them."

That outburst earns her ten solid seconds of silence, a long enough time for John to wonder if the line has been crossed now and he's about to leave this world in a spray of blood and bone shards.

"Hmmm . . ." Martok says finally, his voice a flat monotone. "That is quite a dilemma, is it not? Excuse me, please."

He pushes back from the table and gets to his feet, then walks stiffly across the room and into the hallway. A few moments later, they hear the front door opening and a cold wind whistling through the house.

"Well," Six says when it's apparent that Martok isn't coming back anytime soon. "That went better than I expected."

John gets up, goes out to close the still-open front door, and then comes back to sit at the table again. He and Six sit in silence for a while, listening to snow pattering on and off against the picture window that looks out into the woods.

"Do you think he's coming back?" Six says eventually.

John shrugs. "Probably."

"When he does, do you think he's gonna kill us?"

Another shrug. "Probably."

After a long silence, John says, "That was a lot, you know. It might have been better if you eased him into the whole *working with the ferals* thing."

"I thought he already knew about them."

"Based on his reaction, I'm pretty sure he didn't."

Six sighs. "Yeah, that does seem likely. I was just trying to get out in front of the issue."

He turns to look at her. "Do you know what that actually

means? Because you keep saying it, and I'm not sure it means what you think it does."

Her face twists into a scowl. "It means *fuck you*, okay, John? That's what it means."

John takes a strip of dried meat from the platter at the center of the table, gnaws half of it off in one bite, then spits it out onto his plate a moment later when he realizes he can't chew that much of the rubbery stuff at once.

"Oh come on," Six says. "You're disgusting."

He takes a smaller bite from what's left in his hand, chews, and swallows. He'd like to argue with her, but the wet hunk of meat staring back at him from his plate makes that pretty much impossible.

"Don't worry," he says. "Once Martok comes back, goes *absent*, and pulverizes both of us, you'll never have to worry about my table manners again."

"I guess there's a bright side to everything, isn't there?"

John takes the water pitcher in both hands, fills his glass, and drinks. Grays have a much higher salt tolerance than humans do, and their dried meat in particular needs a lot of dilution.

"We didn't actually lie, you know."

John turns to look at her. "What?"

"Martok doesn't have justification for killing us. We didn't tell him some stuff, admittedly, but we never actually lied."

"Not telling him stuff? That's lying by omission."

"I don't think that's a real thing."

"Trust me. It is."

Six pulls her feet up onto the seat of her chair and hugs her knees to her chest. For the first time since John met her, she actually looks like the child she is.

"I honestly thought he knew," she says. "When he said that thing about not killing our next guest, I thought he knew everything. Between that and him talking about *humans* last night, how could he not have known?"

John scowls. "He knew about the thing *I* confessed to. He definitely knew that Sinta had gotten the idea that he was an enforcer, and I think he probably knew that it was because of what happened with me in Lake Town while the two of you were out shopping. He was okay with that. He was ready to forgive us. Why did you have to start blathering about everything else?"

"I don't know." Six moans and drops her head into her hands. "I panicked, I guess? I was so worked up about not getting stomped for lying that I kind of forgot that they can stomp us for all kinds of other stuff too."

"You mean like beating the shit out of one gray and conspiring to kill another one? Because I'm pretty sure both of those things are a lot further up the punishment scale than telling a fib."

"Yeah," Six says miserably. "Like that."

The truth is that even if Six hadn't blabbed, John has to admit to himself that he probably would have eventually. The conditioning from the crèche is still strong in him. He can see now that he'd somehow been keeping the part of him that was plotting to murder a gray and the part of him that moved through the normal parts of his day and, more importantly, interacted with Martok, in separate parts of his brain. Once the wall between them was breached, though, there was no way he would have been able to keep the truth from pouring through eventually.

"At least he didn't *absent*," John says. "I thought he was going to for a minute there."

"Is that what it looks like?"

John turns to look at her. "You've never seen a gray *absent* before?"

Six shakes her head. "As far as I know, it only happened once in the ten years I was in the crèche. One of the older boys tried to run away. They caught him, obviously. I mean, where did he think he was going to go? You could see from one end of that town to the other. I guess he tried to fight the nursemaids when they brought him back, tried to get away from them again, and . . ."

"And one of them *absented*."

Six nods. "There was a red stain on the porch in the morning. They tried to clean it, but it never really did come out. It was still there when the two of you came to take me away."

John lets that sit between them. What else is there to say?

"You said he wouldn't kill us," Six says after the silence becomes unbearable. "Last night. You said everything would be okay."

John drains the rest of the water from his cup. "I also told you not to do anything drastic. Remember that part?" Her face darkens then, and John remembers abruptly that he's talking to a frightened child. "Honestly, though, I don't think he will, Six. Most grays would have done it already. Most grays would have pulped us before you'd gotten through the second sentence of your little confession. Martok, though? I don't think he has that sort of thing in him. Why else would he have just walked out the door like that? He wanted to get away from us for long enough to settle down, for long enough to make sure he wasn't going to *absent*. Once that's done, he'll come back, and we'll talk."

When Six speaks again, her voice is smaller. "What do you think we'll talk about?"

John leans his head back and closes his eyes. "I guess we're gonna have to wait and see."

It's well past noon by the time Martok returns. John is in the kitchen, standing next to the sink and eating an apple he's just taken from the pantry. Six is upstairs in her room with the door closed tight, which is where she's been since breakfast. It seems silly to John—if Martok has decided that he's done with them, a flimsy wooden door has about as much chance of saving her as a handful of fairy dust—but if it makes her feel better, he finds he's not inclined to argue with her.

"Hello, John," Martok says.

"Hi," John says, and puts the remains of his apple down on the counter. Martok looks . . . tired. His hands hang loose at his sides, his chin dips toward his chest, and his crest is a flat, lifeless gray.

He's not *absent*, anyway.

Martok crosses to the island that takes up the center of the kitchen and lowers himself onto a stool. It creaks under his weight, but it holds.

"Shall I be surprised to still find you here? It occurred to me that you might have fled." He folds his hands together and rests them on the island. "In truth, John, part of me *hoped* that you might have fled."

John feels a cold breeze pass through him at that, but his voice is steady when he says, "Where would we have fled to, Martok? There isn't anywhere safe in this world for a lost bondsman, is there?"

Martok's gaze drops to his hands. "There are humans in the forest, if Six is to be believed. You could have gone to them."

"Maybe," John says. "The problem with that, though, is that I'm not actually human, am I?"

Martok looks up, then down again with a subsonic rumble of a sigh. "No. No, I do not suppose that you are."

John has spent the greater part of his life being afraid—afraid of the nursemaids, afraid of random grays on the streets of Farhome, afraid of nearly everything in this fallen world, if he's being honest with himself.

He's never been afraid of Martok.

If that's about to end, he'd like to at least know what kind of world he's leaving.

"What am I, Martok? I'm not human. So? What am I?"

Martok sighs again, and runs one hand back along his crest. "You are a bondsman, John. You are what we made you to be." He hesitates, then drops his hand back to the island. "Humans? They are very dangerous things." His gaze flickers to the cast on John's left arm. "It seems you may have learned this recently. Even after The Fall, after their civilization was in ruins and nearly all of them were dead, they were dangerous—too dangerous to be permitted to persist, if we were to survive here. And so, we had a choice: wipe the world clean of them entirely, or *change* them into something with which we could coexist."

"Something you could *own*, you mean."

A flush of scarlet blossoms on Martok's crest at that, but his voice remains calm. "Would you rather we had killed them all, John? Would you prefer to never have existed? To end an entire species, to wipe a genetic line from the world for all time—this is a very great crime. Humans, if our reading of the histories of this place are accurate, have done this many times over with little more than a few false tears, but our people are not nearly so cavalier. Despite this, many of us argued for it. The decision was a near thing. The humans of that time, few and desperate though they were, had weapons of fantastic power, and they never hesitated to use them with a savagery that we utterly lacked. It bewildered us, truly, how their technology could have surpassed ours so badly in this one area while lagging so far behind us in nearly every other facet. The fact of it was seen as more evidence that they could not be allowed to live. They were ingenious creatures, clearly, but their genius seemed to be directed almost entirely toward destruction. Our first landing parties were slaughtered wholesale. They butchered us, John. They *ate* us. We could not live on this world with creatures like that running free."

"So you changed us."

"Not at first. First, we dropped spiders. They were directed to kill any adults they encountered, and to take any children. Even then, it was a near thing. The thought that our spiders could be beaten, that they could be faced and killed in close fighting, had never occurred to us, but those humans . . ." He trails off, and a shudder runs through him. When he speaks again, his voice is softer. "We finally succeeded only because the remaining humans were few and scattered, and we were able to produce enough spiders to overwhelm them.

"Once we had an adequate breeding population, the surviving spiders were ordered simply to kill. We hoped they would drive the remaining wild population to extinction." He rubs his face with his hands, then leans forward until his elbows rest on the island. "It was impossible, of course. This was the humans' world. They knew how to hide—and even when they were found, driving creatures to extinction was their specialty, not ours. When the last of the spiders was dead, some remnant of the feral humans still survived."

John has more questions: *What caused The Fall? Was* that *your fault too?*—but he knows he's walking a fine line now, and he doesn't actually want to die under Martok's feet today if there's any way to avoid it. It's probably for the best, in any case. He could use a little time to assimilate this new information before having his worldview flipped on its head yet again.

The silence holds between them then for a full minute before Martok says, "What shall I do with you, John?"

"About that," John says, "Six and I were talking after you . . . left . . . and I think she actually has a point. Technically, we didn't really lie to you, so—"

"*Lie?*" Martok says, his voice suddenly loud enough to fill the house. His hands rise up and then slam down onto the island with enough force to crack the wood as John cringes back against the counter, and Martok's crest flushes a sudden, vivid red. "*Lie?* You think *this* is what I should care about? How can you . . . John, you *struck* Min Hara née Ice River! Can you possibly not know what it means for a bondsman to do violence to one of us? It would be enough to condemn you if you had simply lashed out at some roustabout on the streets of Lake Town, but you . . . you *abused* a feeble elder—one who was my guest, and explicitly under my protection! Do you not understand that I have shamed myself already, by not crushing you underfoot the very moment I knew this? Is it not clear to you that my disgrace *grows*, it *compounds*, every moment that I continue to permit you to live? How do you not see this?"

Martok drops his head into his hands, and his fingers dig divots into the thick, loose skin on either side of his crest. John slowly straightens, his back pressed against the counter.

"Martok," he says, "I'm sorry. I didn't . . . I mean, I knew what we were doing was wrong, but . . . I just—"

"Go," Martok says without looking up, his voice flat and low now. "If you stay, I must kill you. I must . . . No. No, I could not bear that, my friend. Despite all, I could not bear that. I would sooner kill myself. Please. Take Six. Take whatever of our possessions you can carry, and go."

"Martok," John says, his voice barely more than a whisper. "Please. We can fix this. I can . . ."

He trails off as he sees the skin under Martok's fingers begin to tear as the deep red flush on his crest darkens toward black.

Martok is on the verge of *absenting*.

Without another word, John backs slowly out of the room. Martok moans, drops his forehead to the surface of the island, and covers his head with his arms.

John goes.

CHAPTER EIGHTEEN

The woods are different, John finds, when you know there's no house to go back to. The trees seem taller, and the shadows between them deeper. The wind is colder, and the snow pulls at his boots with every step.

Oh well. At least he's still alive.

Martok, after bringing himself back under some modicum of control, locked himself in his room while John and Six hurriedly stuffed clothes and blankets and medicine and food into bags before bolting. John, at the last moment, took an image cube from the mantel that showed a rotating series of images of him and Martok together—Martok grinning as he holds John on one shoulder by the lake in Farhome; Martok crouching next to John as the two of them watch a wrestling match in the south amphitheater; Martok and John posing before a table laden with the feast Martok bought them with the down payment on a roof repair job that they never actually completed.

Six, at the last minute, grabbed a rifle and ammunition that John hadn't known they had. When he asked her where that had come from, she told him they'd bought it in Lake Town. When he asked why she never told him about it, she said, "At first, I didn't trust you. Later . . ."

She never finished that sentence. John didn't push her.

They're farther out than John has been before, past the big rock and slogging through knee-deep snow, chins tucked against a wicked north wind, when Six says, "So what's the plan here?"

"Plan?" John says. "I don't have a plan. My last plan was to not get stomped to death on the kitchen floor. It worked, barely. At this point, I'm just walking and hoping for the best."

They trudge on for a dozen more steps before Six says, "If your feral friends don't show up before dark, we're freezing to death tonight. You know that, right?"

"Yeah," John says. "Seems likely."

Privately, he's not actually so sure that's true. They have their jackets, and they have blankets to wrap up in. He shudders, thinking about how miserable a night out in this would be, but he's spent enough nights without a roof over his head to think it would probably be survivable.

What happens after that, though? They have food for a few days, but they're likely to wear down faster than that if they can't get any real rest. John has been homeless and hungry before. That was in Farhome and *not* in the dead of winter, but still he remembers how cold he got in the deep of the night as his metabolism shut down to conserve what few calories he and Martok had been able to scrounge during the day. They probably won't freeze tonight, but tomorrow night? The one after that?

They're definitely on the clock here.

"Seems like it might have been a good idea to make sure you had some way to contact Dana and Tanner, huh?"

John turns back to look at her. Her head is down, and she's wearing a blanket wrapped like a shawl over her heavy coat. John is actually bordering on over-warm just in his cut-up jacket at the moment from the effort of pushing through the snow. How is she not sweating right now?

"Yeah, well, I hadn't planned on getting kicked out into the snow today—or ever, actually. The idea that I'd be begging a bunch of ferals to take us in never really occurred to me."

As he starts walking again, Six says, "So. Are you working on your sales pitch?"

"My what?" John says without stopping.

"Your sales pitch. You just said it—we're gonna be begging them to take us in. You know them better than I do, I guess, but honestly I didn't get the impression that they were super into charity. It's gonna be a real downer if we find them and they tell us to go die in a hole, isn't it? So, you need to have some idea of what you're gonna tell them to convince them that it's actually a good idea to give us somewhere warm to sleep tonight."

Huh. He hadn't actually considered the possibility that Tanner and Dana might refuse to take them in.

He flashes back to the first time he met them, to the two of them casually discussing whether to slit his throat. There's definitely a very distinct chance that they're going to refuse to take them in.

"Well," he says, "I hadn't really thought about it, honestly. I guess I'm open to suggestions."

After a short silence, Six says, "You don't think about much, do you, John?"

He stops walking again, and turns to face her. "Sorry?"

She stops as well, folds her arms across her chest, and squints her eyes against the wind. "I said, you don't think about much. You didn't think about what would happen after you let Sinta think that Martok was an enforcer. You didn't think about what a terrible idea it was to team up with a couple of ferals to torture a gray. You didn't think about how unfair it was of you to drag *me* into this mess. You see the pattern here?"

John's jaw sags for a moment before snapping shut again with enough force to send a jolt of pain through his molars.

"Drag you? I'm sorry, but I'm pretty sure I remember you being right there with us when we did what we did to Min Hara—and wasn't it you who had the idea to fake being sick? I tried to keep you out of this, Six. You just kept sticking your nose in until I didn't have any choice but to include you."

She glares at him. "That's not how I remember it—and anyway, even if I did, I'm a literal child, John, barely out of the crèche, and you're a grown-ass adult man. Shouldn't you have been looking out for me?"

And that's a step too far. John feels a flush creep up his neck as he opens his mouth to let her know exactly where she can shove *that* particular line of argument, but . . .

Well . . .

Honestly, she's got a point.

As quickly as it rose up, his anger subsides. He shakes his head and says, "Yeah, I guess I probably should have been. Ever since Martok first told me about this stupid plan I've been pretty much focused on my own problems. I guess I didn't have much energy left over to worry about yours. I still don't know exactly why Martok decided to take you on before we came here, but—"

"Seriously, John?"

That stops him. "What?"

"He took me on for the exact same reason he took you on, dummy. I was about to age out, and he didn't want the nursemaids to kill me."

He stares at her. "You think it was . . . charity?"

"Do you have a better explanation?"

"How would he even have . . ."

He trails off then, because of course Martok knew Six was there, knew she was running out of time, and that the nursemaids would hand her over for nothing. They got off the train in that miserable little town for no other reason than to collect her.

"The more I think about it," Six says, "the more I think that all Martok really wanted was a place in the woods where he could keep his little collection of stray bondsmen safe. The whole guesthouse thing was just a means to an end." She sighs. "There was a thing the adults used to say when I was little, before the grays found us. 'No good deed goes unpunished.' It stuck with me, but I never really got what they were getting at." She starts walking again, brushing past John without looking at him. "I think I get it now."

IT'S LATER, CLOSE to sunset, and John is just thinking that they might have to find a place to set up whatever half-assed sort of camp they can manage when Dana finally comes for them.

"You're a long way from home, little man," she says as she appears, seemingly from nowhere, leaning against the snow-coated trunk of a tree no more than a dozen paces in front of them.

John pulls up short, and Six bumps into him from behind before looking up.

"Josiah said he saw the two of you wandering around out here. I didn't believe him—or at least, I didn't believe it was actually you." She pushes away from the tree and starts toward them, one hand on the hilt of her knife. "I think I've made it pretty clear on many occasions that I didn't want you out here looking for us, didn't I?"

The knife is out in her hand now, and John is about to tell her that there's no need to feel threatened, that they're here to throw themselves on her mercy, when Six steps out from behind him and says, "Stop. Now."

John turns to look at her, mouth hanging open.

The stock of the rifle is against her shoulder. One eye squints down the sights, which are centered on Dana's chest.

Much to John's surprise, Dana stops. She raises both hands slowly, and a grin spreads across her face.

"Well," she says. "The first time we met, I asked if you were out hunting. Do you remember that, John? You said you weren't. Tanner believed you, and that's why you're still alive. Is this where I find out that you're a lying little turd? Because I gotta say, ordinarily I'm pretty happy when I can prove that Tanner's an idiot, but I'm honestly a little down about this one."

"We're not hunting," John says. "We're running. We were thinking . . . that is, we were *hoping* you might be willing to take us in."

Dana stares at him blankly for a beat, then bursts out laughing. "Take you in? Like, you want to come live with us?" She lowers her hands and sheaths her knife. "Go home, you idiot. I don't know what kind of spat you've gotten into with your gray, but I'm not about to bring him down on us by helping you run away."

She's started to turn away when John says, "We're not running away. Martok threw us out. We don't have anywhere else to go."

That stops her. She turns back to him. She's not laughing anymore. "Threw you out? That seems awfully cruel of him, doesn't it? Look at the two of you. He must know you won't last a day out here, and from what I understand, pets like you two are expensive to replace. What could you possibly have done to get yourselves turned out into the cold?"

"You know what we did," John says. "You helped us do it."

"Ah," Dana says, and brings one finger to her chin. "Your little torture racket came crashing down on you already, huh? Go figure." She tilts her head to one side and studies them for a moment. "I'd like to help you, little man. Honestly, I would. The thing is, though . . . I don't know that it's in my best interest to get in the way of a gray's death sentence."

"It's not a death sentence if you help us," Six says as she lowers her rifle.

Dana's face hardens. "Maybe not—but old Martok wouldn't have any way to know that was a possibility, would he? After all, he doesn't know about us. Right, John?"

John doesn't answer. Over the course of five seconds, Dana's expression shifts from anger, to dawning realization, to blank fear. When she speaks again, her voice is a flat monotone. "No, he does know about us, doesn't he? He knows, because you told him."

"We told him about *you*," Six says. "Just you. We had to. He knew what we did to Min Hara, and it's pretty obvious we couldn't have done it alone. He doesn't know what else might be out here. He doesn't know you've got a whole community."

"He knows humans don't live alone. He's got to at least suspect there's more than just me, no matter what you told him." Dana closes her eyes and takes a slow breath in, then releases it again. "Fucking Tanner. I told him. I *told* him! I should have cut both of your throats that night at the lake house. Hell, I should have cut John's throat the first time I saw him."

"Yeah, well," Six says. "Water under the bridge, right? No use in cutting our throats now, and we can help each other moving forward. We've got medicine. We've got food. We've got a rifle. We can—"

"I don't care what you've got, you little shit!" Dana presses her fists against her eyes, then throws her head back and says,

"Fuck. Fuck! How long ago did you tell him? How long do we have?"

"Until what?" John says.

"Until the spiders come," Six says. "I get why you're freaking out. I was there when they came for us at Owasco. Martok, though, I don't think he'd—"

"You don't think? You don't fucking *think*?" The knife is out again, and Six brings the rifle back to bear. "You expect me to risk the lives of my family, of my friends, of everyone I know, on what you *think*?"

"Daro Lia née Greatfoot knew you were here," John says, and steps forward to stand between them. "Or at least he must have suspected. He didn't bring the spiders down on you, and he would have had access to the credits to do it. Martok definitely does *not* have the credits, and also he's not a complete shithead. Why do you think he'd—"

"Because Daro did *not* know we were here. He just knew that his pets kept getting mangled out in the woods. Maybe it was bears getting them. Maybe it was cougars. Who knows? Grays are greedy fucks at heart, every one of them, and if they can talk themselves out of spending credits, they'll do it. Martok, though? He doesn't *suspect* that we might be out here. He *knows*. He knows, because *you* fucking told him." She runs her free hand back through her hair, then sheaths her knife and says, "Give me the gun."

Six blinks, then shakes her head and says, "I don't think so."

Dana steps forward. "Give it to me. You're right that killing you isn't going to do me any good at this point—so, fine. I won't kill you. If you really think we can help each other, though, we're going to need to do some trust-building. That starts with you handing over the rifle."

John looks back at Six. Her eyes flicker from Dana to him and then back. She doesn't lower the rifle.

"Six," John says. "Give her the gun."

"You trust her?"

"I don't have a choice. Neither do you. You said it yourself. If they won't take us in, we'll freeze out here—maybe not tonight, maybe not even tomorrow, but soon enough. So? Give her the gun. If she turns around and shoots us with it, what have we lost? She'd probably be doing us a favor."

Six hesitates, then scowls, lowers the rifle, and holds it out to Dana, stock-first. Dana steps forward to take it from her. The weapon was built for bondsmen. It looks like a toy in Dana's hands. She pulls back the bolt and peers into the chamber, then looks down at Six.

"It's not loaded."

"Nope," Six says. "You surprised me, showing up like that. I didn't have time to dig the ammunition out of my bag."

Dana stares her down for a moment, then breaks into a grin. "I like this one, John. She's got balls." She turns away then, and starts off into the trees. After a half-dozen steps she looks back and says, "Come on, if you're coming. I'm not waiting, and I'm sure as hell not gonna carry you."

JOHN ISN'T SURE what he expected Dana's encampment to look like. Houses in the trees? A palisaded fortress? Longhouses with roaring fires in their hearths?

He didn't expect this.

It's fully dark now. The night has brought a clear sky and a fat, silvery moon, but next to none of its light is reaching them here. They've come to the base of a steep hill overlooking a narrow stream, now frozen hard enough to walk across and dusted with snow. The trees are so thick that even leafless they bring a sense of oppressive closeness and block out nearly all of the sky. A slab of rock a dozen meters wide and as thick as John is tall juts out of the hillside at a sharp angle in front of them, and another half-buried boulder leans against the high end, leaving a sheltered space beneath them that's shoulder-high on Dana at one end and shrinks down to nothing at the other.

"Watch your heads," Dana says, then snickers to herself as she ducks under the slab and disappears into the darkness beneath. John looks at Six. She shrugs, and follows Dana down. After a moment's hesitation, John does as well. He's only gone two hesitant steps when light flares, silhouetting Six in front of him. Beyond her, he sees Dana crouched just inside a half-open circular hatch set into the rear of the shallow cave.

"Let's go," she says. "You're letting the heat out."

CHAPTER NINETEEN

"You have power," John says, and squints up at the light panel set into the roof of the tunnel.

"Yeah," Dana says. "What did you think?"

They follow her farther into the hillside. John lets his fingers trail along one smooth gray wall as they walk. He expected to feel damp, cold stone, but this is something else. Metal, maybe? Hard to say. It's dry, though, and neither warm nor cold to the touch. There are closed doors on either side of the corridor, every ten steps or so. The light panels are farther apart, enough so that the illumination is noticeably dimmer between them. John turns to Six and whispers, "Is this what it was like with the ferals you knew? When she called this *the hole*, I expected . . . you know . . . a *hole*."

Six shakes her head. "We lived in tents made out of deerskin and wooden platforms in the trees. The most high-tech thing we had was a compound bow from before The Fall that jammed up half the time when you tried to shoot it."

"Right," Dana says without turning. "That's why the grays

found those guys and they still haven't found us. That's why we're alive and they're not."

The corridor ends in a T. Dana takes the right-hand branch, then stops at the first door on her left, knocks once, and opens it.

"Good," she says after leaning through the doorway and looking around. "It's empty." She steps aside. "You two, in. You can wait here while we figure out what we're gonna do with you."

Neither of them moves. Dana rolls her eyes, grabs John by the scruff of his neck, and shoves him into the room. Six starts to back away, but before she's gone a step Dana has her as well, and she's stumbling past John, and the door has closed behind them with a bang.

"Stay put," Dana says from the corridor. "I'll be back for you eventually." John hears the distinct *snick* of a bolt sliding home, and then Dana's footsteps receding down the corridor.

The room she's left them in is nice enough, as jail cells go. Honestly, it's nicer than anywhere he and Martok had ever managed to hole up prior to coming to the house in the woods. It's a wood-paneled box, four meters wide, three deep, and three high, give or take, with a bed in one corner, a desk and chair in another, and a chest of drawers along the back wall. A single light panel in the ceiling gives off a dim yellow glow; a door on the right-side wall leads to an even smaller room with a sink and toilet that are both almost but not quite too big for them to use; and a steady stream of warm, dry air comes from a grate set into the ceiling.

Six drops her bag on the floor, climbs up onto the massive bed, and says, "This is crazy. I don't mean weird. I mean I literally feel like I'm going crazy. What is this place?"

John drops his own bag next to hers, peels off his jacket, and sits down on the floor with his back to the wall. "That's what I was about to ask you. You're the one who knows all about ferals, right?"

Six shakes her head. "I told you, the ones I was with didn't have . . . well, anything, really. For fuck's sake, they were hunting with stone arrowheads and hand-carved bows." She looks around. "This place? I've never seen anything like it. I'm not even sure the *grays* have anything like this."

"Well," John says. "Let's not go crazy. The grays have electricity and indoor lighting. In terms of high tech, that's pretty much all we've seen so far, right?"

"Maybe. I don't know, though. How deep underground are we? We've got fresh air and dry floors. That takes some kind of engineering. And by the way, where's that electricity coming from? The grays have power cells, but those need fuel, and there's no way these guys are getting a steady supply of that here."

That's a fair point. John has only the vaguest idea of how electricity is generated, but the process as he understands it does in fact involve feeding foul-smelling liquid into a large box on a regular basis. The liquid has to come from somewhere, and he very much doubts this place is on the grays' regular delivery route.

"Okay. Let's say, just for the sake of argument, that this place is every bit as fancy as whatever the grays can pull together, and maybe even more so. If that's true, though . . . if Dana and her people are so sophisticated . . . why did she need to come to us to help her sick kid? More than that, why are they hiding out here at all? Why aren't they busy taking the planet back from the grays right now?"

Six lies back on the bed and folds her hands behind her head. "I don't know. Maybe they're good with tech, but not so much with medicine? Science isn't science, you know. There's different kinds of science, and different kinds of scientists. Also, just because they can build an underground lair doesn't mean they can build weapons. That's totally different tech."

John scowls. "You're doing it again."

"Doing what?"

"Acting like you know stuff that you don't really know. I mean, a doctor isn't an engineer. Obviously. I know that. What I don't know is what kind of gear or knowledge or whatever you need to make electricity without a fuel cell, or to make antibiotics, or to make a ray gun." He holds up his broken left arm, which barely hurts anymore inside the cast. "Or this cast and its osteo-whatevers, for that matter. I don't know what it takes to make any of that stuff, and neither do you."

Six doesn't respond. After a minute or so of silence, John gets back to his feet and paces around the room. The desk is solid polished wood, with a wide, shallow drawer across the front and two more running down the right side. John opens them, one by one. All are empty. The chest of drawers is the same, heavy polished wood with three drawers. He peers into the bottom two. The top one is almost too high for him to see inside, but he opens it anyway, stretches up, and feels around inside with his good hand. Nothing.

"You think this is someone's bedroom?"

Six grunts, but doesn't reply.

"If it is, it seems weird that you can lock the door from the outside, doesn't it?"

He circles back around to his place against the wall, and slides down until he's sitting.

"Six? Don't you think that's weird?"

After another long silence, he says, "Are you asleep?"

"No," Six says without sitting up. "I'm not asleep. I'm just not talking to you."

"You're . . . why not?"

"Why not? Because you're an asshole, that's why not. I'm

trying to be helpful here, thinking things through, trying to figure out what the hell is going on, and you're just worried about your stupid little ego and whether I'm smarter than you are or not. Well, guess what, John? I *am* smarter than you. Okay? Get used to it. The fact that you're older doesn't mean shit, because you've spent pretty much every minute since Martok took you out of the crèche hanging around with him and only him, and as far as I can tell he's the dumbest gray on the planet. And what does that make you, John? The *pet* of the dumbest gray on the planet, that's what. I don't know what's gonna happen here. Maybe Dana and Tanner are gonna decide we're all friends now and we can live here, happily ever after. Maybe they'll come back here five minutes from now and cut both of our throats. I do know one thing, though: Whatever happens, I'm going to realize it's happening before you do, because *you* are a *dimwit*."

"Wow," John says. "That escalated rapidly."

Six doesn't respond. Footsteps approach along the corridor outside, pass by, and recede.

"I don't think they're actually going to kill us," John says. "Do you?"

"What do you care what I think? I'm just pretending to know stuff that I don't actually know, remember?"

John sighs. Apparently Six doesn't have any immediate plans for letting this go.

"Look," he says. "I'm sorry. Okay? That was rude of me to say."

"Yeah, it was. Now say I'm smarter than you are."

"I'm . . . wait, what?"

"You want me to forgive you? Say I'm smarter than you are."

"I'm not sure I want you to forgive me that badly."

Six sits up and stares him down. Her face is fixed in a scowl, but John can see the hint of a smile hiding behind it. "Of course you do. We're maybe about to get murdered. You don't want to leave this world with bad blood between us, do you?"

"We're not getting murdered."

"You really want to take that chance?"

John breaks into a grin. "You know what? No, I don't. I really don't. You, Six, are smarter than I am. Not only are you smarter, you are also better-looking, you smell better, and are much more popular." He pauses. She's still scowling. "Also, you're much, much taller than I am."

That gets a giggle out of her. "Okay. I guess I forgive you—this time. Don't make me regret my decision."

Back in the crèche, there was a disused cupboard just off the kitchen, set low into the wall just to the left of the door that led out to the dining room. It was disused primarily because Rema, who had responsibility for the kitchen most days, wasn't able to bend over without using both hands on her knees to keep her back from giving out on her, and didn't much like either kneeling or getting back to her feet. It was an empty space behind a thick wooden door, a meter or so high and wide and maybe half that deep—which is to say, it was an ideal place for John to hide when he was trying to avoid being tormented by the other children, which, particularly as he got closer and closer to the day when he would age out without a contract, was most of the time.

He didn't understand at the time why the others grew crueler and colder as his time ticked down. What was happening to him might well happen to any of them, after all, and the end that was approaching him likely awaited at least a few of them eventually. He's had the opportunity to ponder the question many times over the years, though, and has come to the conclusion that their behavior was a form of denial. They couldn't allow themselves to believe that John was simply unlucky. That would imply that they might be unlucky too, and might in another year or two find themselves in the alley behind the crèche, face down on the concrete, waiting for a nursemaid's foot to fall. Much better to convince themselves that John *deserved* his fate, whether because of something he'd done, or because of some intrinsic flaw in him that drew an inevitable path from his birth to his death. Much better to think that because they themselves were blameless, they were safe.

The obvious corollary to this, of course, was that John was *not* blameless, and that—who knows?—his flaws might be contagious. And so, as he got older, and the cohorts above him were bonded out, and then those from his own bunk room, and then, finally, in ones and twos, the children a year and then two and then three younger than him, John found himself increasingly alone.

One dank spring afternoon very close to the end of his time there, when he was technically overage already and had begun going to sleep every night with the growing expectation that he'd wake to one of the nursemaids dragging him by the ankle out of bed and into the alley, he was curled up in the close darkness of the cupboard trying to convince himself that maybe they'd just forget about him at some point and he could live there forever, creeping out at night to steal food and poop in the other children's oatmeal, when two sets of heavy footsteps approached from the foyer and then stopped right outside his door.

"It's well past time," a voice John didn't recognize said in the peculiar pidgin of English and rumble-speak that the nursemaids tended to fall into when they were speaking among themselves.

"Why are we still feeding him? He should have been in the midden long before now."

"Oh hush," Rema replied, her voice cracking with anger. "He barely eats, he's so small. There's no need to rush him along. No need at all."

"No need to keep him, you mean," the other voice said. "You do him no favors keeping him about, you know. He knows as well as you what ought to have happened a season ago, and he'll never bond out, no matter how long he stays. He has the stink on him."

"Oh, you've the stink," Rema said. "The boy will bond out, or he won't—and if not, we'll do what we must. All things in time, Nara, and his time has not yet come."

She added something then in pure rumble-speak, too deep for John to parse. The other responded, and then their footsteps receded into the kitchen to leave John alone again, hugging his knees to his chest and imagining his face pressed to the pavement and the weight of a gray's foot on the back of his skull.

That afternoon returns to John in vivid detail as he waits in this bedroom-slash-cell for Dana to come back and tell them what her people have decided to do with him. With it comes the realization that he's spent far too much of his life doing exactly this—waiting passively while someone else decides what's to become of him. Rema was kind to him, more or less, for reasons that John still hasn't fully parsed after all this time. Martok, too, has mostly taken care of him, at least by the grays' standards. He's not as confident that Dana, or whoever Dana is conferring with, will treat him well. Even if they do, though, and somehow he and Six wind up in a tolerable situation here, he has a growing realization that, moving forward, he needs to stop relying on the kindness of others, whether that means grays or humans—because whether it's now or later, he's eventually going to find himself in the hands of someone who is not, in fact, kind.

"On your feet, little man. Walter wants to talk to you."

John's head snaps up. He'd been dozing, back to the wall and forehead resting on his drawn-up knees. He squints up at Dana in confusion as his brain comes back online, then shakes his head and says, "Who's Walter?"

"You mean us," Six says as she hops down from the bed. "You meant to say that he wants to talk to both of us, right?"

"Walter is the person who's going to decide whether you get to keep being alive," Dana says, "and no, he doesn't want to talk to both of you. He wants to talk to John."

"No," Six says, and starts to cross the room before Dana stops her with one raised hand. "There's no way I'm betting my life on whatever John has to say. He's not that smart, you know. He just finally admitted it to himself. If you're only taking one of us, it should be me."

"Don't care," Dana says. "Walter said bring him the little man, so I'm bringing him the little man." Six starts forward again, but stops after a half step when Dana's hand goes to her knife. "Hold up there, kiddo. You have two choices here: you can hop back up on that bed and take a nap while you wait to see what the grown-ups decide to do with you, or you can spend the next however-long face down on the floor, trussed up like a turkey. Your call, but I'd advise you to go with the bed."

Six stares at Dana for a dangerously long time, the muscles in her jaw bunching and relaxing, until finally she folds her arms across her chest and says, "Fine—but if John screws this up, I get to kill him before you kill me."

Dana laughs, then visibly relaxes and says, "Fair enough." She turns to John. "On your feet, my friend. Walter doesn't like to be kept waiting."

CHAPTER TWENTY

This place is big.

John didn't get a full picture of the size of it when Dana brought them in, but he sees it now. They're winding deeper into the hillside, through a mix of clean gray corridors like the one they saw near the entrance, and others that look like they've been dug by hand and braced with just enough timber to prevent a cave-in. As they go, the questions he and Six had been batting back and forth begin to clarify themselves in John's mind. Parts of this place do indeed look like something equal to or maybe even beyond the abilities of the grays. Others remind him uncomfortably of a rabbit warren he once dug up on the property of an elderly Greatfoot matriarch who'd hired Martok for a week's worth of inexpert landscaping work. The people who built the former parts were clearly technological sophisticates with access to equipment, materials, and engineering that were at least the equal of anything John has ever seen or imagined in Farhome.

John is entirely confident at this point that those people were not Dana and her ilk.

Dana's people, John imagines, must have found this place abandoned at some point in the hundred-plus years since The Fall, and then moved in like raccoons making a nest in a hollow tree. The dirty, frighteningly unstable-looking dirt-and-rock tunnels must be their work, expanding the existing facility to accommodate their numbers without having any idea how to do so in a way that the original architects would have recognized.

"Well, here we are," Dana says as they come to a stop in front of a closed door in one of the clean corridors. "Good luck in there. Hope I don't have to cut your throat when you come back out—not because I care one way or another whether you live or die, you understand, but just because cleaning up the mess would be a pain in the ass."

"Thanks," John says. "I think, anyway. You're not coming in?"

Dana shakes her head. "You're on your own here, little man." She turns the knob and pushes the door open, then steps back and waves him forward. "Go get 'em."

John takes a deep breath, then crosses the threshold. Dana pulls the door closed behind him.

The light in this room is dim, provided by a single glowing panel set into the ceiling that seems to have lost half or more of whatever it is that makes it shine. John makes another mental note at that—here's something that clearly needs repair, and hasn't gotten it. More evidence that Dana's folk aren't even able to maintain what they have here, let alone build more of it. The space is smaller than the one where Six is presumably still waiting for him to screw this up and get her throat cut for her. One wall is covered in shelves full of books from floor to ceiling. Books are something John has only seen once or twice in his life—grays don't use any such thing, and only the richest and most eccentric of them are interested enough in human artifacts to have kept any of them around—so this strikes him immediately as a sign of almost unimaginable wealth. Another wall is taken up almost entirely by a black glass screen with an ugly crack zigzagging back and forth down its center, which is honestly less impressive. Directly in front of him is a chin-high desk. Behind the desk sits Walter.

"Well, hello, there," he says, and gets to his feet. "John, is it?"

From the deference that Dana clearly felt toward this man, John had assumed that he'd be a monster. Tanner was the biggest, strongest creature John had ever seen short of a gray, and Dana had never shown him anything more than the barest respect. Walter, he thought, must be taller than Martok, muscled like a titan, and probably had fangs and claws to boot.

The man behind the desk is none of those things.

He's taller than John, at least, but only by a head or so. As he steps out from behind the desk, John sees that Walter is nearly as thin as him as well. His hair is white and wispy, and deep wrinkles line his forehead and cheeks. He squints at John, and a smile creases his face.

"You look nervous, John."

John can feel his face twist into a scowl. "Shouldn't I be? Dana said this interview was going to decide whether my throat stays uncut or not."

Walter laughs, and John is surprised to feel himself beginning to relax. "Oh, you can't take anything Dana says too seriously. She has a dark sense of humor."

"If you say so. She really didn't sound like she was joking."

Walter walks a slow circle around him, eyes running from his feet to his face and back again. "Interesting. How long ago did you come out of the crèche?"

John hesitates, then says, "Twelve years? Roughly."

"Would you say you were average for your cohort, more or less?"

"Excuse me?"

"Considering your fellows in the crèche, would you say you were on the small side? Or about average?" His smile widens. "Or were you a bruiser?"

"I don't know," John says. "I wasn't the biggest. I wasn't the smallest either. I guess I was on the short side of normal?"

Walter gives him another once-over, then nods and says, "Interesting indeed. The only other bondsman I've had the privilege to meet recently was the doctor you sent us. Alph, I think it was? Thank you for that, by the way. It was a remarkable act of trust, and we have been lacking in medical expertise for as long as I've been here. He was nearly tall enough to look me square in the eye. I thought that might have indicated that they were holding the breed steady, but I suppose he's probably a generation or two older than you as well. Or perhaps he's simply a bit of an atavist, eh?" He strokes his chin absently for a moment, then leans back against his desk and folds his arms across his chest. "I was nearly the smallest in my own cohort, you know. That was two generations ago, though—or maybe three? They're still breeding us down, it seems. Come back in another hundred years and you'll be able to carry one of us around in a teacup!" He laughs at that, then sours when John doesn't join in. "So serious! Tell me, John. What must I do to convince you to relax?"

John closes his eyes and rubs his face with both hands. When he looks up, Walter is watching him with a sympathetic half smile on his face. "Well," he says, "I guess you could start by promising that Six and I will still be alive a week from now. That would be helpful."

Walter's smile twists into a grin. "Not exactly reaching for the stars, are you? Unfortunately, if I'm being completely honest, I don't know that I can promise you that. If, for example, your former employer decides to call in the spiders to search for you, I can't promise that *any* of us will still be here tomorrow, let alone in a week. I won't sugarcoat this, John. Your coming here has put us all in a great deal of danger. Dana's attitude toward you isn't coming from nowhere. What I can do, however, is promise you that if you *aren't* alive a week from now, it won't be because one of my people has killed you. Fair enough?"

John hesitates, then shrugs and says, "Yeah. Fair enough."

"Good!" Walter says. "Very good indeed. Now I'm going to ask you some questions, John, and I need you to promise me that you're going to answer them honestly. Can you do that for me?"

John can feel a growl rising in the back of his throat at the condescending tone, but he swallows it down and says, "Yes. I can do that."

"Excellent. We'll start with the easy ones, shall we? What, exactly, has brought your owner to my doorstep?"

"Martok is not my owner," John says, and instantly hates the hint of a whine in his voice. "He's my employer."

Walter shakes his head. "He is not, John. That word, *employer*. It means something—or it used to, anyway. Employers pay their employees, and employees are free to leave their employ at any time. Would you say that fairly describes your relationship with this Martok?" He waits out John's sullen silence before continuing. "No, I thought not. So, you are not his employee. It's tempting to say that you are enslaved, but that's not quite right either, is it? That might have described our relationship to the grays if they had left us as we were when they found us, if we still looked and thought and acted as our mutual friend Dana does. If, in other words, they had left us as naturally free beings and then bothered to put in some amount of effort to keep us oppressed. No, you are neither Martok's employee, nor his slave."

"Fine," John says. "So? What am I?"

Walter contemplates him for a moment, then circles back

around the desk and drops into his chair. "Do you know what a *dog* is, John?"

John hesitates, then says, "Dogs are a kind of wolf, aren't they? I saw one of those once, in the park in Farhome. What does that have to do with me? I'm no wolf."

Walter gives him a wry grin at that. "No, John. You are not. Wolves are wild creatures, exquisitely adapted to live in this world. A wolf makes his own den in the forest. A wolf hunts his own food. Our friend Dana? *She* is a wolf. If you dropped her, naked and alone, into the middle of the wilderness, Dana would have a shelter, a warm fire, and a full belly within the hour. A dog, however, is something else entirely. Many thousands of years ago, humans took wolves and bred them down, made them docile and dependent. They kept them as helpers and companions." He chuckles. "In truth, this may be an unfair comparison. If the stories I have read are even partially true, it seems humans treated their dogs with greater respect and compassion than most grays show their bondsmen."

John ponders that for most of a minute. Walter waits through the silence with a sad smile on his face. Finally John asks, "How many dogs were there, before the grays came?"

"Millions. Many millions, probably. It seems they were a part of almost every human society."

"What about wolves? How many of them were there?"

"Why, they were nearly extinct."

"What about now? Now that the humans are gone?"

Walter nods. "Yes. I think you begin to see. Now, John—tell me about your owner."

And so, he does.

"So," Six says as soon as the door swings open. "Are we getting murdered?"

John shakes his head as he steps across the threshold and the door locks behind him. "Doesn't look like it. Not today, anyway."

"So you didn't talk us into a beheading? Amazing."

"Your faith in me is inspiring, Six. Truly."

Six grins and hops down off the bed. "Ah, I'm kidding. I believed in you. What did they want with you?"

John puts his back to the wall and slides down to the floor, suddenly exhausted as the adrenaline drains out of him. "Honestly? I have no idea. Walter asked a lot of questions about Martok—where he's from, what he's doing here, what his clan connections are . . . that kind of stuff. He seemed really curious about the crèche where I grew up too, for some reason. He's one of us, by the way."

Six's eyebrows knit together at the bridge of her nose. "What does that mean?"

"He's crèche-born. He's a bondsman."

Six stares for a moment, then shakes her head and says, "That's impossible."

"It's not. I saw him. I guess I can't say for sure that he's just like us—he's as tall as any bondsman I've met except for maybe Alph, and older than anyone I've ever seen—but he's definitely not whatever Dana and Tanner are. I'm not sure how many other categories there are out there."

"But he's the boss man, right? Dana sure acted like he was."

"Seems that way, yeah. Anyway, is it so crazy that there might be one of us here? How many times have you reminded me that you spent five years living with ferals? If the spiders hadn't come for them, you'd still be there, right?"

"Sure, maybe. Pretty sure I wouldn't be running things, though. There were three other bondsmen with us, and a couple of kids who were mixed-breed. The humans were nice enough to us, I guess, but even the adult bondsmen got treated like children. I feel like things were pretty loose there, leadership-wise, but no way one of us would have ended up with any kind of authority."

"Well, maybe this group is smarter. Maybe they're more open to seeing the best in people, and not just how tall they are. Maybe that's why they haven't gotten caught yet."

"They haven't gotten caught because they've got this place. We were living loose in the woods, remember? Much harder to stay hidden that way."

"Okay. Maybe Walter was the one who showed them where this place was or how it worked. Maybe he was a builder for the grays or something before he came over?"

Six shrugs. "Doesn't really matter, does it? However he wound up in this position, it seems like he's the one who's going to decide what happens to us. Did he give you any clue as to what that might be?"

John hesitates, then shakes his head. "No. Not really. He did say none of his people would kill us, though. That's something, right?"

Six scowls. "Yeah, it's something. Kinda sad that that's our standard for success these days, but I guess that's who we are now."

John has long experience with enduring boredom. He can't count the number of days he spent alone in some boardinghouse room while Martok was out hypothetically looking for work, but more realistically probably in a tavern somewhere with a bunch of other low-status grays complaining about the way the Greatfoots were keeping them all down. He's passed thousands of empty hours with nothing but a window to stare out of if he was lucky, or a blank, mold-encrusted wall to stare at if he wasn't. He learned long ago to let his mind go blank and just *be*.

Six, it seems, has never developed that particular skill.

She spends the first hour after John's return pacing the room, from bed to desk to door, giving a frustrated twist to the locked doorknob, and then back to the bed before starting again. John follows her with his eyes from his place on the floor, but he's not really watching her. When he's thinking at all, he's thinking about the crows in the street outside their last rented room in Farhome. Now, *those* guys were interesting. There was one with a white feather at the crest of his head who seemed to run things for the most part, but he took a great deal of grief from a pair of smaller birds around the distribution of spoils whenever they came across a particularly juicy bit of carrion. The last day he and Martok were there, a gray dropped a—

"How long do you think they'll leave us here?"

John blinks, and his eyes focus on Six. She's leaning against the bed, chewing at one of her thumbnails.

"Hard to say. Somewhere between two minutes and forever, probably."

"Not helpful," Six says, then stomps into the bathroom and slams the door behind her. A few minutes later John hears the toilet flush, and then water running in the sink. When the door opens again Six says, "Where does their shit go?"

"Uh," John says. "What?"

"Their shit," Six says. "There's no sewer system out here. There's no water mains either. So where does the water come from, and where does it go?"

"No idea," John says. "Does it matter?"

"Maybe," Six says, and closes the door behind her. "Don't go in there for a while, by the way." She crosses back to the bed, hops up, and turns to face him with her legs dangling over the edge. "Anyway, it's another piece in the puzzle of why these guys are hiding from the grays instead of crushing them."

John barks out a short, incredulous laugh. "Really? We're overthrowing the grays with wastewater treatment now?"

Six's face twists into a scowl. "No. That's not what I said. It's just, look, this place is almost like a spaceship, and—"

"You know the grays have *actual* spaceships, right?"

"Do they, though? I mean, I know spaceships brought them here, but that was a hundred years ago. What do they have *now*?"

"They've got the spiders."

That gets John a solid five seconds of silence before Six says, "Well, yeah. I guess you've got me there."

CHAPTER TWENTY-ONE

It's an unknown number of hours later and John is still on the floor with his back to the wall, knees drawn up and eyes half-closed, when the sharp *snick* of the door to the corridor unlocking announces Dana's return.

"Hey," she says, poking her head through the half-open door. "Little man. On your feet. We need you."

"Oh hells no," Six says, and hops down from the bed. "You're not leaving me here again."

"Oh hells yes," Dana says. "We totally are."

John shakes his head clear and climbs to his feet. "What's happening?"

"What's happening is you're coming with me and she's staying put." She turns her attention to Six, who is glaring at her from across the room, arms folded tight across her chest. "Relax, kiddo. You're getting the long end of the stick here. Tanner's bringing your dinner by in a half hour or so. You can eat John's plate too if you want."

"Hey," John says. "Wait a minute. I—"

"You nothing," Dana says, and pulls back into the corridor. "Get moving—and bring your coat with you. It's cold outside."

DANA IGNORES JOHN'S questions as he follows her through the dimly lit corridors, retracing their steps from—how long has it been, actually? John finds he doesn't have a clue. Hours, at least. How long did he spend in a fugue state, huddled against the wall with his mind drifting? It couldn't have been a full day, could it? He's not hungry enough for that.

That being said, he *is* pretty hungry. He hopes Six has enough decency to not really eat his dinner.

Nobody else seems to be out and about, and their footsteps echo hollowly from the corridor walls as they approach the entrance. John stops a half-dozen steps from the closed hatch, folds his arms across his chest, and says, "Where are we going, Dana?"

"*We* aren't going anywhere," Dana says, then turns the lock on the hatch and shoves it open. "*You* are going out there." It's still full dark outside, so apparently it hasn't been more than six or seven hours since they arrived. John has to slit his eyes against the ice-laden gust of wind that whips through the opening. "Get moving, little man. You're letting the warm out."

John shakes his head. "Not until you tell me what's happening. Are you kicking me out? Why? And why me, and not Six?"

"I'm not kicking you out—not necessarily, anyway. I'm sending you out because your pal Martok is out there. He's been wandering around the woods for the last hour and a half bellowing your name loud enough to call the fucking spiders down on us, and you're the one he's yelling for, not Six. We left tracks in the snow when I brought you in. I don't think he's observant enough to find them, but it's better to not take any chances. Find out what he wants, and then get rid of him."

"Get rid of him?"

"Make him go home. What did you think I meant? Kill him?"

"No, I thought . . . doesn't matter what I thought. This is pretty trusting of you, isn't it? What if I bring Martok back here? What if I show him where you live?"

Dana's face darkens. "Then we find out how many arrows it takes to kill a gray. Same thing if you get it into your head to go back with him, by the way. Now that you know about this place, you can't go home again. In fact, let's make sure you don't mention anything about us at all, huh? He knows I'm out here, right? That's all you told him. Just one lone wolf. He doesn't know about the rest of the community we've got here. Keep it that way. Joshua and Mara are out there right now, keeping an eye on him. They'll be keeping an eye on you, too, and listening to what you say. If you try to dip out with him, or tell him about this place, or tell him anything more than he already knows about us, they'll take you both out. You understand?"

John hesitates, then nods.

"Good. Get going. The sooner you get him gone, the sooner you get to find out if your friend ate your sandwich or not."

IF THERE'S ONE thing John has learned from his years of intermittent homelessness, it's this: it is always cold at four AM. It doesn't matter in the end if you're wearing a ragged, bloodstained jacket or a thousand-credit insulated body suit. It doesn't even really matter how cold it is when you're stuck outside for the night. The human body shuts down, metabolically speaking, during the hours when it thinks it ought to be sleeping. Heat stops pushing its way out from the body's core, and like the outer shell of an exhausted star, the cold collapses in.

At least he had Martok's bulk to huddle against during those nights spent in the park in Farhome. The metabolism of a gray is a different animal entirely from that of a human, and while Martok's thick hide allowed him to keep most of the warmth he generated to himself, even on the coldest, wettest nights enough leaked out to allow John to shiver himself to sleep eventually.

John wouldn't mind having someone to huddle against now.

The wind has picked up during the hours he spent underground, and the temperature has dropped. Tiny ice crystals patter against his jacket, coating his hair, forcing him to narrow his eyes to slits. The skin of his face is already cold enough that the crystals stick there for long moments before melting, and five minutes out from the shelter his nose and cheeks are numb.

He crosses the frozen stream, climbs the bank, and starts uphill, away from the shelter and generally back toward the house. Until he reaches the first crest he's pretty certain this is a fool's errand. Even with a full moon overhead behind thin gray clouds, the woods are dark and foreboding, and the odds of him finding Martok out here seem impossibly long. He hears it, though, as soon as he tops the shallow hill: *John! Joooooooohn!*

The voice is distant and John loses it briefly when the wind abruptly shifts around behind him, but Martok's bellowing carries a long way, and after a few moments of listening John is moderately confident that he has a fix on Martok's direction. He tucks his chin to his chest, shoves his hands into his pockets, and starts walking.

As he slogs through the shin-deep snow, pausing every so often to listen for Martok and reorient, John finds himself contemplating the question of whether Joshua and Mara, whoever they are, are really out here somewhere, watching him. He's had enough experience with Dana to know that if they are, they could probably be a dozen paces away from him right now and he'd never know it. He shivers, and briefly wonders whether they'd really have people out in this cold, just standing sentry or whatever they were supposed to be doing when they noticed Martok bumbling around. After a bit more thought, though, he realizes that Dana has never seemed bothered in the least by the cold, so there's no reason to think that the weather would keep these others inside. Probably best to assume they're really there.

That conclusion leads him to the next question: If they are out there, would they really try to kill Martok if John brought him back to the shelter, or told him something he shouldn't have, or tried to go home with him? And if they did, would they be able to do it? Dana seemed to think it was possible when he put the question to her. He remembers her saying a bunch of stuff about pull weights that he didn't understand, but the gist seemed to be that she thought she'd probably be able to get an arrow through a gray's hide, and that if she did that enough times, she could probably take one down. Was that just bravado? For the entirety of John's life the idea of hurting a gray, let alone killing one, was no different than the idea of flapping his arms and flying—not difficult, not improbable, but rather so ludicrous that it didn't bear consideration.

Dana and her friends don't seem to labor under those same preconceptions.

John has to concede that Six has a point. After watching Dana and Tanner in action, it's hard to understand how the grays managed to take the world away from these people, spiders or no.

Martok's bellowing is getting closer, enough so that John finally decides it might be worth the effort of calling back. He waits for the last *Jooooohhhhnnn* to trail off, then shouts Martok's name into the silence that follows. For five long seconds the forest seems to hold its breath, until Martok calls out again, this time with a question mark at the end: *John?*

From that point, it's just a few minutes of back-and-forth

before Martok lumbers out of the darkness to stand in front of him.

"John! My friend! You've survived!"

Martok reaches for him, but John steps back out of his reach and says, "Really, Martok? It was just a few hours ago that you were talking about killing me yourself, wasn't it?"

Martok's arms drop to his side and his face falls. "That was madness, John—a momentary shock to my psyche, from which I have long since recovered. All is forgiven now, yes?"

John gapes up at him. When he speaks again, his voice is slow and deliberate, and he enunciates every word. "You threw us out. In the dead of winter, you threw us out into the snow with nothing but what we could carry."

"Yes," Martok says. "I know. I know. Now, though, I have seen the error of my ways, and come to repentance. Where is Six? Bring her along, and we can be home within the hour. I shall lay out a feast for the two of you, by way of apology. I still have a haunch of roast beast in the larder. I had planned to serve it to our next guest, but since it seems there shan't be a next guest now that I've learned that our business was . . . operating under false pretenses, I think that we could—"

"No," John says. "Stop. I'm not coming back with you, Martok."

Martok flinches at that, and even in the dark of the forest, surprise and hurt are plain on his face. It occurs suddenly to John that this is the first time he's ever said *no* to Martok—or to any gray, honestly. The realization of that sends a shiver of evenly mixed fear and elation up his spine.

"John, please . . . I know that harsh things were said in the heat of passion, but you must understand . . . your actions, your actions were . . ."

"My actions? Listen to yourself, Martok. My actions were the direct result of the way *you* forced me to live. I lied to two Ice

River roustabouts in Lake Town about who you were and what you did because if I hadn't, they would have taken our gear, and your prospects of ever paying the note you took out on my bond would have been even more hopeless than they already were. I couldn't tell you about lying to those two because a bondsman can't lie to a gray without getting his head crushed. Everything that happened after that was as inevitable as the tide.

"You act like I committed some terrible crime that needs forgiveness, but the fact is that I barely had a choice about any of the stuff that's happened up until now if I didn't want to wind up with my head on the block. I've just been reacting to events, trying to keep myself alive day to day. You know who did have some agency here, though? You. You, Martok. *You* chose to take out that note, and wager my life on a whim. *You* chose to bring us here. *You* chose to delude yourself into thinking that a bunch of Ice River grandees would come flocking out into the middle of nothing, to eat your mediocre cooking and listen to you ramble.

"I'm not perfect. I'd be the first to admit that. I've done a lot of stupid things since we left Farhome. None of them hold a *candle*, though, to what you did to me when you took out that note. If you want to blame this mess on anything, you can blame it on that."

The expression on Martok's face now, wide-eyed and slack-jawed, could not have been more incredulous if John had just sprouted wings from his back and launched himself into the night sky. John, for his part, is equally astonished at what he's just said, and a strange admixture of exhilaration and horror is currently bubbling its way up from his churning stomach to his brain. Martok's mouth works soundlessly for a long five seconds, until finally he stammers out, "John, my friend . . . my *brother* . . . do you not love me?"

And the hell of it, of course, is that on some level, yes, he absolutely does. John closes his eyes and breathes in the knife-sharp air. As he does, he flashes back to another frozen night in the woods, this one in the park in Farhome after he and Martok had been evicted from the room they'd been renting because Martok had taken offense at the proprietor's characterization of clan Black Hand as "a rabble of ne'er-do-wells at best and criminals more likely, who never should have been allowed onto the ships in the first place" and poured a tankard of ale over the old gray's head.

It was snowing then, probably harder than it is tonight, and the wind was just as cutting. Worse, John didn't even own a jacket at the time. He was wearing three shirts and two pairs of pants, which constituted the entirety of his wardrobe, and still his teeth were chattering before they'd gone a dozen steps into the darkness. John stumbled on the edge of the sidewalk as they entered the park, his feet already numb, then tripped over a tree root and fell face down into the snow, bare hands scraping on the gravel pathway.

Martok picked him up then, cradled John against his chest, and rumbled, "Apologies, my friend. I forget sometimes what the cold does to you." He carried John into the shelter of the trees, picked a spot under the spreading bare branches of a massive oak, then sat down and curled around him, his chest and arms and massive chin protecting every bit of John but his eyes from the weather.

They stayed that way, barely moving, until the morning. John has never felt safer or more protected than he did that night, either before or since.

John opens his eyes again. The look of pleading on Martok's face is nearly enough to break him.

Nearly, but not quite.

"Go home," he says quietly. "You made your choice, Martok.

You threw us out. Six and I are fine now. Go home, and forget about us."

"So is it true, then? There are ferals in the forest, and they have taken you in?"

John flinches at that, imagining Dana's friends somewhere nearby, and a fat red target on the back of his neck. Are they really there? If so, how close? The wind is howling now. Could they have heard what Martok just said?

"I see," Martok says, and steps closer to John. "I see the truth in your face, my friend. You are afraid." He drops to one knee and leans forward until their heads are almost touching, his voice dropping to a barely audible rumble. "Are they forcing you to this? Is Six held captive, a hostage to compel you to say these ridiculous things? How many of them are there? Ten? Twenty? A hundred?" He waves his own question away. "Bah. It makes no difference. Together, we can save her. Tell me where they are, and I shall—"

"No," John says, and he can hear the weariness in his own voice. "No. Six is not a captive, Martok, and nobody is forcing me into anything. Please, just this once try to really listen to what I'm saying. Six? She's been a captive her entire life. So have I. *So has every bondsman*. For the first time, for however long it lasts, she and I are actually free now." He reaches out, places his numb hand against Martok's mottled cheek. "Please, Martok. *Listen* to me. Go home."

Martok kneels there, frozen, for a long moment, before covering John's hand with his own and nodding. "I hear you, John," he says, his voice barely more than a whisper now. "I understand." He gets to his feet and takes two steps back. When he speaks again, his voice is theatrically loud. "I understand now. You and Six have chosen to live a life of solitude here in the forest." He takes another step back. "This wounds me grievously, and I fear for your survival. However, I must respect your choices. I shall not trouble you again."

He *winks*.

Martok Barden née Black Hand, would-be innkeeper and erstwhile enforcer, in the middle of the night, in the middle of the woods, almost certainly within full view of two heavily armed humans who are undoubtedly searching for any signs of collusion between the two of them, screws up his face, and he winks.

John has no idea what to say to that. He watches in slack-jawed astonishment as Martok turns and disappears into the darkness.

CHAPTER TWENTY-TWO

Six has, in fact, eaten John's sandwich.

"You were gone for a long-ass time," she says with a shrug. "I thought you were dead."

John glares at her as he strips out of his jacket and tries to rub some life back into his numb fingers.

"It was our own food," Six adds. "They literally fed us from our own packs, and then acted like we ought to be grateful for it."

"Did they feed *us*?" John asks. "Because it seems like they fed *you*."

"Oh, quit crying," Six says, and hops down off of the bed. "I saved you a snack." She tosses a brown lump of something to him. He tries to catch it, but his fingers still aren't working properly and it winds up bouncing off of his chest and dropping to the floor, where it breaks into four smaller pieces and a scattering of crumbs. It's a chunk torn from a protein brick, he sees now. He drops to his knees and scrapes up as much as he can.

"Thanks a lot," he says as he grimaces and brushes grit off of the largest piece. "You're a real friend."

Six breaks into a grin. "Fine, you big baby." She reaches back onto the bed and comes up with two thick strips of dried beast. "I was saving these for later, but I guess you can have them."

She crosses the room in three strides and holds the meat out to him. John glares up at her, then mutters, "Thanks," and takes it.

"So," Six say as John stuffs a handful of protein brick into his mouth and chews. "What was this trip about? You were gone for a long time. Did they have you begging for our lives again?"

"Not exactly," John says around a mouthful of goo. "Martok was wandering around in the woods, looking for us. They wanted me to make him go away."

"Huh," Six says. "Looking for us to kill us?"

"Nope. He wanted us to come home with him."

Her eyes widen. "No shit? Are we going?"

"No," John says. "We're not going."

"Why the hell not?"

John bites off a hunk of beast, chews deliberately, and swallows. "I'm confused. Weren't you the one who was raised by ferals and hated being a pet? You're where you wanted to be now, right? Why would you want to go back?"

"Honestly? These guys seem a lot shittier than the ones I lived with. I know I was just a kid and I might be remembering things as nicer than they really were, but I'm pretty sure they never threatened to cut my throat, for one thing."

"Yeah," John says. "That's fair enough. Along those lines, though, Dana made it pretty clear before she sent me out to talk with him that we weren't going back to Martok—not now, or ever. We know about this place now. Can't take any chances on the grays finding out about it."

"Great." Six climbs onto the bed and flops back so that only her dangling feet are visible. "So where does that leave us?"

John finishes the last of the protein brick, then tucks the rest of the dried beast into a jacket pocket. "Not sure," he says. "But I'm guessing it mostly depends on what Walter thinks we can do for him."

TIME PASSES SLOWLY in their cozy little prison, marked only by the lights dimming to a dull silver glow at night and coming back up in the morning. Meals come regularly for the first two days. On the morning of the third, breakfast is late, and when Dana finally shows up to feed them, all she brings with her are two hard biscuits and a strip of some unfamiliar meat, dried to the consistency of boiled leather.

"Hey," Six says as Dana turns to leave. "What about our fruit? I need a lot of fiber in my diet, you know."

Dana rolls her eyes. "The fruit is gone. So is everything else you brought with you. From now on, you eat like the rest of us."

"Hold on," Six says. "That's bullshit. We took everything we could grab when we left the house. Our bags were stuffed with food."

"Yeah," Dana says with a mocking half grin. "They sure were."

She walks out the door, latching it behind her before Six can come up with a reply.

"Well," John says when she's gone. "That sucks."

"Sucks?" Six says. She's pacing back and forth now, working herself up from anger to red-hot rage. "That's all you've got? They stole our food, John! They ate it all themselves!"

"What did you expect?" John takes a bite of his biscuit, scowls, and then chews slowly. "If *this* is the sort of thing they're living on," he says when he's finally able to swallow, "I'm kind of amazed they let us have any of what we brought at all."

Six puts her back to the wall and sinks down next to him. She tears off a chunk of the meat, makes a face, and says, "This *sucks.*"

"Sucks?" John says in a singsong voice. "That's all you've got?"

She elbows him in the gut, hard enough to hurt. "This isn't funny. We're literally in prison here." She chews and swallows, then mutters, "We should have stayed with Martok."

"Martok was going to kill us, Six."

"Whatever. You said he forgives us now, right? So, we can go back. We just need to get out of here."

John turns to look at her. "Get out of here? You mean, you want to try to escape?"

"Considering that since we got here we've been threatened with murder, locked up like prisoners, and now starved? Yes, I think escaping would be a fine idea."

John finishes his biscuit in silence, then washes it down with water from the bathroom sink. When he comes back, Six is sitting in the desk chair, swiveling back and forth with a sour expression on her face.

"Okay," he says. "Say we wanted to escape. How are you proposing we do it?"

THEY SPEND THE next three hours brainstorming options. During that time, they come up with dozens of scenarios, ranging from the simplistic (jump Dana when she brings them their dinner, disable or kill her, and flee, hopefully avoiding any of the other ferals on their way out the door) to the baroque (make dummies of some sort to put in the bed, crawl into the air vent, hope it's big enough for them to squeeze through, squirm their way to freedom). Some of their plans are plainly ridiculous. Some, if John squints hard enough, almost seem plausible.

The only problem is that every one of them carries a probability, ranging from "very likely" to "absolutely certain," of ending with Dana murdering them both.

"Look," Six says when John finally points this fact out to her. "This is a no-risk, no-reward kind of situation we're in. How do you think things end if we stay here? I don't know what I expected when we decided to throw in with these guys—maybe that they'd treat us the way the ferals I grew up with treated me, I guess—but it's pretty clear at this point that these people have no intention of just letting us join their little clan. They took our gear. They took our meds. They took our food. Right now I'm pretty sure someone somewhere is asking what else there is to take from us, and if the answer is *nothing*, I'm even more sure that same someone is going to suggest that there's not any point in keeping us around anymore."

John shakes his head. "Walter promised me they wouldn't kill us."

"I'm sure he did. You never tell the people you're gonna kill that you're gonna to kill them. Once they know that, they've got nothing left to lose, and people with nothing left to lose are dangerous. What you do is you keep stringing them along until you've got everything you want out of them, and then you chop 'em up and hang 'em up to dry. What was that meat Dana brought us this morning, John? It sure as hell wasn't roast beast."

John stares at her, his jaw working silently, then says, "You . . . you think they fed us *people*?"

"I'm not saying they did," Six says with a shrug. "I'm not saying they didn't either, though."

John hesitates, then digs his knuckles into his eyes and says, "Look, I think we're getting a little punchy here. We don't have any reason to believe that these people have any intention of killing us, let alone chopping us up and turning us into jerky. Walter is one of us, remember? Why would he do that? We just need to calm down and be patient. I'm sure they'll figure out what they want to do with us at some point."

"Uh-huh," Six says. She crawls up onto the bed, rolls onto her side, and pulls the blanket over her head. "I just bet they will."

DINNER THAT NIGHT is two biscuits and a bowl of red beans to split between them. Breakfast is just a biscuit.

"They're starving us," Six says when Dana latches the door behind her. "They're not even gonna do us the courtesy of murdering us. They're just gonna let us starve to death."

John takes a bite and chews. He's not any happier about these developments than Six is, but he's been hungrier than this plenty of times, and he's not quite ready to panic yet.

"This isn't starving," he says around his third and final mouthful. "Starving is no food at all. If they wanted to kill us, that's what we'd be getting." He swallows, washes it down with enough water to fill his stomach for the moment, and then says, "This is what you get when it's been a long winter already, and there's at least another six weeks to go before we've got any hope of a thaw. Did you never wonder why Dana and Tanner were willing to work with us? I mean, did you not think about what an insane risk that was for them? I don't think it was just Dana's sick kid. I think they're the ones who are starving here, and they were willing to risk bringing the grays down on them for a shot at a share of Martok's food."

"Maybe that's true," Six says darkly. "Maybe they're so hungry that even you're starting to look appetizing."

John closes his eyes. "Not that again, please. If they wanted to butcher us, they'd do it now, before we get any skinnier."

"Maybe," Six says. "Maybe that's exactly what they're about

to do. Maybe we should be picking out one of those plans we talked about and trying to make it work before they go through with it."

John rubs his eyes and says, "Okay. Which one? The air vent is too small for you to fit through, let alone me. Jumping Dana works in principle, but unless you smuggled another weapon in here somehow I don't think we've got a chance in hell of pulling it off. I'm not sure we could—"

"The virus one," Six says. "That's the move."

That stops John for a moment. "The virus one?"

"We talked about this last night, remember? I fake sick—we already know that I'm a pro at that—and you tell Dana it's something super-contagious. They can't risk us spreading it, so they toss us out into the snow. We run home to Martok, and live happily ever after."

Oh. He remembers this now.

"Yeah, we talked about this. We talked about the fact that Dana took our jackets and boots. We'd freeze to death before we got home. Also, it's probably more likely that they'd just lock us in here and wait for us to die rather than taking the chance on us contaminating the rest of the facility on our way out."

"Maybe. Maybe not. We'd have a chance, anyway."

"We've got a chance here, Six! You don't know they're planning to kill us! You don't even have a good reason to think that!"

"Whatever. This is happening, John. When Dana comes around with our boiled shoelaces or whatever else they're planning to feed us for dinner, I'm gonna be deathly ill, and you're gonna back me up."

"No," John says. "I'm not."

Six shoots him a poisonous glare. "Yes, you are."

"Look, Six. Right now I think our chances are better waiting it out here than trying to find our way home out there with nothing between us and the weather but what we've got on our backs. If that ever changes, we can talk about this again, but I don't—"

He's interrupted by the sound of the lock opening. He turns to the door as Six drops face down onto the floor and lets out a theatrical moan.

"John," Dana says as she steps into the room. "We need—Hey, what's up with her?"

John turns back to Six, who's twitching now, mouth open and drooling and eyes screwed shut.

"No idea," he says. "You need what?"

"Something just came up. You need to come with me." Six moans again, and a spasm runs the length of her body. "Does she, uh . . . need some help or something?"

"No," John says. "She gets this way sometimes. She'll be fine in a few minutes."

"You sure?"

"Yeah, I'm sure."

Dana shrugs. "Okay, then. Let's go."

WHEN JOHN IS ushered into Walter's office this time, there are two bondsmen waiting there, not one.

"Hello, John," Alph says with a wry half smile. "How is your arm progressing?"

John stares at him, slack-jawed, then says, "Uh . . . good, I guess?" He shakes his head, looks down at his hand, and flexes his fingers. "Miraculous, honestly. I can hardly tell it was broken."

Walter gets up from his seat behind the desk and comes around to stand next to Alph. John doesn't remember thinking of the doctor as an old man the last time they met, but seeing the two of them together now, it's obvious from the stoop of his shoulders and the lines on his face that he's nearly as old as Walter himself.

"The grays took a great many things from us when they came here," Walter says. He leans back against the desk and folds his arms across his chest. "We cannot deny, however, that they did bring us a small number of gifts, even if they are not well distributed. Medicine is one such thing. Human science was advanced beyond theirs in a number of areas, but in medicine they were our clear superiors even before The Fall. Did you know, John, that the lifespan of a gray is limited almost entirely by senescence?"

"That, and happenstance," Alph says. "Intra-gray violence may be so rare as to border on insignificance, but they are still just as subject to accidents as any other creature."

"Well, certainly," Walter says. "My point was that maladies like cancer or infection are almost unknown among them. It is nearly unheard-of for a gray to die of anything other than either misadventure or extreme old age."

"I did know that, actually," John says. "Martok used to boast all the time about how amazing gray medicine was. He told me once that if only they had arrived here a little sooner, they might have been able to prevent The Fall."

Alph barks out a short, sharp laugh, then shakes his head and says, "Yes, John. No doubt they would have. However, this is not why we were hoping to speak with you today."

"Are you gonna kill us?"

That gets him a long moment of silence.

"No," Walter says finally. "I told you the last time we spoke that while I could not guarantee you would not be killed, it would not be one of my people who did it. Do you not remember this?"

"He remembers," Alph says. "He does not believe."

"I believed you," John says. "Six didn't. I was asking for her."

Walter smiles. "When you return to your room, you may reassure your friend that under no circumstances do we intend to kill you. There are very few of us left in this world, you know. We can hardly afford to run around killing one another."

"There might be very few ferals," John says. "There are plenty of *us*."

"Plenty?" Alph says. "Setting aside the question of whether we should make a distinction between wild-born humans and bondsmen, do you have any idea how many humans there were on this planet before The Fall?" He waits for John to shake his head, then says, "Billions, John. Billions. How many bondsmen are there now? A hundred thousand? Maybe two? Either way, a tiny, tiny fraction of what there once were."

"Be that as it may," Walter says, "you are safe here—or at least as safe as any of us."

Alph steps toward him. "On that note, John, we would appreciate it if you told us what words may have passed between you and your former employer when you last saw him."

"Martok?" John says, and takes a half step back.

"Yes. You met him in the woods four days ago. What did he say to you?"

"Nothing," John says. "I mean, he tried to convince me to come back with him. I told him that wasn't going to happen. Then he left." He turns to Walter. "Your people were watching us, right? Couldn't they hear us?"

"No one was watching you," Walter says. "Dana sent you out alone."

Of course she did.

"Okay," John says. "Anyway, that's all he said. He said he had forgiven me for my terrible crimes, and that we should come home with him. I told him no. That's all."

"Did you tell him that we held you prisoner?"

"No," John says. "No, I didn't. Why?"

"Have you wondered what brings Alph our way, John? His last visit required Dana breaking your arm to bring it on. What do you suppose prompted this one?"

John looks from Walter to Alph, then back again. He hadn't wondered, actually . . . but now he does.

"Martok summoned me," Alph says. "I assumed that there had been some setback with your arm. Imagine my surprise when I arrived to find that you had gone."

"I don't . . . what did he want with you? Is he hurt? I've never heard of a medico who treated grays and humans both."

"No, Martok is well, and you are correct that I could not have helped him if he were not. He summoned me because he hoped I would serve as his messenger. He asked me to tell you this: 'I have spoken with Chairman Sinta. He has consented to help us. Be ready in two days' time.' He stated most clearly that I was not to allow 'the ferals' to know why I had come, or to hear my message."

"So," Walter says. "You understand now why we must speak with you. Tell me, John—what does this message mean?"

John opens his mouth to say that he has no idea, but the words catch in his throat before he can say them.

He does know, doesn't he?

"Spiders," John says, as a shiver runs from the base of his spine to the back of his neck. "Martok is sending in the spiders."

CHAPTER TWENTY-THREE

Everyone knows *of* the spiders. Almost no one knows all that much *about* them.

The grays discuss the spiders, when they do, in the same way humans once discussed chemotherapy—as something expensive, painful, and dangerous, but sometimes necessary if life is to be preserved.

The children in the crèche, on the other hand, talked about the spiders constantly.

When he was six years old, John got it into his head that the spiders the older children whispered about, the ones that came for you in the night, the ones that could kill with a touch and would follow you to the ends of the Earth, never tiring, never relenting, and the spiders who lurked in the high corners of the bunk room spinning webs and eating flies, were one and the same. One crisp autumn night he woke to see one of the latter kind hanging in midair, legs splayed wide, caught in a bright beam of moonlight as it slowly descended from the ceiling toward his bed. He watched for a long, breathless moment as it dropped and twisted, silver light glinting around it. It was just a hand's-breadth above his thin woven blanket when he started to scream.

By the time Rema turned the lights on and stomped through the door demanding to know what had happened, half the children in the bunk room were either screaming, crying, or both. It took thirty seconds and an earsplitting bellow to reduce the cacophony to a scattering of muffled sobs.

"Now," she said. "What is this nonsense? Has one of you died?"

A half-dozen fingers pointed to John, who was still quietly hyperventilating with his blanket pulled up over his chin. When Rema finally coaxed him into stammering out some semblance of what had happened, the old gray laughed, hunched over, and tousled his hair with one thick, three-fingered hand.

"Silly boy," she said. "You'll not see the spiders dangling over your bed if they ever decide to come for you. They're one with the darkness, you know. One with the night. You won't even feel their touch before you die." She straightened then, and looked around the room. "All right, now. Back to sleep, all of you, or you may have a visit from the spiders tonight after all."

John did not go back to sleep. In truth, he was sure in that moment that he would never sleep again. He spent the rest of that night curled on his side, staring out the window at the fat silver moon. When the spider reappeared, a spindly black shape climbing up the thick glass of the window in short, manic bursts, John reached out and cupped his hand around it, let it crawl up onto his palm. He watched it for a moment, turning his hand into the light to see it more clearly as it crept over the pad of his thumb. Its feet were sharp, pricking his skin as it stopped and turned and raised its two front legs, as it seemed to look into his eyes.

With a savage grin, John clapped his hands together and crushed it.

"Wow. So WHAT did you tell them?"

John shrugs. "I told them the spiders are coming."

Six shivers and pulls the blanket tighter around her. She's sitting on the edge of the bed, legs dangling, blanket wrapped around her shoulders like a shawl. John has rolled the desk chair to the center of the room and is spinning in slow circles, toes occasionally brushing against the wheeled feet to keep him moving.

"You don't know that," Six says. "Martok never said anything about spiders, did he? And anyway, Martok doesn't have the credits for a roast beast sandwich, let alone an infestation. He must have meant something else."

"Alph said Sinta was involved. Sinta has enough credits for anything he wants."

Six scowls and looks away. That's certainly true enough.

"You've seen the spiders," John says finally. "Could they get into this place?"

"I was a child, John. I was seven years old."

"You were traumatized. You definitely remember what happened that night."

"Really? You're, what, a brain doctor now?"

John spins around once more, then says, "No. I'm not a brain doctor. I'm right, though, aren't I?"

Six glares for a long moment, then says, "Look. I have nightmares, okay? I have them all the time. I do remember . . . things. I don't know, though. I don't know which of them are real, and which are just shit that my brain made up because everyone I loved got murdered and I didn't know how to process that." She sighs, pulls the blanket tighter, and flops onto her back. "I remember stuff. Most of it can't possibly be true, though—and the parts that could be? I don't want to think about them."

John lets that hang between them. After a silence long enough that he starts to think she might have fallen asleep, Six says, "They came at night. They always come at night, right? We were camped in the trees then, on platforms built into the branches. I woke up hearing the screaming. It was far away at first, on the other side of the settlement, but it spread like a wave, closer and closer." She falls silent again, and John hears her breathing, faster now, verging on ragged.

"This part . . . ," she says. "This is the part that I don't think is real. This is the part that I think comes from the nightmare. I was on a platform, maybe three or four meters off the ground. The woman who took care of me—her name was Ariane—she was there with me. When the screaming started, she pulled me close, wrapped her arms around me, and whispered for me to be still, whispered that it would be okay. She was trying to cover my eyes, trying to keep me from seeing, but her whole body was shaking and I could . . . a leg came up over the edge of the platform, thin and black and tipped with a claw that dug into the wood like it was loose sand. Then another and another, and Ariane wasn't breathing anymore and she was squeezing me so tight that I couldn't breathe either, and then there was an *eye,* and it *saw* me, John. I mean, it looked into me and it knew who I was, *what* I was, and . . ."

She takes a deep, shuddering breath, then lets it out slowly. When she speaks again, her voice is a dull monotone. "Anyway, the next thing, the thing I'm pretty sure was actually real, was that I woke up in Ariane's arms and she was cold and stiff and smelled like shit, and two grays were down below arguing over how they should get me down and whether I'd been too contaminated by feral ideas to be worth the trouble. Eventually they called up to me that if I didn't come down on my own, they'd burn the tree, and I came down, and they bundled me into a trundlecar and hauled me off to the crèche."

John waits through a long, heavy silence, then says, "I'm sorry that happened to you, Six. You didn't answer my question, though. Can they reach us here?"

Six barks out a harsh, grating laugh. "If half of what I remember is true? Yeah, they can reach us here." She rolls over and pulls the blanket over her head. "They could reach us anywhere, John. Those things could reach us on the far side of the moon."

It's later, and John is dozing in the chair when the click of the door latch snaps his head up from the desk. He turns to see Dana closing the door behind her.

"Hey," he says, and digs his knuckles into his eyes. "What time is it?"

"Late," Dana says. "Or early, depending on how you want to look at it. We're about five hours from sunrise."

"Huh. So it's too early for breakfast, and you already brought our dinner." He looks her over. "Also, you've got no food. Why are you here, Dana?"

"Is it true?"

John blinks slowly, then says, "Is what true?"

"You know what, little man. Don't fuck with me right now. I'm not in the mood. Are the spiders coming?"

John blinks, rubs his face with both hands, and says, "I don't know, Dana. Maybe? Probably? I don't know what else that message could have meant."

"Message?"

John stares at her blankly, then says, "Didn't you talk to Walter? Isn't that why you're here?"

Dana's face hardens. "Walter doesn't tell me anything unless and until he thinks it'll serve him for me to know it. I overheard him talking with the bondsman doctor. I didn't get most of it, but I heard the tone in their voices, and I definitely heard Walter say 'spiders' more than once. So?"

John sighs. "When you sent me out to talk to him, seems like maybe Martok got it into his head that Six and I needed to be rescued. I swear, I told him we didn't, but when he gets an idea it's really hard to get him to let it go. Then, when you took me to see Walter earlier, Alph told me that Martok sent him to get a message to me. He said Chairman Sinta had agreed to help us, and we should be ready in two days. That's all. Nobody actually said anything about spiders—but honestly, I can't imagine what else he could have meant. It's not like he and Sinta are going to try to come in here and get us out themselves."

"No," Dana says. "I guess not."

"Can you fight them?" Six asks. John turns to look at her, but all he sees is one leg dangling off the side of the bed. He'd almost forgotten she was there. "The ferals I was with couldn't, but it seems like you've got a lot of stuff here that they didn't."

"Do we?" Dana says. "I admit we've got a good setup, but we didn't build it, and as far as fighting goes, you've seen what we've got. I don't know what they teach you about the humans who survived The Fall, but I'm telling you that they had weapons that make that rifle you gave us, which is now probably the most lethal thing we have, by the way, look like a pointy stick—and at the end of the day they couldn't fight off the spiders, so I really don't think that's an option for us."

"So you run," John says. "That's your only choice, right? Hand us back over to Martok and run. It's probably too late to stay now that Sinta knows you're here. He'll want to clear you out no matter what you do with us, just to keep you away from Lake Town. If Martok gets us back, though, I don't think he'll be inclined to chase after you, and Sinta should be happy as long as you're not his problem anymore. You've got two days, more or less. You could get pretty far if you start now. I get that it would suck letting go of this place, but it's better than dying."

Dana stares at him blankly, then says, "Run? Run where, John?"

"Anywhere," John says after a moment's hesitation. "West. South. It's a big planet, right?"

Dana shakes her head. "They really don't teach you anything, do they? There is no west, little man. There is no south. Why the fuck would you think we'd be hanging around here, right on the edge of the grays' territory, if we had anywhere to go? Start walking west from here and you hit the end of the world in about an hour and a half." She puts her back to the wall and slides down to sit on the floor. "Just out of curiosity, what do they tell you in your crèche schools about The Fall?"

John shrugs. "Not much. Mostly that it was the result of hubris, that humans had overburdened the world with their industry and their numbers and they brought The Fall down on themselves . . . and, of course, that we should be grateful to the grays for taking in the survivors. That's why we owe them service. If they hadn't come by just when they did, we'd be extinct."

"Hubris, huh? I guess that's one way to look at it." She leans her head back against the wall. "The rest of the planet is dead to us, John. Some things can still live out there. Mold. Grass. Maybe some kinds of bugs? People who go out there, though? They don't come back—or if they do, they don't live for long afterward. The only part of the world that's still survivable, as far as we know, is a circle a few hundred klicks across, centered on Farhome. You really think *we* did that?"

John stares at her, then shakes his head and says, "I don't believe you."

"You don't, huh? I can take you to the edge if you really want to see it. We could be back before dawn. It's something. Live trees, then dead trees, then a bunch of dead animals that don't ever rot, then nothing but scrubland as far as you can see. It's probably snowed over now, so maybe not as impressive, but still."

John opens his mouth to respond, lets it hang that way for a moment, and then closes it again.

"Yeah," Dana says. "I think you're starting to get it."

"Okay, but . . . but even if that's true, even if there's a wall of death or whatever west of here, it doesn't mean the whole *world* is dead. Maybe there was some kind of local disaster, and we're right on the edge of it. You said yourself that nobody goes out into . . . whatever is out there. For all you know, everything might be fine over the next hill."

Dana gives him a tight-lipped smile. "I guess you're right. We don't have any way to know what's happening beyond where we can see. The humans right after The Fall, though? They did. They had long-distance communications and flying machines and eyes in the sky and all kinds of stuff that you can't even imagine. They knew what happened, and now we know what they knew, because we kept histories. You don't have to believe me if you don't want to, I guess, but I'm telling you: This is it. This little patch of green is all that's left of the world."

"Okay," John says. "Fine. Let's say I believe that. Let's say it's true that something killed the entire damn planet except for this little bit. You think it was the grays that did it? I've lived with the grays my entire life. The tech you've got here is more impressive than anything I've ever seen in Farhome. What you're talking about . . . that's god-level stuff. It's impossible."

"Look, I have no idea why the grays live the way they do, but, John, they have *starships*, for fuck's sake. They literally came here from another *star*. Do you have any idea how big it is out there? How far it is from here to wherever their actual home is?"

John hesitates, then shakes his head. This wasn't a topic they covered in the crèche.

"Well, I don't really either," Dana says, "but it's a hell of a long way."

"Forget about starships," Six says. "They've got the spiders."

"Yeah," Dana says, a hint of bitterness in her voice now. "That too."

SCHOOL IN THE crèche was a winter thing. The children weren't able to go outside in the cold, and it was easier for the nursemaids to teach them history or writing or math than to try to keep them entertained in the bare common rooms. John liked school, for the most part. It was easier than summer work details when they would pile into trundlecars and head out into the country around Farhome to pick fruit or plant seeds, and it was more closely supervised than the outdoor play periods that so often ended with John being tormented by one thick-skulled bully or another.

Deep in the darkest part of the winter John turned twelve, Rema decided that John's cohort of six boys and five girls needed to learn about The Fall.

"Many years ago," she said as the children sprawled around her in a loose circle on the floor, "this world was filled entirely with bondsmen like yourselves, and no people at all. Can you imagine?"

John glanced over at the girl sitting next to him. She was leaning back on her hands with her legs stretched out in front of her, head tilted to one side and eyes half-closed and shadowed by a mass of wavy dark hair. Her name was Nali, and John had been fantasizing on and off for the past several weeks about actually speaking to her. He was going to do it, he resolved, was going to lean over and whisper something about the trail of goo hanging down from Rema's left eye or the way the tip of her long gray tongue poked out of her mouth when she said *bondsmen*, when Rema stomped hard enough to set the floor dancing and said, "And you, John. What do you think of that?"

John's head snapped around and his heart lurched into an uneven staccato rhythm. Rema was staring at him, her crest beginning to flush red.

"He was just telling me," Nali said. "He said how lucky we were that the people came into the world just at our moment of greatest need. He said that if only you'd come a tiny bit earlier, The Fall might never have happened at all."

"All that?" Rema said, her thick-lidded eyes narrowing. "This boy whispered all that into your ear just this moment, even as I was speaking?"

"He did," Nali said. "Your lesson was so moving, he couldn't help himself."

Rema huffed air through her nose and muttered something in rumble-speak, then looked at John and said, "Yes, well. From now on, boy, you must keep your opinions to yourself during lessons—no matter how well-founded they may be."

"Yes, Rema," John said. He didn't dare look at Nali again. He intended to thank her for saving him from a punishment cycle at best, and more likely a beating. He took two days to work himself up to it, though, and by the time he did she'd been bonded out, snatched away by a minor Greatfoot functionary. John never saw her again.

CHAPTER TWENTY-FOUR

When Dana is gone, Six sits up on the bed and says, "We have to get out of here, John. We can't be here when the spiders come."

"Why not?" John says, and begins spinning the chair around slowly with one foot again. "They won't hurt us. The whole point of this is that Martok wants to get us back, not kill us."

Six shudders and pulls the blanket up around her shoulders. "You have no idea how awful those things are. Even if they don't straight-up kill us, they'll drug us and carry us away, and they're not too fussy about dosing. There were other bondsmen in the camp when they came for us, you know. Only two of us came out of it alive."

"I feel like fifty-fifty is better odds than we'd have trying to take Dana down."

Six gives him a withering glare, then says, "You're a real coward, you know that?"

"Am I?" John says. "Aren't you the one arguing that we need to run away right now?"

"I'm saying we should try to *do* something. You're saying we should sit here with our thumbs up our asses while we wait to see what Martok or Sinta or Dana decides to do with us. How is that not cowardly?"

"I'd argue that it takes real courage to accept your fate." He looks up at her, head tilted to one side, then says, "How many times have you seen bondsmen get put down?"

Six opens her mouth to respond, then hesitates, shakes her head, and says, "A few. Too many. What does that have to do with anything?"

"It's almost always ugly, right? Screaming and crying and begging and then one gray pinning the poor bastard to the ground while the other does the job."

Six glares at him, but doesn't answer.

"So, when I was a kid," he continues, "there was an older boy in the crèche. He was probably the most annoying person I've ever known. He was big enough that he didn't come in for the kind of abuse that I got, but he used to say the weirdest stuff—I remember once we were at dinner and the stew had meat in it for once, and he pulled a lump of it up on his spoon and said, 'This is balls, you know. Pig balls, specifically. They're feeding us pig balls.' I—"

"Were they?"

John hesitates, confused, then says, "What?"

"Were they feeding you pig balls?"

"What does that matter? The point is—"

"Seems to me like it matters a lot. Was this kid a shit-stirrer, or were y'all just persecuting the only honest man in the crèche?"

"It doesn't . . . I don't know, okay? They were little chewy lumps in thick brown sauce. They could have been anything. That's not the point, though. The point is nobody liked him. Nobody but me, anyway, and I only liked him because having him around meant that I wasn't quite at the bottom of the social heap. I guess he was just as unpopular with the grays as he was with us—"

"Makes sense, if he was calling out their cooking all the time."

"—because he never bonded out," John says, finally realizing that talking over her is the only way he's going to get through this story. "Eventually the nursemaids decided they had to put him down. Not sure how this worked where you were, but in my crèche they made us watch when they did that. I guess it was supposed to instill respect or fear or something like that.

"Anyway, the way it happened was that a couple of the nursemaids would come at dawn and pull the condemned out of bed and then drag them, kicking and screaming, down the stairs and out to the alley behind the building, while the rest of us followed behind in a sort of a funeral parade. This kid, though? He was sitting on the edge of his bed waiting for them when they came, already cleaned up and dressed. When they came into the bunk room, he said, 'It's about time,' and then walked right past them, down the steps, out the door, and into the alley. We followed after, nursemaids and kids alike, and when we'd all gathered around, he knelt down, put his head to the pavement and said, 'Do it.'

"Now, would you say he was a coward? Because I've spent the last fifteen years thinking he was the least cowardly person I've ever known."

"Okay," Six says after a lengthy silence. "You're a coward *and* a liar."

John shoots her a mirthless grin. "Why do you say that?"

"Come on. He was sitting on the edge of his bed, dressed and ready to go? How did he know that day was the day? Had he been sitting on the edge of his bed every morning for the past six months, just waiting for them? And then he actually said *do it*? Not only are you a liar, you're a shitty, melodramatic one."

John laughs and gives himself a spin. "Maybe. I still think it's a fair question, though. Who's the real coward? The one who goes kicking and screaming into the night? Or the one who sees what's coming, understands there's nothing to be done about it, and faces the foot with a little bit of dignity?"

"It's a dumb question," Six says. "There's no dignity under a gray's foot—and trust me, nobody faces the spiders with anything other than screaming."

John doesn't have an answer for that. After a long silence, Six puts her back to him and pulls the blanket up over her head. John shrugs, draws his feet up onto the chair, and wraps his arms around his knees. As if in response to the silence, the lights draw down. John sighs, closes his eyes, and tries to sleep.

DESPITE HIMSELF, JOHN wakes in the coal-black darkness from a spider-haunted dream and begins chewing over escape plans. Taking Dana down still seems like the only remotely plausible option. Is it really possible? He remembers Tanner pinioning Min Hara. He hadn't thought anything or anyone could do that to a gray—even a decrepit wreck of a gray like Min. Tanner is bigger than Dana, but not by much. If she's remotely that strong, he and Six would be better off trying to tunnel through the walls than fighting her.

What if they don't take her head-on? What if they arrange some sort of ambush? John imagines himself pulling the grate off of the air vent above the door. They've already established, by climbing up onto the door and peering through the slats, that the vent narrows quickly to the point that neither he nor Six could possibly use it as an escape route. The first half meter or so is wide enough for him to squeeze into, though. He sees himself crouching there, waiting for Dana to bring their breakfast, then dropping down onto her when she opens the door.

And then, what?

Getting flung to the floor and beaten to death, probably.

What about weapons? Is there something in the room that he could turn into an improvised bludgeon? Or what about a blade? The desk drawers slide on metal rails. He imagines himself prying one loose, sharpening it to a fine edge against the concrete floor. Then, when he pounces on Dana from above, he'll actually have a way to—

It's just at that moment that the latch clicks, the door swings open, and all of his plans become moot.

"Come on," Dana says. She's framed in the light spilling in from the hallway. She's dressed for the weather, in leather and fur, and she's holding John's and Six's jackets in one hand.

She's holding their rifle in the other.

"Get these on," she says, and tosses the jackets onto the floor. "It's time to go."

"KILLING US ISN'T going to help," Six says. "Us being dead won't keep the spiders from coming. If we're alive, though, if you let us go, we'll tell Martok this was all a scam. There aren't any ferals here. We just ran away and hid for a while. We won't tell him anything about your place, about you and Tanner. He won't want to waste the credits then, he'll call the spiders off, and things can go back to what they—"

"Shut up."

Dana's voice is as cold as the wind cutting through their too-thin pants and tattered jackets. Six looks like she'd like to keep going, but in the end, prudence wins out. She shuts up.

John, for his part, is thinking about his stoic almost-friend from the crèche. Despite her skepticism, the story he told Six was true, more or less. The boy's name was Arn. John can't swear to the part about him sitting up on the edge of the bed waiting for the nursemaids—Arn was three years older than John, and so in a different bunk room—but he remembers the parade, remembers Arn walking out to the alley under his own power and then turning to the nursemaids, stone-faced, and putting his head to the ground. Did he really tell them to *do it*? John remembers it that way, but whatever he said was low and bitter and some of the younger children were crying—so again, he can't be sure.

Mostly he remembers thinking that he was seeing his own future, and wondering whether he'd be able to keep it together long enough to make a memorable end.

He's not in line to be stomped to death now, anyway. Will the rifle be easier? Depends on Dana's aim, he supposes, but he can't imagine it could be worse.

"It doesn't make sense," Six says, her voice softer now and on the verge of cracking. "If you kill us, you'll just make Martok angry. He won't forgive that. He'll hunt you down."

"You think so?" Dana says. "I killed a bunch of Daro's bondsmen. He didn't seem to think that was worth raising a finger, let alone bringing in an infestation."

"That's because Daro is trash. Martok is different."

"The grays are all trash," Dana says. "There's no point in even trying to tell one from another. They're genocidal fucks who murdered an entire planet just so they could build their little settlement here. They stole our world from us, and they've been trying ever since then to wipe out the few of us who managed to survive The Fall. You may think Martok liked you, but grays don't like bondsmen. They don't respect bondsmen. They can't, because they don't think bondsmen are people. When a gray likes you, it's not the way you like your friends or your family. It's the way you like your shoe, or that sandwich you had for dinner."

They walk on for another five minutes in silence, stumbling in the darkness, teeth chattering and bodies shaking, until Six finally trips over a root and falls to her hands and knees. When John reaches down to help her up, she shakes him off.

"No! No, just leave me here! Why are you doing this to us? This is stupid! It doesn't make any sense!"

"It does," John says wearily. "It makes perfect sense. Martok is bringing in the spiders to get us back, so she can't let us stay. She can't let us go back to Martok either, though, because we know about their hidey-hole. So, what do you do?"

Six looks up at him, tears beading at the corners of her slitted eyes. He offers her his hand. After another moment's hesitation, she takes it, and lets him pull her to her feet.

"Come on," Dana says. "We're almost there."

John has never been a particularly philosophical person. He's spent most of his life alternating between boredom and desperation, with not much time in between for studied contemplation. He's interested to find that he seems to be getting that way now, though, in what are almost certainly his final minutes. He should be afraid, he knows. What's about to happen is likely to be painful, at least for a second or two, and it carries a finality to it that he hasn't really contemplated before. Still, he finds himself thinking about Dana and Tanner and the little community they have in the woods—a *human* community, as Dana has repeatedly emphasized, with children and old people and a shared purpose that doesn't revolve around the needs of the grays—and contemplating the fact that what he's doing now might actually be the first really meaningful thing he's done in his life. He's not just being marched out into the woods to be murdered. He's giving his life to help save the last human community on Earth.

"I have a kid."

John glances back at Dana. She's trudging along behind them, rifle clutched across her chest, looking nearly as miserable as Six.

"I know," he says. "That's why you broke my arm. Remember?"

"Yeah," she says, eyes fixed on the ground in front of her. "That was for her. So is this. So is all the stupid shit I've done since I met you. You . . . you can't understand what that's like, being a parent. You'll never be one, and you never had one. It changes you, you know? Suddenly all that energy that used to go into yourself gets turned around and poured into her, and you'd do anything, say anything, sacrifice anything to keep her safe."

"Great," Six says, her voice dripping with bitterness. "I mean, that's really inspiring. Do you have a point?"

"My point is that's why I'm doing this. I wanted you to know." She stops walking. "This is far enough, I think."

John stops as well and looks around, his heart suddenly racing. The big rock is behind them, he realizes. They're no more than a hundred meters from the house. He looks up. The clouds are breaking, and the first pale light of dawn is starting to creep over the horizon.

"You don't have to do this," Six says quietly. She's stopped next to John, but she hasn't turned to face Dana and her eyes are fixed on the ground in front of her. "Just let us go."

Dana's face twists into a grimace. "You know, I was thinking she was the one for this, but I guess it's gonna be you, little man." She walks up to John, shoves the rifle into his chest hard enough that he staggers a half step back as he cradles it with both arms, and then backs away. "Put it right here." She taps her chest, just left of center. "If I'm still breathing after that, put another one in the back of my head." She closes her eyes, breathes in deep, and then lets it out slowly. "Please don't fuck this up, okay?"

John stares at her, numb hands clutching the rifle. "I don't understand."

"I've thought this through," Dana says, "and this is our only chance. You'll tell them I was a lone wolf, a survivor from Owasco, maybe, and there aren't any other humans out there. I was the one who beat that old gray bastard. I was the one who broke your arm. I was the one who tricked you into running away. You weren't really running away, though. You were hunting, and you got me. Congratulations. No need to waste credits on the spiders now. There's nothing more to see here."

"John?" Six says, but he's not hearing her. He's entirely focused on Dana. He raises the rifle, sights down along the barrel, settles the crosshairs on a discolored patch of leather over her left breast. His finger slides from the guard to the trigger. He breathes in, then out. His finger begins to tighten.

"Do it," Dana says.

Off in the distance, a wolf howls.

CHAPTER TWENTY-FIVE

Do it.

John thinks of Arn, of the look on his face when he knelt and put his forehead to the pavement. His focus drifts up from Dana's chest to her face. Her eyes are open now, hard, locked on his.

"John?" Six says. "This doesn't seem right."

John shoots her a quick glance. "Really? Five hours ago you were trying to convince me that we had to kill her, first chance we got."

Dana's eyes narrow. "You were what, now?"

"That was different," Six says. "We needed to get out then, and she was in our way. This, though? This just feels like murder. It feels like something the grays would do."

Dana turns on her. "What the fuck, Six? Two minutes ago you thought I was gonna kill you, and that apparently wasn't okay. Now you've got your chance to kill me, and that's not okay either? Seriously, what do you people want?"

"Maybe nobody kills anybody?"

Dana tries to grin, but it twists into a grimace. "Sorry, sweetie, but if nobody kills anybody, then your fucking owner kills *everybody*, including my baby girl. That's not gonna work for me. If you don't have the stones for Plan A, that's fine. Give me the rifle back, and we'll go with Plan B. I still think that's a worse bet, but it's better than nothing."

She holds her hand out and takes a step toward him. John tightens his grip on the rifle and says, "Stay back!"

Dana laughs. "Or what? You'll shoot me?" She takes another step. "Do it." One more, so that she's almost close enough to grab the barrel. "Do it, or give me the gun."

John breaks and runs.

"Hey!" He hears the rush of footsteps behind him, then a surprised grunt and a thud. He risks a glance back to see Dana sprawled in the snow with Six wrapped around her legs. Dana kicks at her, but Six covers up and clings on. "John! Get back here, you little shit! Seriously! What the *fuck*?"

"I'll fix this!" John yells. "Wait here! I'll fix this!" He stumbles then, almost goes down, spends a frantic moment as he struggles for balance contemplating the thought of how absurd it would be if he accidentally shot himself now, and decides that he really needs to give his full attention to running. *Thanks, Six. Hope she doesn't beat you to death.* Ahead of him, he can just see the lights of the house rising from the snow through the last ranks of trees.

THERE ARE TWO trundlecars in the yard in front of the house. The one Sinta gave to Martok that day in Lake Town is parked in the same spot next to the porch where it's been since they came here, buried in so much snow that it's just a vaguely car-shaped white lump. Behind it, a bigger, newer, cleaner model sits, with clear tracks leading back down the driveway to the road and just a light dusting of snow covering the windows.

That can't be good.

John approaches the porch at a slow walk, rifle clutched across his chest. Sinta is here. Who else could it be? John had hoped to talk to Martok alone, to convince him to stop this lunacy. Is it too late now? Are the spiders already here?

It occurs to him now that he has no clear idea how the grays' spiders are transported, or even how big they are. Six described them as gigantic, but those were the memories of a traumatized child. For all he knows, they could be no bigger than a real spider.

All things considered, it's probably better not to know.

He creeps up the stairs, crosses the porch, then hesitates with his hand on the doorknob. The first sliver of sun is just creeping up over the horizon, adding a deep red glow to the sky over the bare, snow-crusted trees. It stops him. He's probably about to die. Before he does, he wants to see the sunrise.

His reverie is interrupted by the sound of Dana's voice in the distance, shouting his name. He sighs, shoots a quick glance over his shoulder, and turns the knob. Time to go.

He finds them seated at the dining room table. Martok has his back to the entranceway. His head is thrown back, draining the last dregs from an ornate wooden tankard. The gray sitting across from him is hunched over his plate, just shoving a hunk of rare roast beast into his mouth. He looks up as John pushes through the door and steps into the room, and their eyes meet.

"Hello, Chairman Sinta," John says. "I'm happy to finally meet you."

"Martok," Sinta says around a mouthful of food. "Is this your bondsman?"

Martok's head snaps around, and his eyes widen. "John?" He slams the tankard down onto the table and pushes to his feet.

"You've come home! Huzzah!" He's taken two strides toward him, arms spread wide, when John levels the rifle and says, "Stop there." When he sees the sudden, heartbreaking shock on Martok's face, he adds, "Please. Please, Martok. Step back."

It's not until this moment that John realizes what he's come here to do. Once again, it seems, some part of his brain has found a way to bypass his conditioning until the moment of crisis. Min Hara is a human sympathizer. If what Alph told John is true, Sinta is all that stands between Min Hara and the levers of power in Lake Town.

The thought that Min Hara's first official act might be to demand that Martok turn John over to him does flit across his mind, but John waves it away. He told Dana he'd fix this, and his one tenuous route to doing that sits across the breakfast table from him.

Sinta stands, both hands planted on the table and crest beginning to flush. He's a giant, John sees now, nearly a full head taller than Martok, and wider across the shoulders as well. He says something in rumble-speak. John misses most of it, but catches a few individual words: *madness*, *unacceptable*, *destroyed*.

"No," Martok says, and holds one placating hand out toward Sinta while reaching for John with the other. "You misunderstand, good Chairman. John did not threaten me. He would never! He has spent long days now in terrible captivity. He is frightened and disoriented." He turns back to John. "Hand me the rifle, my friend. You are home now, and have no more need of such things."

John shakes his head and takes one slow, cautious step backward to stay out of Martok's reach. "No. Please. I need to know what's happening. Have you summoned the spiders?"

"Madness!" Sinta says, and comes out from behind the table.

Martok turns to face him. "Good Chairman, please! I tell you truly, John means no harm! Only give me a moment!"

"Nonsense," Sinta growls, and shoves Martok aside, sending him crashing into the still-laden sideboard. "Such disobedience from a bondsman *cannot* be tolerated, not for a single moment! I shall—"

John pulls the trigger.

The bullet strikes home. Sinta takes up so much of the room that John could hardly have missed if he'd tried. A puckered hole appears in the wrinkled hide of Sinta's belly. All three of them stand frozen for a moment in the aftershock of the report. Sinta looks down at the wound, touches it with one finger, and then looks up at John. "You—"

John fires again, striking Sinta in the chest, then works the bolt once more and gets off a final wild shot that grazes the gray's shoulder before the Chairman rips the weapon from his hands, twists the barrel until the metal nearly snaps, and casts it aside. It's time to run. John knows this, but now, belatedly, a lifetime of conditioning kicks in to keep his feet rooted to the floor as Sinta snatches him up by the neck and lifts him until their faces are nearly touching.

"You wretched creature," Sinta growls, in a register so low John can barely make out the words. "When the spiders have finished with—"

"Put him down. Good Chairman, please, put him down." John can't turn his head to look, but he's able to cut his eyes far enough to see Martok standing with arms held out, palms up, beseeching. "His time with the ferals has crazed him, clearly, but John is my friend, sir. Please—"

"This creature attacked me!" Sinta bellows, and shakes John so hard that he can feel the bones in his neck grinding against one another as his vision fades. "He attempted to do *violence* to my *person*! I shall not put him down—not in one piece, at any rate. I shall—"

Martok takes two quick steps forward and strikes Sinta a thunderous overhand blow to the face.

Things happen quickly now.

John drops to the floor, forgotten, and scrambles back against the wall as Sinta's eyes roll back, his crest flushes fully, and he lets out a long, wordless bellow. He stomps first one foot, then the other, hard enough to crack the floorboards, then turns to Martok with arms spread wide.

Sinta is *absent*.

It takes John a stunned, uncomprehending moment to realize that Martok is very much *not*.

The two grays circle one another, Sinta smashing furniture, flailing his massive arms and howling, while Martok, moving with bewildering grace, manages to stay just out of the bigger gray's reach, all the while making sure to draw Sinta as far as possible from John. The heavy table flies into the wall as Sinta blunders into it, then turns his attention briefly to stomping it into splinters. Martok takes advantage of the distraction, slipping around behind Sinta and kicking out the backs of both the Chairman's knees in quick succession. Sinta bellows and falls, and Martok is on him with a speed and nimbleness John has never seen in any gray, let alone his bumbling employer, wrapping one thick arm around Sinta's neck and locking the other behind his head, driving him face down onto the cracked floor, then *squeezing*. Sinta falls silent, but his arms and legs keep flailing until finally something gives way, and with a sickening *crunch*, the Chairman falls still.

Martok holds on, panting heavily into the silence, for another minute or more before pulling back and letting Sinta's head drop heavily to the floor, hanging loose on a shattered neck. He pushes himself up, turns Sinta's slack face toward the wall, then stands.

"John," he says, his voice low and weary. "I am truly sorry to have shown you that. Are you well?"

John shuts his gaping mouth with an audible snap, swallows, and says, "I don't . . . you're . . . you're actually an enforcer?"

Martok gives a noncommittal rumble, comes over to where John cowers against the wall, and kneels. "Clearly not, my friend. Enforcers can command nearly any price for their services. You have learned this firsthand recently, have you not? Enforcers certainly do not live hand-to-mouth, shuffling from boardinghouse to boardinghouse, lacking the credits for a decent sash."

"But . . ."

"I *was* an enforcer. Before I came to this place. It was the earnings from that work that let me buy passage on the ship. When I realized the game you had played, convincing Sinta that I *am* an enforcer, I thought perhaps you had somehow learned my secret, but it seems this is not so, yes?"

John looks up at him, starts to speak, then shakes his head and says, "I don't understand."

Martok rumbles out a sigh, then turns to settle next to John with his back to the wall. "How to explain? This work, this . . . *violence* . . . you could not understand how corrosive it is to one of my people. Your forebears apparently did violence to one another constantly, without the slightest care or consequence, but for us this has never been so. There are some few of us—very few—who can do this without becoming *absent*, but even for such a one, there is a price to be paid." He lets his eyes sag closed, and John can almost see the combat hormones draining out of him. When he speaks again, his voice is bonelessly weary.

"I tried for years to harden myself to the work when I was young. My clan is . . . perhaps not as wealthy and highly regarded as I have led you to believe. The credit I could earn plying this trade turned the fortunes of much of my extended family for a time. I learned very quickly, however, that I could not support them all, and there would be no end to their demands as long as I continued there—and even if this had not been so, the work was killing me. No matter how great the rewards may have been, I could not bear the price. So, I forsook my family and clan. I came to this place and took up the life of a vagabond."

Martok closes his eyes again and lets his head droop forward until it almost touches his pulled-up knees. He holds that pose for long enough that John begins to wonder if he might have dozed off. Just as John is thinking of getting to his feet, though, maybe trying to find out what became of Dana and Six, Martok says, "Have you ever wondered why I took you from the crèche?"

John hesitates, then says, "I always assumed that you wanted a friend, and I was the closest thing to it that you could afford."

Martok laughs, leans his head back against the wall, and gives John's leg an almost-painful squeeze. "Yes, there is that. You know me too well, my friend." He pulls back his hand and draws his knees closer to his chest. "The day after I came for you, you were to be put down. Did you know that?"

John shakes his head. "I knew I was close. I didn't know I was that close."

"You had a caretaker, Rema was her name. Do you recall her?"

John nods.

"I had done a bit of work for your crèche the year prior, patching a leak in the roof and clearing some rubbish from the grounds. When she had paid me, I asked Rema to inform me the next time one of her charges failed to bond. She thought I was in search of cheap, disposable labor, and let me know in clear terms that she disapproved of such things. Nevertheless, though, she called me—and when she did, I came for you." He leans his head back again, and turns his gaze to the ceiling. "I had formed a notion, you see, that if I could save one of you, it might balance the scales for some small part of what I had done before. I had felt increasingly haunted by the shades of those I had harmed, and I thought this act of charity might quiet them."

John waits for him to go on. When he doesn't, he says, "So . . . did it work?"

Martok looks down at him again. "Much to my surprise, it did. It was a small gesture—there are many crèches in Farhome, and all of them had children who had failed to bond—but it was something." He smiles. "And, of course, you became a blessing in my life, entirely aside from whatever purpose I'd originally imagined you might serve for me. I would have done more, would have saved others, if I thought I could manage to feed another mouth. I had hoped that this venture might allow me to do much more, eventually. Six was in a similar position to yours, you know. If we had not taken her, she would be long dead by now. My plans, foolishly ambitious though they may sound, were to eventually make it so that in Lake Town at least, no bondsman would ever again die under a nursemaid's feet."

John returns his smile, in spite of himself, then abruptly remembers Six speculating about something almost exactly like this.

Maybe she really is smarter than him after all.

The feeling of warmth fades quickly, though, when his gaze falls back to Sinta's broken neck.

"So," he says. "What happens now?"

"Now?" Martok says. "Now we do our best to make this a place that the gentry of Lake Town will truly wish to visit when the grime of the town becomes too much for them. The good Chairman had already transferred the credits needed to bring the spiders to our corner of the forest to my account prior to his unfortunate demise. However, with Sinta's departure from the political scene, Min Hara's faction will likely take control of the

Ice River holdings now, and Min is broadly known to be a human sympathizer. So, I do not believe any further actions against any feral humans who may or may not inhabit these woods are necessary now, do you?"

"No," John says. "No, I don't believe they are."

"I am pleased that we agree on this point. The resulting savings should give us funds enough to clear your bond, and to invest a bit into our property besides. Any new business is a risk, of course—but I am surprisingly optimistic about our prospects."

John's jaw works soundlessly for a moment, until finally he manages, "That all sounds wonderful, but Martok . . ." He hesitates, then screws up his courage and says, "*If* I come back, if we really try to do this together, it can't be like it was. You've said a million times that you think of me as a friend, as *family* even. Now . . . now you've actually got to live that. We need to be *partners*. Not employer and employee. Not . . ." He stops himself before saying, *Not owner and pet.*

Martok sits silent, watching him, for long enough that John begins to wonder if he's overplayed his hand. When he finally speaks, Martok says, "Hmm . . . what you say borders on sedition, my friend." He tilts his head to one side, considers for a moment, and then bares his tusks in a grin. "However, as I've just dispatched the Chairman of the Western Province, it seems I have little room to criticize your orthodoxy. It will be as you say."

"Thank you," John says. "Since you mentioned it, though . . ." He gestures toward Sinta. "How do we plan to get around that?"

"A fine question," Martok says. "The answer, as I see it, depends on whether anyone other than Min Hara himself who might be in a position of authority in Lake Town is aware of my . . . peculiar status. If the answer is no, then I was of course *absent* when the good Chairman met his end. One cannot be held responsible for things done in that state. This is a bedrock principle of our laws."

"And if the answer is yes?"

"In that case, I suppose it will depend upon whether they cared enough for the good Chairman to find and engage another enforcer to deal with me. Min Hara certainly will not take this course, but I suppose Sinta must have had his supporters." He climbs to his feet, and offers John a hand up. "The expense would be immense, of course. Those in my former profession generally prefer to avoid interfering in one another's business if it can possibly be avoided. The Chairman was powerful, but I suspect in the end that he was not so well loved. My guess is that this will be seen as a simple misfortune, much like the one that brought our beloved Chief Administrator to his current seat."

John takes Martok's hand and lets himself be pulled to his feet.

"So . . . this is it, then? It's over?"

"Oh, on the contrary," Martok says. "For us, I think perhaps it is just beginning."

John finds Six and Dana crouched in the snow a dozen meters into the tree line, waiting for him. Six has fresh, vivid bruises on her face, a bloodied ear, and what looks to be a broken nose, but seems to be well otherwise. Dana is unmarked, but furious.

"Tell me why I shouldn't kill you," she says when John stops, close enough to speak with her but far enough that he thinks he's got a fair chance to make it back out of the trees if she comes for him.

"You're safe," John says. "How's that? The spiders aren't coming—not now, or ever."

Dana stands slowly and glares down at him. "Really? That's

fun. You just went in there and talked some sense into old Martok and . . . Sinta, is it? Just talked them right down off of the ledge, and now everyone's happy. Is that what I'm supposed to believe?"

"Believe what you want. Sinta is dead, though, and Min Hara is next in line for the chairmanship. As long as his faction holds power, I don't think you have anything to worry about."

Dana laughs. "Dead, huh? So those shots we heard—that was you killing Sinta? And Martok too, I guess? I'm not sure I'd trust that rifle to take down a deer, but you used it to kill two grays with three shots. Is that right?"

"I didn't kill anyone," John says. "Martok killed Sinta." He turns to Six. "Turns out he really is an enforcer. Neat, right?"

Six shakes her head. "You're not doing much to boost your credibility here, John."

John starts to reply, but neither of them are looking at him any longer. Six's mouth has fallen open, and Dana is staring past him, her face an even mixture of fear and fury. John turns to see Martok shuffling toward them through the snow at the edge of the trees. He stops two paces behind John, spreads his arms, and says, "Six, I am very happy to find you safe." He presses his palms together then and bows, a formal gesture John has seen between grays, but has never imagined could pass between a gray and a human. "And greetings to you and yours, friend. Will you join us for a meal? My breakfast was interrupted, and I think we may have important things to discuss."

CHAPTER TWENTY-SIX

The summers here on the western fringe of the habitable world are short. The snow lingers in the shadows of the trees until May, and by September the wind is already beginning to bite again. John always found himself dreading the next winter almost before the old one was over when they lived in Farhome, but here he finds that the pace of the seasons agrees with him. The forest seems to know that its time is limited, and the riot of life that erupts there during those few warm weeks is even more vital somehow because it's on a short clock.

He's perched on top of the big rock one soft, hazy July morning, thinking about the work he needs to do that afternoon in a desultory way but mostly just appreciating the fact that he's free and alive in a place like this on a day like this, when Dana's head pops into view, followed shortly by the rest of her as she vaults up to crouch beside him.

"Hey there, little man," she says with a grin, then settles in next to him and leans back on her elbows. "Hiding from your chores this morning?"

John shrugs. "Pretty much. You?"

"Yeah, same."

After thirty seconds of companionable silence, John says, "How's Miri?"

"Good," Dana says. "Thanks for asking. Took her forever to totally shake whatever that infection was last winter, but she's thriving now. I gave her a bow for her birthday. She took to it like a fish to water. She keeps up this way, she'll be a better shot than I am before she loses her last baby tooth."

"Oh . . . is that good?"

Dana laughs. "You really don't get parenthood, do you? Yeah, it's good."

John picks up a flake of stone, turns it over once in his hand, and then rears back and tosses it. He can't get much into the throw from a sitting position, but it still rises up over the canopy and then drops down through with a satisfying rustle of disturbed leaves.

"What about you?" Dana asks. "How's the hotel business going?"

"It's not a hotel," John says. "It's a luxury wilderness retreat."

"Whatever. How's business? Is the new staff working out?"

"Yeah, they're fine. I mean, they're all children and they make me feel like I'm a hundred years old, but they seem to understand that they won the lottery here, and they're hard workers. We've got two guests today, which means we've got three associates waiting on each of them hand and foot. That's one reason I can spend my morning hanging around in the woods. Other than riding herd on them, there's not that much for me to do."

"Any more of them ready for re-wilding? Your friend Ani has been pushing for us to reoccupy Owasco ever since she came over, and Walter is thinking about letting her give it a shot. If we're going to do that, we could really use some new blood."

It takes John a confused moment to realize that she's talking about Six, and then another to process the question. "Not sure," he says finally. "These ones are all pretty green still. I'll ask around, though."

"Thanks. Let me know how it goes." She reaches up to scratch idly at the back of her head, then says, "Hey—you got the steel Tanner was asking about? We've got fifty kilos of venison to trade."

"Tomorrow, I think. Martok's planning on making a run up to Lake Town. If he ever manages to quit flapping his tusks with those Ice Rivers long enough to make the trip, he'll get it then."

"Good enough. Don't wait too long, though. We've only got the one freezer, and it's pretty much full."

"I'll let him know. Martok loves venison. He won't want to let it spoil."

"Thanks."

John looks up. A hawk circles lazily above them. *He's not hunting*, John thinks. *He's just enjoying the morning, same as we are.* A minute or so later, the bird proves him wrong by folding his wings and diving into the canopy. When John looks away, Dana is climbing to her feet.

"I'd better get back," she says. "Miri's probably shot Tanner by now." She walks to the edge of the rock, then pauses and looks back at John. "Tell me something, little man. Do you think this can last?"

John turns that question over in his head. Does she mean the morning? The weather? The summer?

No, he knows what she means.

"I don't know," he says finally. "Min's old, but even old grays can live a long-ass time. And when he's dead or deposed, we'll still be fine as long as his faction holds power."

"Will they?"

"Who knows? Sinta's people are on the outs now, but they

could come back. The Greatfoots could decide they care about what's happening in Lake Town after all and come push them both out. If that happens, we're probably right back where we started, except with at least a couple of grays in Lake Town who know that you're here. Or, who knows? Maybe something worse than the grays will come out of the dark before that happens, and just go ahead and kill them and us both."

Dana laughs. "Wow. You're a real ray of sunshine this morning, aren't you?"

"Yeah," John says. "I am, actually. I've been thinking a lot about this lately, and here's what I've come to: It's a fact that we'll all be dead at some point. That's the truth. On the other hand, it's also a fact that we're *not* dead today. I'm trying really hard these days to practice some gratitude for the second thing, and not let the first thing fuck that up."

She looks him over, head tilted to one side and hands on her hips. "Huh. When did you become a fun-sized Zen master?"

John squints up at her. "I don't know what that means."

Dana laughs again, then shakes her head and says, "No, I don't guess you do. Those crèche schools really do suck." She watches him for a moment more, then puts one hand to the rock, hops off the edge, and disappears.

"I'll see you tomorrow?" John calls after her.

"Sure thing," she replies, voice already fading with distance. "Bring the steel."

"Bring the venison," he says, but she's already gone.

SUMMER TURNS TO autumn, and autumn to winter. The morning of the first heavy snow finds John in a hunting blind three meters up in an old oak tree, shivering in his heavy jacket and waiting for some unlucky animal to cross his path. Dana is good for the occasional shipment of meat, but their guests are hungry, and her price has risen sharply as the weather has worsened. He's been there for three hours now without seeing anything bigger than a crow and is thinking about packing it in for the day and telling Martok to spend some of the massive pile of credits he's been accumulating on a haunch of roast beast from Lake Town, when a shadow catches his eye, moving slowly through the trees fifty or sixty meters distant.

He takes two deep breaths to settle his nerves, then brings the rifle up and puts his eye to the scope. It takes him a moment of searching to find his target.

It's not a deer. It's a wolf.

John settles his sights on a spot at the base of the animal's neck, and slides his finger from the guard to the trigger. A wolf doesn't represent much of anything in the way of useful meat, of course. Dana would trade for the fur, though—and if nothing else, it's a competitor for whatever venison is out here. He breathes in, breathes out.

The wolf raises its head, sniffs the air, and then turns to look directly at him. John's finger tightens on the trigger, but doesn't quite apply enough pressure to trip it. He's remembering that long-ago meeting in the park in Farhome, and suddenly he's sure this is the same wolf. It can't be. Rationally, he knows this. That was years ago, and three hundred klicks away, and how long does a wolf live, anyway?

Doesn't matter. That wolf could have taken him, but it didn't. Maybe it recognized a fellow traveler, another creature who'd had a world that he'd once owned taken away from him.

Maybe it just wasn't hungry that night. Either way, John realizes, he's got a debt to repay.

He lowers his rifle. The wolf watches him for a moment more, then turns and trots away.

The sun is a hand's-breadth above the horizon now, sharp and bright and cold in the southern sky. John stands and stretches, then stoops to gather his gear.

It's time to go home.

ACKNOWLEDGMENTS

There are a great number of people without whom this book would never have come to be. I'll start with whoever is currently running this simulation, because it's been glitching in an entirely positive way for some years now from the perspective of my literary career, and I'm one hundred percent here for it. On the actual-real-person side of things, I am as always deeply grateful to Paul Lucas and the good folks at Janklow & Nesbit, without whom I would most likely be selling oranges under a highway overpass right now, and to my West Coast friends, Sean Daily and his colleagues at Hotchkiss Daily & Associates. Huge thanks also to my editor, Michael Homler, whose ongoing support and encouragement almost certainly has as much or more to do with where I am today than anything I might have done, and to all the wonderful people I've been privileged to work with at St. Martin's Press.

In addition to the people whose job it is to be nice to me, there are a surprising number of others who have been willing to help me along entirely for free. I am eternally grateful to the following folks, in no particular order:

Therese, Kim, Jonathan, Aaron, Sarah, Craig, Max, and Nick, for helping me to see what did and didn't work with the early drafts of this book, and for allowing me to steal all of their grape tomatoes and cheese.

The good folks at Lift Bridge Books in Brockport, The Dog Eared Book in Palmyra, and Another Chapter in Fairport, for stocking my books, hosting my events, and generally being some of the best people I have ever been fortunate enough to know.

My friends at our local Barnes & Nobles (all three of them) who have been nothing but kind to me ever since *Three Days in April* came out half a lifetime ago.

Karen, for teaching me that I needed to know more stuff before I could write what I know.

Jack, for teaching me that despite my best efforts, I still don't know nearly as much stuff as I think I do.

Jennifer, for inexplicably continuing to put up with my nonsense.

Kiran, for his insightful criticism of both this book and of me, personally.

Claire, for her artistic insights, and for providing me with abundant motivation to keep working.

Heather, for hooking me up with the folks at Sundance Book Emporium and Fallout Shelter.

Mickey, John, Jon, and the other Jon, for being my oldest friends and biggest fans.

Tabones, for reminding me to keep my priorities straight when ranking the best days of my life.

Maggie, for reminding me that accomplishment means nothing without struggle by flopping across my arms every time I try to sit down and write.

Freya, for being the weirdest dog I have ever had the privilege to encounter.

I'm sure there are many other people who contributed to the creation of this book in ways both large and small. If you're one of them, I hope you'll forgive me for forgetting to call you out. As you know very well, I'm not nearly as smart as I look.

Now, on to the next one, right?

ABOUT THE AUTHOR

JustTeeJay

EDWARD ASHTON is the author of the novels *Three Days in April*, *The End of Ordinary*, *Mickey7*, *Antimatter Blues*, *Mal Goes to War*, and *The Fourth Consort*, as well as several short stories that have appeared in venues ranging from the newsletter of an Italian sausage company to *Escape Pod*, *Analog*, and *Fireside Fiction*. He lives in a cabin on the shore of an inland sea, where he enjoys wandering the woods with a neurotic hound, teaching quantum physics to sullen graduate students, and whittling. You can find him online at edwardashton.com, or on Instagram, BlueSky, and other assorted social media platforms @edashtonwriting.